RELENTLESS ENEMY

KEITH GOAD

BQB

Virginia

Previously self-published as *By The Same Relentless Enemy* in 2017 under ISBN978-0997194234

Now published in the United States by BQB Publishing
(an imprint of Boutique of Quality Book Publishing Company, Inc.)

www.bqbpublishing.com

ISBN 978-1-945448-87-4 (p)
ISBN 978-1-945448-88-1 (e)

Library of Congress Control Number 2020944324
Book design by Robin Krauss, www.bookformatters.com
Cover design by Rebecca Lown, www.rebeccalowndesign.com
First editor: Caleb Guard
Second editor: Andrea Berns

To Stephanie,
now and always
the love of my life

Deep within humans dwell
those slumbering powers;
powers that would astonish them,
that they never dreamed of possessing;
forces that would revolutionize their lives
if aroused and put into action.

—Orison Marden

Other books by Keith Goad

The Invictus - Volume 2 of the Relentless Enemy series
(releasing in the fall of 2021)

CONTENTS

1

UNSEEN, UNCONSCIOUS, AND UNHARMED

Chicago, Illinois: 1982

It was past midnight. The small boy stood at the top landing of the staircase, his body rigid, his trembling hands clutching the wooden posts of the railing. He was listening to the adults in the living room below, their hushed voices changing in cadence.

"Does he know? Did he see? Oh, dear Lord, I can only imagine what it would've been like for him." Judy Walsh's words came in fits and starts.

Slouched in an easy chair, staring at the living room carpet, her husband, Jim, held his forehead in his hands. "I don't know, Judy. I just don't know. I convinced the sheriff to let me get Craig the hell out of there before it became a circus." Jim looked up at his wife. "We both know how Andy was. I wouldn't think that guy could have an enemy in this world." He looked down at the carpet again. "There was absolutely no reason for this."

A seasoned police officer, Jim had seen his share of shocking crime scenes, but nothing had prepared him for what he'd seen several hours earlier. His brother-in-law, Andrew

Henriksen, had been murdered inside the Lutheran church he led in Cedar Township, Iowa. It was unlike any crime scene Jim had seen before. Andrew had been mutilated, slashed, and bludgeoned in a fashion that had shocked even the most hardened police investigators.

The crime had occurred as Andrew's only son, Craig, lay apparently unconscious on one of the pews. The ten-year-old child was unharmed. It wasn't clear, either to those who initially found Andrew or to Jim once he arrived on the scene, whether the boy had witnessed any of the carnage that unfolded. This was the same child who now clutched the upstairs railing of the Walshes' modest three-bedroom home in suburban Chicago. He was listening, trying to understand his aunt and uncle's discussion.

Judy sobbed quietly. "In a way, I'm glad my sister isn't alive—I wouldn't want her to see this. It's awful, Jim, just awful."

Judy Walsh was normally straightforward and matter-of-fact, not prone to exceptional displays of emotion. A sandy-haired woman of average height and build, she was always neat and measured in her appearance. But the news of her brother-in-law's violent death had caused her to come undone in these early morning hours.

Jim was trying to think of what to do next, to think of anything else he could to get the images of the crime out of his head. "What now, Judy? What is this kid supposed to do now? Jesus, he's only ten years old." Jim asked the question aloud, but inside he knew full well how his wife would reply.

"He's got to stay with us, Jim." Now her voice was calm, steady, and determined. "We're the only family he's got now."

It had been just Craig and his father since Judy's sister died four years earlier from an aggressive form of cancer.

Since then, Craig and his father had been nearly inseparable. Andrew ministered to the residents of their small community and was highly regarded and trusted by all. It was a kind of throwback to the days when a minister was truly involved with the members of the church. It wasn't uncommon to find Andrew at dinner with a different member of his congregation each week, always with Craig by his side. Craig was old enough to see the connection his father made with the members of their community. The congregation thought the world of their minister and constantly sought him out for advice and counsel on their concerns. Craig adored his father, and he seemed to understand, even at such a young age, the positive influence his father had on the lives of others.

This is what made the event the Walshes were discussing that much more unbelievable. The Andy Henriksen they had known had been a devoted husband and a kind and giving person. But somehow, just hours earlier, either through random violence or calculated hate, a murderer had ended his life.

Jim didn't respond to Judy about Craig needing to stay with them. He knew that she was right, that Craig staying with them was the most logical course of action. But he refrained, knowing that his confidence and experience was in crime and police work. On matters of family and children, Jim knew his wife was the authority.

Breaking the silence, Judy went on. "So, are the police going to need to take more statements from Craig, or try to get him to remember something about the killer?"

"I think I got them to understand that if the time comes when Craig can remember anything about the killer, we would work something out. That is, if they can find the guy."

"Which makes it even more important that he's here with

us in Chicago, and not anywhere near Cedar Township," Judy quickly added. "He could be in danger there."

Jim's eyes swept up and locked with those of his wife, both understanding the common ground they had just reached. Judy knew in her heart that the boy should be with the only remaining family he had. Jim understood that Craig needed to be protected, far away from Iowa, and with a family whose experience was rooted in protection, lest the crime prove to have been calculated, not random. Jim returned his gaze to the carpet.

As much as Judy tried, she couldn't dispel the shock she was feeling. "Jim," she started slowly and deliberately as she gathered her courage, "tell me exactly how he died." She covered her mouth as she waited for her husband to answer.

Jim's mind drifted back to when he arrived at the crime scene. He remembered the startled expressions on the deputies' faces. Craig's father, Andrew, was lying facedown in a pool of blood. Two deep puncture wounds that Jim saw on Andrew's back were what he presumed had been fatal. Jim again felt a rush of shock fill his chest as he recalled a deputy lifting up the side of the body. The state of the face and chest was shocking. The face was bludgeoned. The chest looked equally horrific. The place where a white T-shirt had covered the torso was unrecognizable. Only the staining of blood and a chest cavity having been hollowed out through repeated slashing and stab wounds remained. Never had Jim seen anything like it at a crime scene before.

"Judy . . ." Jim started, trying not to relent. He met his wife's eyes again as she stood in front of him, her expression unchanged, awaiting his reply. Jim dropped his head. "It was almost like an animal attacked him. He'd been slashed and beaten. His skin"—Jim took a long, slow breath—"his skin looked like it'd been ripped off in places."

"Could it have been some animal, some . . . thing?" Judy asked.

"No." Jim closed his eyes and shook his head. "No, a man did this. He had to have been powerful and determined."

Jim was clearly rattled to a degree that belied the nature of his profession. A homicide detective for several years with the Chicago Police Department, he was an imposing man, nearly six foot four. His hair was cut very short in a military style, and he had a square, rugged jawline that matched his personality. He was normally serious, dispassionate, and to the point. That had changed when he received a call early in the afternoon at his Chicago precinct from the sheriff in Cedar Township, reaching out to the next of kin. The sheriff knew Andrew Henriksen well, and he knew that Andrew was related by marriage to a Chicago detective.

As he sat in a chair in his living room late that evening, Jim was now trying to recount for Judy the scene with which he was met when he arrived in town. Andrew Henriksen had been attacked near the front altar of his church. There were signs of a struggle, but no evidence of a weapon or device that had been used to kill him. Andrews's body was being photographed by a sheriff's deputy. When he witnessed the state of Andy's body, Jim was startled to the point of nearly losing his balance.

While at the crime scene, he learned that the first responders had found Craig unconscious on a pew near the front of the church. Several pews had been upended, possibly during the significant struggle, covering the one where Craig had been lying, possibly obscuring him from view. When he regained consciousness, the police on the scene took the boy out of the main sanctuary, away from his father's body.

As Jim described the events at the church, tears began to slowly roll down Judy's cheeks again. "Okay, Jim. That's enough." She tried to regain her composure before continuing. "But how, Jim? How is that little boy upstairs right now, not a hair on his head having been harmed? How can you explain that?"

"I don't know, dammit!" Jim's voice was loud as he shot an impatient stare at his wife. He quickly glanced toward the second floor before recovering and lowering his tone. "I don't know, Judy. It doesn't make any more sense to me than it does to you. All I know is that if he's going to stay with u—if that's what you're saying—he's going to have issues. You and I need to be sure what we're signing up for. Are we?" His question was half to state the obvious, half to test Judy's resolve.

"You know as well as me, Jim, that Andrew's parents died when he was young too. There's no one Craig can go to. No relatives he really knows like he knows us. We've got to be here for him, Jim. Danny can help too." She looked up toward the bedrooms upstairs. "I know they're not real close, but this will be their chance." She fixed her eyes on her husband again. "We've got to be there for him."

Upstairs, clinging to the railing, Craig could only assemble bits and pieces of the conversation. His father was gone, that much he understood. He had died in a tragic way that seemed to alarm an uncle that Craig had only known to be steady. It was also clear to Craig that he was now left completely alone. Alone, except for the relatives in whose home he now took shelter.

"Sounds like something bad's going on, huh?" Danny Walsh appeared behind Craig, having emerged from his bedroom groggy and tired. Startled, Craig spun around, clutching his shirt and gasping heavily.

"Relax, Craig, relax. I didn't even know you were here until Dad's voice woke me up. What the heck's going on, anyway?"

"My dad . . . " Craig started, almost panting. "He died. I mean, somebody hurt him. I mean . . . " The young boy was searching for words, his eyes growing bigger as reality became more and more clear in his mind. "He's dead, Danny."

"What? Jeez, are you sure? What the . . . holy crap." Danny stood in stunned silence.

While he'd seemed physically calm up to that point, Craig now began to shudder, his eyes wide as saucers. Danny was twelve years old, big for his age, and observant. While he didn't quite understand exactly what had happened, why, or when, he realized immediately that Craig was in some kind of shock.

"It doesn't make sense, man. Your dad, I mean, he's a good guy. Who would want to mess with him? Do you know who did it? Were you there?" Now Danny seemed oblivious to Craig's trauma as his intense curiosity rushed out in a series of questions. Craig squeezed his eyes shut and grimaced. "Danny, I . . . don't know . . . I didn't see . . . " His voice trailed off. He was shivering all over now.

"Hold on—just calm down. It's cool." Danny said, moving closer and patting his arm, trying to reassure the younger boy. "Craig, I'll help you figure this out. It'll be okay. I'm sure that things seem crazy right now, but you're safe. You know Dad's a cop. It'll be safe here. I'll help you out," he said, "Don't worry, man. I'll help you out."

2

THE RELUCTANT OBSERVER

Chicago, Illinois: Eighteen years later

Sergeant Eric Hammond signaled to his colleague from the doorway of a dingy Chicago apartment. "Walsh—Walsh, can I see you over here for a second?" Hammond's tone was terse and hushed.

His words were directed toward two uniformed Chicago officers standing at the center of the apartment, just short of the bedroom door. Between them stood a tall, strong-looking man wearing a dark tan, three-quarter-length trench coat. As Detective Daniel Walsh turned to see who was calling him, a couple of quick sideways head jerks from Hammond let Walsh know that his superior and good friend had brought to the scene something Danny needed.

"Hey, listen, guys. I'll be back in a minute," Walsh told the two officers.

The apartment was large for this area of Chicago, but with his long strides, Detective Walsh reached the door quickly, and Hammond pulled him over near a corner.

"You know, Danny, it ain't that easy pulling this stuff off for you," Hammond said.

The two were huddled close. At six foot two, Hammond

was nearly as tall as Walsh but slimmer and lacking Walsh's football-player-type body.

"Eric, relax, man. We'll be quick—you know that. You gave Forensics the wrong address, right?"

"Yeah, but don't make me lie like that again. And don't put my ass in a sling just 'cause you wanna phone a friend— again—on this one." Hammond drew even closer to Walsh as his voice lowered in volume. "I can't argue with results. You know that. When your guy started helping out with these scenes a couple of years back—well, I get it that he's got some kinda knack for sensing shit. But you gotta dial back being so bold about it. I've got him tucked away and waiting downstairs, and I'll help get him in here on the down low. But then you get him out fast. Got it?"

"I get it," Walsh said. "Don't worry. It'll take no time, and no one will be the wiser. So, how was he? Did he give you any static when you told him we were pulling him in again?"

"Danny, it's clear he doesn't like being any part of this stuff. He ain't no damn cop. You know that."

"I know, pal," Walsh replied, tapping his colleague's shoulder in mock reassurance. "I try not to drag him into our world too much, but I think we'll need him on this one."

Walsh noticed that the two officers in the middle of the apartment were watching his animated dialogue with Hammond in the corner. He quickly turned to engage them. "So, listen, gents. I've already got a guy from Forensic Services here who'll be able to get to work on this until an FS investigator arrives. But I'm gonna need the two of you to step out and start canvassing the building."

Hammond knew this was his cue to leave the apartment and retrieve the person whom Walsh was anticipating. As Hammond left, ducking under the yellow crime scene tape at the entrance of the apartment, one of the street officers began to protest. "Walsh, come on, man. We got other units coming that can handle all that. Plus, you told us a few months back, the next time you caught a slash and burn 'round here, you'd let us in on the process. What went down in that kitchen is epic."

"Guys, another time. I'm guessing the whole building's keyed up with us being here. Discreet." Both officers shot a look of annoyance toward Danny and then turned to talk among themselves. As they did, Danny took a few moments to survey the crime scene again. Then, quicker than he would have imagined, they all heard the sharp snapping of fingers that called at their attention. It was Hammond, who had reappeared at the door. Standing behind him was another man dressed in khakis and a dress shirt, holding a black attaché bag and wearing a dark baseball cap that read *Chicago Forensic Services* pulled down over his forehead. Hammond directed the two officers out of the apartment as he brought the new person in. "Come on, boys, come on. Let's make a little room in here and have you two watch the front and start working the halls. Can't let things get cold."

As the two officers filed past the new arrival, they were more preoccupied with their annoyance with Walsh than with who had arrived from the FS. "Ah, come on, Walsh. This is bullshit, man!" one muttered. The other waved his hand dismissively at Walsh as they exited.

Danny sought to placate them as they slipped from the apartment. "Guys, all right. I owe you one here. I get it."

With the other officers now gone and the new arrival approaching Walsh, Sergeant Hammond asked, "So, you two are good now, right? Let's make it snappy."

"No problem, Eric. I'll ping you in a few minutes," Danny said, addressing Hammond by his first name.

As Sergeant Hammond shut the door of the apartment behind him, Detective Walsh let out a measured exhale and slowly turned toward the man who had just walked past him to stare through the living area and into the kitchen.

"So . . . do you have enough to work with, here?" Danny asked.

Craig Henriksen stood a couple of paces from Walsh, closer to the interior of the apartment. Henriksen was twenty-eight years old with full, wavy brown hair, cut short. Just shy of six feet tall, he walked with a slight stoop, and as his shoulders slumped forward, his body language spoke of someone with the grim realization of what he was there to do.

He walked slowly through the dark interior of the apartment into a well-lit kitchen. His eyes moved around the room, focusing briefly on the contents it held and what remained of a graphic crime scene. A pool of drying blood had formed on the vintage 1970s kitchen table, and blood spatters stained a wall near the cabinets. But there were only limited signs of a struggle. Aside from a couple of overturned chairs— one clearly being where the victim had been seated—there was little other indication of a fight to match the amount of the victim's blood that had been spilled. As Craig's eyes surveyed the scene, they followed from where the victim had sat to where he had ultimately landed near the base of one of the table legs next to an overturned chair. The body's shape could be seen through the old, thick sheet that now covered it.

"Why do you continue to drag me into these things, Danny?" He turned his head and leveled his gaze at his cousin.

"We're not going to have this debate right now. We don't have much time. And I need you to, you know, do your thing." He paused before declaring, "You've got the gift, and I've got the way we can use it."

Craig drew a heavy sigh, his slight build slackening even more as he leaned forward. Closing his eyes, he began to knead his forehead with one hand, pulling the baseball cap from his head with the other. "And it has nothing to do with it being you that gets to catch a break on a case, right?" Danny looked down, avoiding Craig's eyes, and remained silent, knowing not to push his cousin too much.

Relenting as he always found himself doing, Craig said, "Let's just get on with this. I don't want to spend all night here. I've got to be at work early tomorrow." He turned and continued scanning the kitchen, his expression pained.

"So, what can I get for you? Do you need the shades drawn more, lights dimmer, the door—"

"No," Craig interrupted. "You know I can make this work the way it is. Just watch the door and the hallway until I'm done."

The two men had never tested whether what was about to happen would be visible to anyone else. The nature of that had always been so spectacular, and haunting, that they had never dared take such a risk.

Danny still hadn't answered Craig, who turned his head to stare impatiently back at his cousin. "Right. Absolutely. You've got it," Danny said, moving toward the closed apartment door but maintaining a view of the kitchen.

Craig took a slow, deep breath, opened his eyes wide, and zeroed in on a particularly thick bit of blood spattered on the wall. He moved slowly over to it. "How long has it been again?" he asked.

"Um, I'm guessing about an hour, maybe two. You still able to—"

Danny cut his question short when Craig raised his hand, asking for silence as his eyes fixed on a bloodstain on the wall about belt-high near the end of the table. He moved in closer and reached out toward the wall, touching the hardening bloodstain. He began to rub it purposefully, grimacing as if he were somehow causing it pain. Danny strained his eyes to see more clearly. Only a few lamps illuminated the apartment as the early evening twilight could be seen settling through a patchwork of thick, ugly curtains that hid the windows. While Danny watched Craig, he thought he saw the hardened blood begin to liquefy beneath Craig's fingertips.

Craig continued to rub the bloodstain slowly, his mind momentarily wandering. *Why would someone do this to another person? What causes such rage, such violence?*

Craig guessed there were probably many people who'd be curious to know what happens during violent encounters such as the one that occurred in the apartment. They might even imagine an ability that enabled them to turn back time, to view how the violent situation had unfolded, even if the insight gained was fuzzy. Craig actually had this ability. But for him, it held no appeal.

His mind was drawn back to the apartment as the color and tone of the room began to change, as though a thin, grayish-red fog were descending and thickening in the kitchen. All the tangible things that he and Danny had seen moments ago—the table, the blood spatters, the overturned chairs, the body on the floor—were enveloped in mist. The only things left visible in the room were Danny and his cousin. And then the sound they had heard before started again. A muted, pulsating sound. It was though they were hearing a human heartbeat through a stethoscope.

"It's beginning," Craig said breathlessly. He stopped rubbing the bloodstain but continued to hold his hand against it. His heart started to race. He'd never gotten used to this.

He turned to observe the kitchen, which seemed to have completely transformed: he and Danny remained the only visible objects within the grayish-red veil that permeated the room.

But now, a ghostly black silhouette in seated position emerged in the middle of the room where the dining table had been. The shape had the look of an older man. It was the shadowy form of the murder victim. Only the hazy black shadow of the victim was visible. No other furnishings—chairs, tables, cups—could be seen. While no other sound could be heard but the faint pulsating, Craig and Danny stood in rapt silence, nonetheless, taking in the movements of the black figure against the slow-moving fog that had filled the room. It was like watching an eerie mime performance: the shadow moving and interacting with invisible objects.

Craig maintained contact with the bloodstain on the wall as he and Danny watched the victim's silhouette react to what may have been a knock at the apartment door. The aged victim appeared to move sprightly out of the frame of the kitchen for a few moments, returning to the kitchen with a slower-moving male visitor, whose silhouette was slightly larger. It had the movement and mannerisms of someone significantly younger than the victim. "Danny, it doesn't look like there was a problem between these two."

"Wait . . . " said Danny.

The two shapes seemed to talk and interact normally, but every time the victim's silhouette appeared to look away from the visitor, the visitor's hands and fingertips twitched. He looked impatient or anxious. "See, the new guy is getting antsy," noted Danny.

Over the next five minutes—although it felt like much longer—the visitor grew more animated, now clearly feeling irritated. At first, it seemed as though the victim was trying to calm the visitor, but then he turned and shuffled over to a kitchen cupboard and seemed to remove something while keeping his back to the visitor. Meanwhile, the visitor was scoping the kitchen and apartment as if trying to see if anyone else was nearby. Having retrieved something from the cupboard, the victim returned to where the table would be, sat back down, and with a resigned motion, his head hung low, pushed the object toward the visitor.

"This is taking too long," Craig complained as he remembered Danny's caution that they had only limited time.

"Shh." Danny held up his hand. "Here it comes." As if his request was a signal to the two shadows, the visitor talked animatedly to the victim while moving slowly behind where the victim was seated. Then, in one quick motion, he ripped a closed fist across the victim's throat. The fist must have held a knife; Craig and Danny could both see the victim's throat being slashed. Blood, visible in the recreation as black droplets, flashed from the victim's neck and spattered against the wall and onto the floor. One of the black, shadowy sprays of blood landed where Craig now held his hand firmly in touch with the bloodstain on the wall. The victim clutched at his throat as he collapsed onto the floor.

"Oh, Jesus." Craig reflexively squinted his eyes and looked toward the floor, trying to avoid seeing the final moments of the gruesome assault as it replayed before him. After all, he knew he was only there to unlock a view into the past. Danny was the one who would peer into it for clues.

"What's he doing now?" Danny muttered, daring not to blink.

Craig snapped his attention back to the scene: the black silhouette of the now-dead victim on the floor, his assailant seeming to rummage through the cabinet the victim had opened just a few minutes earlier. The assailant held something in one hand as he dug around the cabinet with the other. He looked over toward the victim's silhouette on the floor. In an act of apparent disgust, he spat on whatever he held in his hand, then hurled it furiously toward the ground as he lunged toward his victim and delivered a punishing kick into the dead man's side. He then drifted over to the edge of the apartment, pushed upward on what was probably the window, and disappeared from the re-creation, apparently down the fire escape.

Now the scene was still, leaving only the black silhouette lying motionless on the floor. "Is that enough? Can I stop?" Craig asked Danny.

"Yeah, yeah. Sure. Thanks." Danny's eyes were darting back and forth, his mind no doubt busy trying to piece together what he had just seen, searching for clues.

As Craig removed his hand from the wall, the reddish veil that had filled the kitchen area immediately receded, like fog burning away in the early morning sun. The black silhouette on the floor vanished, replaced by the actual body covered with its heavy, dark sheet.

It was over. Neither man seemed surprised by what they just witnessed. They'd learned of Craig's ability during their years growing up together. It was something they'd both kept secret—an ability to see, in shadows and silhouettes, muted actions and movements from violent past events.

Craig heaved a deep sigh. He had begun to feel lightheaded, having stooped over during the entire re-creation. As he rubbed his forehead again, he and Danny heard voices coming down the hall from outside of the apartment.

"This one *was* close," remarked Danny. The re-creation

had almost lasted too long. The forensics team might have entered the apartment at any moment, and neither Craig nor Danny knew what they would've seen.

As he had done before, Craig stared curiously at the hand that had been touching the bloodstain on the wall, as if it wasn't even his. His power to do these things had always been a mystery, even to him.

Danny cut his introspection short. "Craig, listen. Put this on," he said. He withdrew a dark, fire department baseball cap from his trench coat and pushed it onto Craig's head. Then he shuffled Craig from the kitchen toward the front door.

"Seriously, Danny? You drag me down here, and now you're going to just push me out?"

"Yeah, go down out the front, and Hammond should probably be there. He can take you back over to work. It's all good—you just have to get outta here, you know?"

Before Craig could say anything else, Danny ducked his head under the tape across the door just as two members from Forensic Services were about to come through it. As Danny pushed Craig past them, one of the examiners cast a puzzled look at the civilian in the firefighter's ball cap who was passing by. Danny greeted the team, ushering them into the crime scene as he called to Craig, who was now slowly making his way down the hall toward the stairs.

"Hey, thanks again for helping get this all sealed up. Sergeant Hammond out front can take care of that other stuff for you."

With that, Danny retreated back into the apartment. There was an electricity now. The men from Forensics began setting up, and Danny felt a rush from having the insight that only Craig's power could provide. He directed the forensics team around the crime scene and quickly shared with them his hypothesis about where they needed to look for clues. Danny's mind leapt ahead to the police ceremony later in the week and thought this chance to quickly solve another case couldn't be more perfect.

———◆——◆◆◆——◆———

Craig emerged on the street, where several Chicago police cars were parked. He glanced around but didn't see Hammond. As he stared up toward the third floor of the shabby apartment building where he'd just been with Danny, the juxtaposition of his time there kept him transfixed for a moment. It always seemed surreal, his ability to channel the wrongs of the past and make them visible before his cousin's eyes. He shook his head in disbelief at the scene that he had actually created. *For what reason? How am I able to do this? And why?* These questions haunted him, but he always felt obligated to help his cousin.

The early evening sky had given way to a veil of low, gray clouds matching Craig's mood. *Great,* he thought, realizing that he would need to make it back to work either by cab or the L. None of the officers had yet taken notice of him as they busied themselves interviewing the residents who approached the apartment building. To avoid getting wet and delayed—or even worse, being identified as a faux member of Forensic Services—he quickly turned and made his way down the street.

As he walked ahead, his eyes scanned the sidewalk and the street in all its normalcy, save for the arrival of the police on the scene. There couldn't have been a more stark contrast between the two realities Craig had seen with his own eyes only minutes apart. In the aftermath of these experiences, he felt confused and out of place. Most of all, he felt alone.

3

TACTILE TRANSFERENCE

"So, these images have returned again? How has that made you feel?"

Craig stared out the window of Dr. Janet Burris's third-floor office, watching a light rain fall on the suburban Chicago neighborhood. As he listened to her words, he slowly closed his eyes, knowing where their conversation was headed. Again.

"I've told you before," he began calmly, his eyes still closed. "They aren't just images or visions in my head, or whatever. I *make* them appear. It's not that I want to. I mean, I don't know how or why I can do it." He opened his eyes and fixed them on his psychologist. "That's what I'm always hoping you can help me with."

Dr. Burris remained silent for several moments, rotating the pen she held between her thumb and forefinger, her lips pursed. She was middle-aged, short, and slightly stocky. Plain but professional. Her wire-brush hair was speckled with gray, and it seemed that she could have looked this way a day, a month, or a year ago. Altogether, her appearance looked to have been constructed and maintained to be as little distracting as possible for her clients. She held herself perfectly upright, glancing down to occasionally scribble on the notepad she kept on her lap.

"Craig, you know I want to help you in any way I can with this. But it always comes back to this point, doesn't it?" She removed her glasses and continued: "You always talk about how you initiate these images, somehow creating them. But that's where we get bogged down, isn't it? Let's focus on what you are feeling, what you are doing at the time, or what behaviors seem to bring them about." She leaned forward, staring plaintively at Craig.

But this was exactly the point in their sessions where, despite his desire for some type of professional insight, he always felt the need to step carefully to avoid sharing too many specifics about what his abilities allowed him to conjure. He only shared a highly sanitized version of what he could see. And when pushed, he never completely admitted that the images appeared anywhere other than in his head. Even if his therapist believed him, Craig worried that sharing the whole truth might somehow place him at risk: legally, ethically, or clinically.

Dr. Burris wasn't the first therapist Craig had sought out over the years. In the various clinical discussions he'd had as an adult, the term "loner" had come up on more than one occasion. His personality and the unusual way he had grown up were the basis for that. He also knew that not opening up more and agreeing to be vulnerable with someone like Dr. Burris, who would be ethically bound to keep his ability secret, only made him feel resigned to letting them see him as an outcast.

"I don't know," Craig replied, looking out the window again. "Really . . . I just don't know." He knew this answer would only serve to shut Dr. Burris out, wasting any chance of true engagement with her. Consistent with her reaction in their previous sessions, Dr. Burris looked back down at her notepad and repositioned her glasses on her nose.

The previous night's events were still fresh in Craig's

mind, and he wanted to try to go further this time. After a long moment of silence, he sighed and started cautiously. "Doctor—"

"Please, as we discussed before, just call me Janet."

"Okay, then," he continued, his eyes now fixed on the base of her chair. "Janet, what do you know about . . . tactile transference?"

Dr. Burris's eyebrows rose slightly. "Tactile transference?" she repeated.

"Yeah," Craig continued, "something about the ability to extract memories or feelings—"

"From an inanimate object or device," she finished in a clinical tone. "One that often has some strong emotional connection to a person, serving as a subconscious trigger to images and feelings so strong that they can seem almost real to the one experiencing it." She sounded as though she was trying to convince Craig of this definition rather than understand his experience. "Yes, I'm familiar with the general concept. Why?"

Craig wondered where she had heard of the concept. When he had attended community college, he read about a Roman myth in which a military leader could summon the strength of his slain soldiers by touching the wounds of their dead bodies. Craig had roughly translated the Latin term as "touch-taking" or, as he interpreted it further, tactile transference. But to Craig, Dr. Burris didn't look like the type who was well-steeped in Roman mythology. He answered her question with his own. "Well, have you ever heard of someone who was able to manifest images or sounds so that others could see and hear them?" He let the question hang in the air between them.

Dr. Burris stared at him dispassionately. Several moments

passed, and Craig felt increasingly exposed by his statement. She finally broke her gaze and went to scribbling in the notepad as she replied, "In short, no."

But then she stopped writing and looked at him again, removing her glasses and tilting her head as if she felt for him. "I have to be honest with you, Craig. A good number of people who thought they could do those things happened to be suffering from extreme psychosis or . . . dementia, or . . . "

"I get what you're driving at, Janet. But we've known each other long enough that I would hope you don't think I'm losing my mind."

"I don't, Craig. But let's try, for once, to get at the heart of these instances. Tell me again about your first experience with this, when you lost the family pet when you and your brother were young—"

"He's my cousin, not my brother," Craig interrupted testily.

Dr. Burris flipped back through her notes, clearly checking his statement against earlier versions of the story he had told. As the pages flipped in her hands, his mind drifted back to the same memory she had made him visit before, a place where her notebook could not go.

———————◆◆◆———————

He was young, only a few years after beginning to live with Danny and his family. Maybe twelve years old, he thought. They were in rural Kentucky, and he and Danny had wandered off to an old, abandoned barn on the property of one of Danny's uncles. It seemed unusually warm for early fall, and the barn offered a shadier place to explore. The sun was getting low. And when they entered the barn, rays of sunlight were spliced as they showed through the cracks and slats of wood. A dusty haze hung in the air. Craig could almost smell the scent of straw as the images floated through his mind. Both he and Danny didn't expect to find the fresh carcass of a large German shepherd crumpled against the inside wall of the barn.

Both he and Danny had been fascinated by the graphic nature of the scene and with how such a large, dominant dog could be summarily killed and left this way. There were even fresh spatters against the wall where the dog's innards had been cast off.

"Wow. What the hell do you think could've done that to the dog?" Danny enjoyed using expletives liberally when he was away from his mother and, especially, his more disciplinary father.

Craig had drawn close to the dog, standing over it and staring at it.

Danny stooped and picked up the dog's large front paw. "Hey, look at this. The rigors haven't even set in all the way on him! This must have happened pretty recently."

"And look at this." Craig pointed to a large smear of blood and clumps of fur stuck to the splintering wall where the dog must have been pinned. Craig moved closer and gingerly touched a clump of bloody fur.

Suddenly, the inside of the barn grew even dimmer, as if someone had blocked out the natural light that had been illuminating the inside. Both boys let out a breathless *"What?"*

Craig's hand froze, almost as if to brace himself for whatever seemed to be happening.

The barn was now quite dark, but the boys could still see one another as they exchanged bewildered looks. Before either could speak, they saw a bright-gray, ghostlike image—clearly that of the German shepherd—enter their field of vision from near the barn door. While neither boy could hear anything, they could see from the outline of the image that the dog was aggressively barking at something. From a direction opposite the dog, but still between Danny and Craig, a large humped-over gray silhouette came into view and stopped as the dog got closer, poised in a defensive growl they could not hear.

"Are you seeing this, Craig? What the hell?"

"I don't know, Danny; I just don't know how this is happening."

Craig was growing increasingly alarmed while Danny ignored the supernatural nature of what he was witnessing and grew more intrigued. "It looks like this dead dog, right? But what the hell is that thing?"

The large, humped shape then seemed to stand upright on its back legs, and it became clear to both boys that it was a bear. Craig and Danny remained frozen as the silent encounter played out in silhouettes. Seemingly content to avoid the dog and leave the barn, the bear dropped back onto all fours and made for a place in the dimness where the barn door would be. The dog kept barking but moved aside, appearing to give the bear a wide berth. But then, in a quick flash, the dog lashed out and bit the bear on its back leg. The bear spun around, rising again on its hind legs before moving with surprising speed to crash down and attack the dog.

Even though they watched the events in a shadowed and muted way, the scene before their eyes still made the boys tremble.

"Danny, I don't like this. Why won't it stop? Why are we seeing this?"

Danny shook his head in confusion and looked away from the scene, toward Craig, when it dawned on him. "Craig, it's your hand. I think it's that shit you're touching!"

"What?" Craig looked at the place where he was bracing himself against the barn wall, realizing his hand was resting on clumps of fur and flesh. "Ahh!" he exclaimed as he quickly withdrew it.

The moment he did this, both silhouettes dissipated like thick vapor and vanished. At the same time, the darkness that had filled the barn lifted as if someone was dialing back a dimmer switch. Breathing hard, Craig cradled the hand that had been touching the wall with his other hand, looking at it as if it were something foreign.

"Danny, what . . . what the heck just happened?"

———◆◆◆———

As Craig recalled the scene now, Danny's mouth still moved in his mind's eye, but instead he heard Dr. Burris's words: "So why do you believe the images were so real and vibrant in your mind, Craig? Was it because you were close to the dog?"

Craig drifted back to the present. "Doctor, I just need to know that you're willing to go there with me when I need help in understanding this. That you'll be there for me when I need you to be."

"Have I *not* been here for you? Craig, I juggled my schedule to get you in here this afternoon, just as you wanted, didn't I?" Dr. Burris suddenly seemed more animated and empathic than Craig was used to. Now he felt bad for inconveniencing her, especially since he wasn't up for indulging her questions.

"I know, I know. I appreciate—" Craig said before Dr. Burris interrupted.

"And speaking of those time slots, I'm afraid yours is up for today."

Feeling tired and resigned, Craig got up from the armchair. "Right . . . right."

Dr. Burris stood as well, approaching him differently than she had in the past. She reached out and cupped one of his hands in both of hers. "Craig, please tell me that you will look a little deeper with these episodes and come back next time ready to open up with me more. I can only help you if you will let me."

She seemed genuine. Craig nodded once and then, as if to convince himself, nodded again before saying, faintly, "Thanks," and walking out the door. Out in the waiting room, while scheduling his next appointment, his attention turned to a television that sat on a corner table. It was tuned to the late afternoon local news.

An arrest has already been made in yesterday's grisly slaying of a Franklin Park man. Detective Daniel Walsh met with the media briefly late today. "Thanks to the cooperation of the other apartment residents and some quick follow-up on leads, we were able to apprehend . . . "

Craig didn't need to listen to any more of the broadcast. He was becoming increasingly familiar with the arc of the news stories about Danny's police work: they reflected the fact that Danny usually cracked a case much faster than his superiors or the media would have suspected.

He was relieved to get away from the television as he made his way out of the building and onto the suburban sidewalk. The cool autumn air was refreshing, and as the sun descended toward the horizon, he shook away the unfulfilling residue of his session with Dr. Burris.

He soaked up the moment, taking a long, deep breath as he tried to decompress from what was itself supposed to be a decompressing therapy session.

When his cell phone buzzed in the pocket of his Oxford shirt, it startled him, and he nearly jumped. He flipped the phone open and answered, feeling as if he knew who it would be.

"So, what'd you think? You see the news? We got this guy!"

"*You* got him," Craig said, correcting his cousin.

"Listen, Craig. I'm sorry I had to push you out like that, but we had to act fast if we wanted a chance at getting him." Danny quickly changed the subject. "What're you up to?"

"Not a thing," Craig said, "You know how my days go, nothing near the excitement level that you have going on."

"You're funny. Well, you're going to have something going on soon, pal. You're gonna meet me and Emma for dinner later this week."

Standing on the sidewalk, arms crossed with the phone at his ear, Craig watched the sun slip lower. "Oh, really . . . " He drew out his response, his mind finally getting some distance from the unusual events of the previous night, and the frustration and depression he had been feeling all day. "So, it must be true then that you might actually feel something for this one, huh? How long has it been now? A couple of months? Why the reluctance to bring her around? Thinking it's almost time to trade her in for someone new?"

"Oh, don't be such an ass. I know my track record with the ladies might seem to follow a pattern."

"Ya think?" Craig inserted.

"Just wait 'till you meet her. She's not the typical club hopper you always say I gravitate toward."

"Go on." Craig still wasn't buying it. "What does she do, then? Let me guess. Um, bartender? No, wait, pawnbroker. Or—"

"How 'bout a goddamn elementary teacher, pal? She's

great. You'll see. Let's catch up over breakfast at Monk's. Let's say, day after tomorrow. Then we can figure out when to go for dinner. You in?"

"Yeah, uh, sure. Can't wait to meet her."

"Great, I gotta go. And Craig, thanks again for helping last night. Really. Thanks, man."

The call over, Craig put his phone back in his pocket, lowered his head, and proceeded down the street to his car, glancing up occasionally to take in the final rays of the setting sun.

4

DETECTIVE WALSH

Danny surveyed the gathering buzz of people as they slowly filed into the police auditorium. It provided him a moment of introspection before he would begin to interact with others. A satisfied smile curled across his face as he stood proudly on the auditorium's stage in his official police dress uniform.

"Walsh, why do you have to be bigfooting the rest of our awards?" The voice came from a man also dressed in an official uniform, just off stage. Recognizing the voice, Danny held his smile as he turned to greet him.

"What?" Danny replied, jokingly. "I've got no idea what you're talking about, Hector."

Hector Ramirez reached Danny and stuck out his hand. "C'mon. I've been waiting years now to make detective, and you've gotta charge your way into today's ceremony determined to be named Senior?"

Danny grabbed his hand to shake it. Ramirez leaned in, and they embraced each other, using their free arms to smack each other on the back.

"It's a good day, my friend." Danny said.

Hector was someone Danny had known for several years. A good patrol officer, he had been working hard in his precinct to reign in narcotics trafficking. His work and dedication would pay off today, as he was slated to be named a detective during the quarterly Command Change and Awards ceremony that the Chicago Police Department hosted at its headquarters. It was the same ceremony where Danny would also be recognized with his promotion to Senior Detective.

"So, this is my first one of these outside the academy. How's it supposed to go?" Ramirez asked.

Danny looked away from his friend and back out at the gathering audience. "You and I just got to stand up here and wait for the superintendent to call each of us over. And then, bask in the recognition and enjoy the fruits of our hard work."

"I guess some of those fruits taste pretty sweet to you right now, don't they?"

"How do you mean, pal?" Danny asked.

"What I mean is that it couldn't have come at a better time to wrap up that southside murder. And in a day, no less? Right before you're set to get promoted to senior."

Indeed, the timing couldn't have been better, thought Danny. Still, he demurred.

"It's all about the hard work, Hector. It pays off."

"Yeah, sometimes it's also about the pedigree you got. And speaking of that, it looks like your pedigree just walked in."

Danny narrowed his eyes and looked out to see his mother and father arrive in the auditorium. They slowly snaked their way through the crowd toward their seats in the front. As they did, they were quickly recognized by other, older officers and retired police personnel. Danny watched again and again as his father would catch the eye of others, heads would turn, and hands offered up to greet him as well as his wife Judy.

Danny watched, and as he did, his smile became a little more muted while a hint of anxiety seemed to move across his face.

Danny felt lost in his thoughts for a moment. Ramirez interrupted. "Right, Walsh? I mean, it must be great having your old man here today with the reputation he laid down during his time."

Danny knew all too well the reputation his father had built up during his time on the force. It was something constantly in the back of Danny's mind, the pressure of a standard that had been set and tied to Danny's last name.

"Walsh?" Ramirez said.

Danny's name was repeated yet again, but this time not by Ramirez.

"Walsh! So, are you ready for all this, son?" It was the superintendent of police who had joined the two of them on stage. A large, imposing man himself, he was also in his dress blue police uniform. His jacket was covered on one of its breast plates with ribbons and insignia, and he wore the trademark checkerboard, peaked service cap that covered his graying hair.

Ramirez seemed to take the cue that the Superintendent had come up specifically for Danny. He excused himself and moved to the opposite side of the stage, where others were gathering to be honored.

"Yes, sir. Definitely. I'm honored to be able to step up in this role for the force."

"You've been Johnny-on-the-spot with closing out your cases over the past couple of years. Not sure I've seen someone catch fire quite like it."

It was true. Danny had enjoyed a meteoric rise in notoriety and respect across the force for his effectiveness with resolving even the most puzzling of homicide cases. But it was owing much to when Danny started to get Craig involved in his cases. After having mixed success once he joined Homicide, Danny had decided to see if Craig's unique ability to re-create images might be useful in reconstructing crime scenes. There was no doubting that they had, even if Danny had to keep Craig's involvement in his success a secret.

"Just trying to wrap cases up as best I can, sir."

"Keep it up, son. You've had big shoes to fill." he said, nodding in the direction of where Danny's parents were getting seated. "But so far, no one can argue with the results."

"Thank you, sir."

The superintendent nodded and began to walk away. "See you in a few minutes at the lectern."

As he walked over to greet a few others near the stage, Danny glanced out at the audience again. Catching the eyes of his parents, he nodded stoically, to which they nodded in reply.

Danny walked over to join the dozen or so officers that were to be honored during the ceremony just as the Superintendent took to the lectern.

"To my fellow law enforcement members gathered here today, as well as the family and loved ones of those that will receive recognition this morning, I'd like to welcome you."

Following the ceremony, Danny was among a throng of people in the hallway just outside the auditorium. Jim and Judy Walsh made their way over to him, his mother wearing a wide smile.

"Hey, Mom."

"Daniel, I am so proud of you! Congratulations, dear." She met Danny in a warm embrace. Jim Walsh was right behind her.

"So? What do you think, Pops?" Danny asked.

Barely managing to grin, Jim Walsh responded "Well, I'd say it's about time."

"Oh, Jim." Judy feigned elbowing him in the ribs, encouraging him to lighten up.

"Nah, I'm just joking, son. It's good to see. I'm happy for you, if this is what you were aiming for."

"Aiming for?" Danny looked puzzled. "Of course. I mean, you of all people know how hard it is to make a mark in this line of work."

"Oh, absolutely." Jim agreed as he shook his head.

It caught Danny off guard as to why his dad might challenge his motivation for wanting to be promoted, let alone not even offering his hand to Danny in congratulations.

Danny was about to probe his father's reaction when Jim changed the subject.

"Where's Craig?"

Danny was surprised. "Excuse me? What do you mean?"

"I mean your cousin. Where is he?"

"I, uh, didn't invite him."

Judy Walsh furrowed the corner of her brow while Jim asked the obvious.

"What do you mean, son? Craig's family. I'm sure he'd want to be here to support you. Besides, he's been here in the city with you now for a few years. I'm sure he knows how important this would be to you."

"Ah, c'mon, dad. You know Craig. The police thing isn't exactly his speed. Besides . . . "

"Well, maybe Danny's right." Judy sought to smooth over a disagreement before it started.

"You probably need to give that some better thought next time, son," said Jim.

Feeling guilty, Danny sought to explain more when the conversation with his parents was interrupted.

"Detective Walsh," the voice called out.

Danny turned to respond but watched as an older man in uniform pushed past him and greeted his father.

"Jim Walsh! Why, I thought that was you I saw down front. How the hell are you?"

As Judy turned and joined in greeting an old colleague of his father, Danny slowly walked away from them as he muttered to himself: "I guess he was looking for the *elder* Detective Walsh."

Danny now stood by himself, lost in his thoughts. After his father called him out, he regretted not inviting Craig.

But at the same time, he wanted today to himself. He knew that he had become reliant on Craig more in the last year or so in solving cases. How much of his success and notoriety was owed to Craig's involvement, and how much would he have been able to accomplish on his own? He worried what the answer to that might be. He had grown to rationalize Craig's involvement as nothing more than any other investigative tool he might use to solve cases and bring killers to justice. Maybe that's why, subconsciously, he'd rather Craig didn't attend a day like today. Danny was convinced he was a good investigator. He just wasn't sure he could be an exceptional one without Craig's help.

"Big day today, Danny. You're coming into your own, aren't you?" A voice brought Danny back into the present.

Danny's current and continued superior officer, Eric Hammond, had come up alongside of him.

"Oh, hey, Eric. Thanks, man. I appreciate it."

"Catch you in a little bit of deep thought?"

"No. Everything's fine. Just, you know, the old man. Can't ever seem to figure him out."

"What's to figure out? I'm sure he's pretty damn proud of you today."

"Let's just say it's hard to see that sometimes, is all. And to figure out the little thing he'll say."

"How so?"

"Well, I was gonna explore that with him just now. Until someone calls out to 'Detective Walsh' from across the room, and it's not me they're looking for." Danny jabs a thumb behind him to draw Hammond's attention to the small group of officers surrounding his father.

"Ah, c'mon, Walsh. You know how these old timers are who are still around, or retired, and come to these things. They know how your old man still walks around with a few pieces of shrapnel in him."

"Yeah, yeah, I know."

"They respect who he is and how he did it. The old-fashioned way. No short cuts with your old man."

"Right. I know how my Pops did it." Danny stared at Hammond and what he wondered he might be insinuating.

"Anyway, big day for you and for the big, blue family with everybody getting recognized. Speaking of that, where's your boy?"

"Who's my boy?" Danny asked, visibly irked.

Hammond remained dispassionate. "You know who. I figured, since he's a relative, he'd probably be down here at this thing when you get recognized."

"He had to work," Danny said, tensing up.

"Oh, right. Got you."

"Listen, Sergeant," Danny addressed Hammond in a more formal way, purposely, "there's nothing you need to worry about with Craig's involvement in what we try to do. He's about as good in his core as anyone you'd find."

"Oh, c'mon, Danny. Lighten up. I'm not trying to get under your skin. You're just annoyed with trying to figure

out what's going on inside that head of your old man's. I told
you several years ago, that's something you shouldn't waste
energy on."

Danny's body language seemed to relax.

"As for your cousin, it's like I've said from the beginning.
I don't need to know the details of how he fits in with your
family or your work. And I don't want to know."

Danny took a deep breath. Hammond picked at the two
areas that Danny was stewing about: his father and Craig's
absence. Hammond went on.

"I just know that you've gotten damn good at your job,
Danny. Around the same time as when your cousin started
showing up at some crime scenes."

"So?"

"The way you've performed has allowed you to establish
quite a rep. That's both good and bad."

"The good part, I get," Danny said. "But the bad?"

"Yeah, bad in that you've got to keep it up. The department
has come to rely on you." Hammond went on to explain. "It
recognizes the value you're bringing with being able to find and
help catch all the bad guys out there. Once that expectation is
set, it's going to be awfully hard for people to dial that back.
You know?"

Danny pursed his lips and looked away from Hammond.

"That's a pressure, whether you're ready to acknowledge
it or not. It's also the type of thing that can make you a target.
Certainly for those with bad intentions. Whether they're
criminals or others on the force."

Danny started to laugh but noticed Hammond did not.

"So, what do you think the good part is?" Danny asked,
trying to pivot. "Distinguishing myself with my work; showing
I can be the man with this stuff?"

"No, just catching the bad guys will do," Hammond said as he sought to pull Danny away from self-interest.

"Well, yeah." Danny agreed.

He started to look over at his father when Hammond drew his attention back.

"I know your old man casts a long shadow, and that always seems to be on your mind. But you've gotta remember what this is all supposed to be about."

Danny started to open his mouth, then decided to remain silent and nod.

"Listen, I've got to run. But we'll catch up later." As Hammond walked off, he called back to Danny. "This is good stuff, detective. Proud of what you're doing for us."

As Hammond disappeared from the hallway, Danny glanced around. There were a number of people gathered in the hallway having conversations. His father was still surrounded by former colleagues and friends. Danny was left to himself and a growing sense of self-doubt.

5

GREY, PARKER, & HARRIS

Monk's Coffee Pot wasn't far from Craig's modest apartment at the edge of Wicker Park. On a typical early autumn morning like this, Craig wouldn't mind walking the few blocks to meet with Danny. But this morning was a little tougher. Craig hadn't slept well the past couple of nights. Both the re-creation with Danny and the session with Dr. Burris had left him feeling confused and dissatisfied, robbing him of his usual morning energy.

It was nearly 7:30 when he entered the coffee shop, scanned the large sitting area, and spotted a two-seater near the front. He figured he'd wait for Danny to arrive before ordering, but as the minutes dragged on, he felt increasingly awkward waiting at the table by himself.

He looked around. Observing the other patrons made him feel more engaged with life. Some sat by themselves, passing time with a newspaper as they sipped their morning coffee. Others in pairs: business colleagues starting their workday before going to the office. A couple embraced and kissed as they rose to leave their table, parting for the day. Everyone seemed to be involved with something, or someone. Glancing down at the table, Craig tried not to think that if it weren't for meeting Danny here occasionally, he would probably be one of the few in the coffee shop who stood out as being alone.

Then Craig noticed a young woman sitting by herself

toward the back of the shop at another two-seat table. He caught her eye, but she quickly looked down at a few papers in front of her and stirred her coffee. He kept staring at her. She was pretty, and he was sure he had seen her before. Dressed in business casual—dark slacks, modest heels, and a brown knit top—with auburn hair that fell to her shoulders in thick curls and waves. She had a beautiful, tanned face, and eyes that almost seemed to sense the weight of Craig's stare. She peered back in his direction from the corner of her eye as her head bent down toward the papers.

Realizing he'd been looking at her for an uncomfortable period of time, Craig began to worry that it might seem like he was leering at her. Danny still hadn't arrived, and to avoid appearing odd sitting alone and staring down some pretty girl, he got up to get a coffee despite not being a coffee drinker.

He walked over to the counter where the thermoses of prepared coffees were arrayed and picked one that sounded interesting. Repeating *Colombian Blend* in his mind, he began pumping it into a cup, still watching surreptitiously to see if the young woman might be looking at him again. She was, and his heart beat faster with excitement—maybe there was a connection.

He knew he had to get back to the table before someone else took it, but he was trying to focus on several actions at once: finish filling the coffee cup, adjust the sleeve so he could hold it, and peek again to see if the woman was still watching him. As he spun around to head back toward his table, his mind distracted, he collided with the customer behind him. It was a man in work clothes and hard hat, who had been sprayed by the contents of Craig's cup that had spilled onto his shirt and pants.

The man stepped back in annoyance, grimacing as the hot liquid landed.

"Oh, jeez," said Craig. "I'm so sorry."

"What the fuck, pal? Watch where the hell you're going!"

Craig's preoccupation with the girl vanished instantly, replaced with the embarrassment of having screwed up. "I'm sorry," he repeated. "I didn't realize you'd snuck up behind me there. Let me help you get some napkins or something."

"Dude, I've got it. But get your head out of your ass, huh?"

Craig grew irritated as the man's rising voice called attention to his clumsiness, just as he thought he'd captured the girl's attention.

"Whatever." Craig's shook his head dismissively. "It shouldn't be such a big deal . . . " His voice trailed off.

The man's eyes grew wide, and he stepped in front of Craig in an aggressive posture. "Are you kidding me? You've got a lot of fucking nerve to be annoyed at *me*, you know."

Craig just wanted to go sit down again and try to be inconspicuous, but the man's over-the-top reaction was making that increasingly hard. Now he was barring Craig's path, clearly intent on creating an issue between them. "Listen, asshole," the man growled, "maybe someone needs to teach you some manners." He reached an arm out and gripped Craig tightly by the shoulder. He was taller than Craig, thin but athletic. In an instant, the man's grasp tightened and he seemed about to pull Craig toward him.

Alarmed, Craig instinctively dropped what remained of his coffee and grabbed the man's hand with both of his own, digging his thumbs into the palm in the soft spot near the thumb. Keeping his grip, he stepped back and twisted the man's wrist up above his head in a painful joint lock. The man's knees buckled, and he bellowed in pain so loudly that it startled Craig. He released the man's hand.

He froze for a fraction of a second, both worried that he'd broken the man's wrist and surprised that the technique had genuinely worked as well as it did. He could see that the man was about to lunge at him, escalating the confrontation into a full-blown fight. Wide-eyed with fear, he watched as the man came at him again, this time with both hands.

Suddenly, a muscled arm in a thin jacket sleeve grabbed the man by his collar and drove him against a wall. It was Danny. "You got a problem here, buddy? Going after my friend like that?"

Danny's large frame and imposing strength kept the man firmly pinned. Rather than pursue what would be a lost cause and try to wrest free from Danny's grip, the man began to complain. "What the hell is it with you, man? Let me the fuck go!"

With one arm still bracing the man, Danny grabbed his wallet from inside his coat, flipped it open, and held his police shield just inches from the man's face. "See this, buddy? This is what's with me. I need to make sure you stop causing problems in this nice place. Now, why don't you just move along and get outta here—walk it off. Go on into work and get yourself cleaned up."

By now, all activity in the coffee shop had stopped, the customers taking in the back-and-forth between Danny and the angry man. Craig stood apart from them awkwardly, feeling like a coward because his cousin had to rescue him. He didn't dare turn to see the pretty girl's reaction to what had unfolded.

"All right, all right, I'll leave. But it was this asshole and his mouth that started all of it. You gotta talk to him too, you know."

Danny released him, and the man straightened himself and prepared to leave.

"Go on, there. Mosey along, buddy."

Danny seemed to enjoy the moments when he could use both his position of authority and his physical strength to control a situation. He kept talking loudly and drawing a lot of attention—unwelcome attention in Craig's view. He tended to resent Danny's help in these situations; it always seemed to make things worse and make Craig look like a weakling.

As the man left the coffee shop, Danny turned to Craig, already joking, "I can't leave you alone for a second, now can I?"

Largely ignoring Danny's comment, Craig headed back over to the table.

"Craig. Hey, what about coffee?" Danny said as though the confrontation had never happened.

Back in his chair, Craig flashed his cousin an exasperated look and signaled for him to forget the coffee and just sit down. Danny followed Craig back to the table as an employee emerged to pick up the strewn coffee cup and towel up the area.

"Why do you always have to do stuff like that?" Craig asked, so quietly he was almost inaudible.

"Well, someone's got to. Hey, there's one thing for sure— that judo stuff you learned when we were younger really seems to work."

"It's called *aikido*." Craig corrected him as he scanned the back of the coffee shop where the girl had been seated.

"Well, whatever the hell it's called, it works. But maybe

you need to focus just a little bit more on what the second move would be, huh?"

Craig ignored Danny's sarcasm, taking note instead that the girl he'd been trading glances with was now gone, probably having slipped out the side entrance during the scuffle. Staring off into space, he felt deflated.

"Uh, you're welcome there, Craig . . . Earth to Craig."

Craig shook his head slightly. "What's up, Danny?" His tone reflected his annoyance with his cousin following the events at the crime scene, now compounded by yet another insinuation that Craig couldn't take care of himself without Danny looking out for him.

"Hey, guess what," Danny said, seeming not to notice Craig's displeasure. "The good news is now official, my friend. I'm gonna be the new senior investigator for the precinct."

"Wow. That is good news. Congrats, Danny. Really, it is. How do Jim and Judy feel?"

"Mom and Dad, they're good with it. Of course, Dad was all, 'It's about time, boy.'"

"Well, your dad's never been the sentimental type."

Danny leaned toward Craig and lowered his voice. "Listen. You know how much I appreciate your help with these cases. I, um, I'm gonna need to know that I can still count on you now and then. You know what I mean?"

Even if it came out as a question, it sounded more like a demand.

"Wait. Hold on. You know I don't like anything about any of this. I don't like that I can do it, and I don't like that it's this big secret . . . and I don't like . . . " His voice was rising now, to the point where Danny gestured with his hands for Craig to lower it. Craig resumed more quietly. "I don't like feeling like some sideshow freak. Heck, Danny. I worry that it's only a matter of time before we slip up, get noticed by somebody, and then it's *me* who gets in trouble for interfering, or worse. I could get locked up in some psych ward because they can't explain what the hell this stuff is all about."

"Craig, just listen. You and I are the only ones who know you can do this, and that's the way it's always gonna be. Tell me that you don't get satisfaction when you help me get these scumbags. Seriously, man. Think about the justice you help bring. And you know that you shouldn't worry about getting in any kind of trouble. Remember—I'm a cop, and I've got your back no matter what, just like I always have. Now I need you to have my back."

Craig let him finish pleading his case, as usual. Although Danny may not have been trying to guilt Craig into feeling that he ought to help him, given all he and the Walshes had done for him, he couldn't help but interpret it that way.

He sighed and looked out the window. This was always the part of Danny's argument with which Craig had the toughest time. While Craig may have hinted at his supernatural ability to Dr. Burris in their sessions, he and Danny were thus far alone in knowing this secret. That, coupled with how much Danny's family had helped him, made Craig feel like he owed his cousin.

"Follow me for a minute on this, Danny. You wanted to make senior detective, or investigator, or whatever. Well, now you've got it. Whatever edge I gave you, it's gotten you where you want to be. This should be it, then."

"C'mon, Craig. I need you to help me *stay* in the role. Besides, you know how much easier it will be to get you on scene now? It won't be nearly as awkward as it's been before with Hammond or the others around."

At the mention of Sergeant Hammond, Craig recalled

several uncomfortable encounters with him near crime scenes with Danny. His eyes narrowed. "So, what exactly have you told Hammond about my being there?"

"Nothing, Craig. Listen. Don't worry, all right? Eric's good people. He just thinks you've got a little intuition, a little sixth sense that I can use. And he doesn't ask questions, so long as we keep getting the bad guys." His tone turned more serious. "Which is another reason I need to know that you're on board. I can't go letting people down now. The department has a ton of faith in me. And my dad? Well, you know what a hardass he is. I need him to know that I'm every bit the cop he was. You know? It's really important that we know we can count on you."

Danny's use of "we" caught Craig off guard. He wasn't sure if Danny meant those in the police force or his aunt and uncle. But he didn't really want to ask him what he meant.

Seeming to notice the tension his request was creating, Danny changed the subject. "Anyway, once you meet Emma, you'll want to keep me in good standing and all. She's really awesome."

"So, Emma is this mystical, everyday girl who's captured your heart, huh?"

"Yep!" Danny's eyes lit up. "Craig, she'll blow you away. She's beautiful and funny . . . and *smart!*"

"You're saying this won't be one we have to sound out the menu selections for?" Craig chuckled.

Danny rolled his eyes and shook his head. "Dude, you're killing me. Just you wait and see. What about tomorrow night? If you don't have plans, let's do Santori's."

"Yeah, okay. I can probably make tomorrow work." Craig didn't want to sound like he was completely devoid of a social life. "But listen. We aren't done talking about the other stuff. I know we won't be able to talk about it at dinner, but I'm not letting it go."

"Craig, come on. Simmer. One thing at a time. Meet my beautiful new girlfriend first, okay? Let's do seven tomorrow."

He stood up and clasped his hands together. "Listen, I've gotta bolt. And I truly appreciate what you can do and how you've helped me. Okay?" With that, he spun around and was gone, leaving Craig by himself at the table.

◆—◆◆—◆

Meeting with Danny had made Craig late for work. While he never really looked forward to his job, this morning he felt even worse. As he rode the L downtown, his mood matched the overcast sky against the downtown Chicago skyline. His mind wandered between thoughts of the recent crime scene re-creation, the unfulfilling therapy session, feeling used by Danny, and missing out on a chance to connect with the girl at the coffee shop. All of it coupled with the daily grind of a job he didn't really care about. *Senior staff accountant at a midsize accounting firm?* Craig thought to himself. There had to be something else in the world for him.

The lobby of the high-rise that housed Craig's firm was busier than usual. He was at the end of several waves of people standing in line for the elevators. He noticed that two of the four cars that went to the twentieth floor and above were out of service. He closed his eyes in resignation. Since the accounting firm of Grey, Parker, & Harris was on the twenty-first and twenty-second floors, he knew he'd be even later.

After several groups of people had entered one of the two operating elevators, he unsuccessfully tried to wedge his way

onto the next one to arrive. "Are you kidding me?" he said as
the doors closed, the occupants trying to pretend they hadn't
seen him as they squeezed on.

Just then, he heard a cheery voice from behind him. "It
just isn't your day yet, is it?"

He turned. It was the girl from the coffee shop. "Oh, hey.
Hi!" He squinted one eye closed and asked, "From Monk's,
right? Yeah, I know. My rhythm's a little off today."

He hadn't had time to get nervous, and his start to the
conversation belied how tightly he was normally wound when
trying to make a good impression.

"Oh, I don't know. It's not every day that someone gets
one of Chicago's finest as their personal bodyguard."

"That? Oh, right. He's my cousin. I was meeting him there
this morning. He tends to have a few . . . impulse issues."

"Impulse issues with law enforcement? Now I'm definitely
feeling safer."

She was funny, Craig thought, but he was starting to feel
his usual nervousness and unease creep in. Not knowing
where he should take the conversation next, he opted to be
general. "So, I'm Craig. I work in national accounts on the
twenty-second floor."

A single ding announced the arrival of the only other
elevator in service. They made their way onto it by themselves.

"I thought you looked familiar," she said as the doors
closed and they started up. "Henriksen, right?"

"How did you know?" Puzzled, Craig was nevertheless
pleased that somehow she knew his name.

"Oh, I guess I just have a knack for linking faces and
names."

Craig was feeling more and more at ease with each word
she spoke. "But wait. I thought it was, like, you're either a

names person or a faces person. You can't be both, can you?" he said playfully.

"Well, I guess that makes me special, then, doesn't it?"

"I guess it does. Miss . . . ?"

"I'm Lauren," she said as she reached out and shook Craig's hand.

Her hand felt soft and warm. The doors opened at the twenty-first floor.

"Well, this is my stop," Lauren said as she started off the elevator.

"Wait." Craig said, not wanting to miss another chance. "Lauren . . . what?"

"Harris. Lauren Harris." she said.

Craig furrowed his brow as he thought aloud. "Harris. Where have I heard that name before?"

As the elevator doors closed, Lauren said, "I don't know, maybe in the title of your accounting firm. Maybe?" She flashed Craig a devilish smile as he suddenly understood.

⸻ ◆◆◆ ⸻

The next morning, Craig woke before his alarm went off. Maybe it was because of his encounter with Lauren Harris the previous day, but his mood had shifted: he had nervous but positive energy that was unusual for him. As he moved about his apartment getting ready for work, he found himself thinking through daily activities that normally took no time at all. He was careful to make sure he was clean shaven, but not to the point where he might nick his cheek and make it bleed. He paid extra attention to how he styled his hair; he lingered on his choice of dress shirt and even took extra time to iron the wrinkles from his slacks.

He was out of the apartment and headed toward the L

well before seven. As he rode downtown, he found his mind running through possible lines he could say to Lauren when he got to work, rehearsing what would come off as most natural.

As he approached his building, he almost forgot to buy the newspaper he would pretend to read as he waited for her in the lobby. He didn't want to seem like he was stalking her, so he had thought through how he could look natural passing time before heading to his floor. Maybe he could even act as if he was waiting on a friend.

At around 7:45, he noticed her walking toward the building with a throng of others arriving for the day. It was warm, and the sun was shining through the clouds, illuminating the people as they came through the revolving doors. Craig thought Lauren looked just as lovely as yesterday; today she wore a dark, conservative dress with a jean jacket over it. As she came through the door, she seemed to spot him immediately—and his mind went blank. He couldn't remember any of the phrases he'd rehearsed, so instead he pretended to be engrossed in his newspaper. Out of the corner of his eye, he saw her approach and stop several feet in front of him.

"So, no coffee today?" she said.

Craig looked up, feigning surprise. "Oh, hey! Lauren, right? Two days in a row now, I guess."

Lauren's smile suggested that she knew he'd been waiting in the lobby in the hopes of catching her on her way in. "I just started going to Monk's when I moved into Wicker Park a few weeks ago. I thought I might see you there again."

Surprised to hear that she'd actually been looking forward to seeing him, Craig didn't know how to respond. "So, Lauren, how do you know my name, and how are you related to Jeffrey Harris?" he awkwardly plowed ahead with one of his rehearsed phrases.

"Well, *Mr.* Henriksen, since you seem to have taken to your brother's line of inquiry . . . "

Craig didn't want to correct her on his relationship to Danny and disrupt their playful banter.

"Let's see. I've told you how I'm good with names, so that explains the whole knowing who you are thing. As for Mr. Harris, I just call him Dad."

Craig cocked his head. "Dad? Really? Wow, okay. So I should probably be *really* nice to you."

"You mean you *weren't* going to be nice to me?" she shot back with half a grin.

"Oh, I've got a ton of questions now, for sure."

"Uh-huh," she encouraged him.

Craig felt his confidence soar. "Lunch. That's it," he said, as if the idea had just dawned on him. "I've at least got to buy the boss's daughter lunch. Are you busy today?"

Lauren crinkled one eye shut, looking genuinely unsure. "Hmm—" she started before Craig jumped in again.

"Or not. I mean, I totally get it if you can't." And just like that, Craig felt a rush of embarrassment. Had he overstepped?

"No, it's not that," she said, apparently trying to put him at ease. "I've just got meetings stacked up before and after lunch. Plus, I've got to be out of town the next few days, and I'm trying to wedge a bunch of work in before I go."

Part of him was happy that he'd gotten up the courage to catch up with her before she left. Another part was disappointed; it seemed like she was going to be too busy, or maybe not interested enough, to have lunch with him.

She nodded her head as if to convince herself. "No, wait.

Yes, we could totally do lunch if you're okay with just staying here and eating in the cafeteria. Would that work?"

Craig's eyes lit up. "For sure, yeah." Then, trying to not seem so eager, he continued, "Then I can get a little more background on this whole good-with-names thing and your dad running the place."

"That's fair enough. So . . . Craig . . . " She extended her hand to shake his as she had done yesterday.

Craig shook. "Lauren—"

"Lunch then. Noon sharp? I've got to get upstairs now to get prepped for a meeting."

"Yup, got it. I'll get out of your way and . . . " He tried to remember what he told her about what he was doing in the lobby. "I'll finish reading my paper."

Her face was in full smile as she nodded. "Okay, then. See you soon."

She turned, flashed her fingers in a small wave, and was in the elevator before Craig could think through their brief conversation.

As he looked down at the paper he had folded in half in front of him, he smiled at himself. He'd been holding the paper upside down the whole time they were chatting.

◆◆◆

There were some reports Craig could have worked on that morning, but his mind was abuzz with his upcoming lunch. He'd always been very shy around women, which made it hard to find a way to strike up a conversation. Lauren's reaching out to him first had removed that initial pressure, and Craig was intent on making the most of this chance.

Right at noon, he met her at the cafeteria entrance, and they both went about getting their meals. For Craig, a sub sandwich and chips. Lauren had a decidedly healthier angle: a salad of mixed greens, an apple, and kale chips. After they had each paid, they headed to a quiet part of the cafeteria and found a table with a nice view of Lake Michigan.

At Craig's prompting about how she had known his name and when she had come to work for her dad's accounting firm, Lauren opened up and shared liberally. She was a psychology major just a few years out of Northwestern. She had a myriad of interests that hadn't yet lined her up for a reliable full-time job, and her father had suggested she work at the firm until she could land something more permanent. She'd been working in HR, which explained her connecting faces of the firm's employees with their names and work groups. Craig's information had stuck out to her—although she didn't yet share why.

He'd finished most of his sandwich while Lauren had made little progress on her salad. She had been talking most of the time as Craig listened intently, offering more questions that led Lauren to share even more of her history. "So, you can probably tell that I've been spending way too much time in the HR file room by myself. I haven't given you a chance to tell me the big 'Craig backstory' yet. So what about you? Has accounting always been what you wanted to do?"

Craig almost choked on the last bite of his sub. "Oh, God, no. I mean, don't get me wrong, GPH is great," he said, affecting a mock formal tone that made Lauren chuckle. "And I'm sure your dad does a wonderful job leading this place. But no. I guess I just always thought a profession like this would be a safe bet. One where I could always be sure to have a decent job."

"So, that's fulfilling to you?" Her voice trailed up, making it into a question.

"Oh, I don't know. What's fulfilling, really? I mean, I like to hear about people who have some perfect job for their personality and all. But how many people do you know who can really make that happen?"

"So, you don't think everyone was put here for a purpose, a calling or something? Ah, come on, Craig. You've just listened to me ramble on for the better part of our lunch. Now it's your turn to share."

Craig had never done well when the tables were turned this way. Opening up just wasn't part of his nature. He wanted to be able to share with Lauren, but he remained guarded. He ignored her invitation and tried to direct the conversation away from himself. "But really. Do you know anyone who's living out their life *exactly* as they dreamed?"

"Oh, I was *so* close to learning more about you, wasn't I?" she said. "Okay. Yes, sure. I have a girlfriend from college who's making a real run at playing folk music on her guitar in small clubs throughout the city. She's really good, but she's broke and constantly working odd jobs to pay her bills. But you know what? She loves it."

"Folk music? Yikes. And she actually gets hired by clubs around here?"

"Hired, or plays for fun." said Lauren. "But she enjoys it. Isn't that all that matters?"

"Hmm. Not sure if I buy that."

"Well, then, let me show you. She's actually playing a small club near the art school tonight. Come along, and you can see for yourself."

A first date so soon? Craig thought. But then he remembered his promise to have dinner with Danny and meet his new girlfriend. "Aw, crap. I can't do it tonight."

Lauren smiled. "Think you'll hate the music that much?"

"No, it's just I have to meet the guy you saw me with at the coffee shop tonight for dinner. He's my cousin, and he works—"

"CPD with the impulse issues, right?"

"Right. But how about doing something else this week? It doesn't have to be folk music."

"Okay, but only if I get to learn more about the elusive Mr. Henriksen. I'll tell you what. I'll go out with you"—Craig hoped his eyebrows didn't visibly rise like they felt they had— "so long as you pick the spot. And it has to be a place that appeals to you, someplace where you'll be comfortable opening up. Whether it's a baseball game or a comic book shop."

They both laughed.

"Or whatever. I just want you to pick somewhere you really like so I can get a better idea of who the real Craig Henriksen is."

The idea actually sounded inviting to Craig. He didn't hesitate with what sprang into his head first. "Okay, then how about the Field Museum some late afternoon?"

Lauren nodded. "Interesting. Sounds good. It's been years since I've been there."

"All right then, how about tomorrow?" Craig wanted to lock it in before she changed her mind.

"Oh, wait. I've got to be up in Evanston the rest of the week helping the firm recruit. But I could do Saturday. Does that work?"

Saturday was further away than Craig had hoped for, but their lunch was coming to an end, and he couldn't think of any alternatives.

Lauren glanced at her watch. "Oh, gosh, I've got to get

back upstairs. Here." She scribbled her cell phone number on a napkin and gave it to him. "Just call me Thursday and let me know what time you want to meet."

He took the napkin as she got up to leave. She touched his hand, and he looked up at her. "I get to hear more about you this weekend, right?"

"Right," he agreed.

As she turned and hurried out of the cafeteria, Craig, unblinking, watched her leave. He looked at the number on the napkin in his hand and smiled.

For the rest of the day, he felt energized. He pushed through several projects with ease, struck up conversations with people on his floor that he hadn't talked to before, and took notice of just how nice the late autumn day was. The effects of his lunch with Lauren and the promise of meeting up with her over the weekend made the tension of the past few days seem to disappear.

6

ROTINI AND RED WINE

As he rode home on the L that afternoon, Craig hadn't yet thought much about meeting Danny and his new girlfriend for dinner. He'd been pulled into so many "auditions" of Danny's girlfriends that it only served to highlight that the women his cousin chose, while always attractive, were usually a bit dim and crude. This time, perhaps buoyed by his lunch with Lauren, Craig felt like he was heading into the dinner with fresh eyes. *Who's to say that Danny hasn't gotten his act together this time?* he thought.

By the time he arrived home, he barely had a chance to shower and change before making his way back outside to hail a cab and travel north to Santori's Restaurant.

When Danny's father was a beat cop in the area, he'd gotten to know Arturo Santori well. And as Craig pursued his career in Chicago and Danny progressed through the police force, Arturo treated them like family; Santori's had become a familiar rendezvous for dinner. It was probably for this reason—and because Danny always liked to be noticed—that he chose this setting to introduce Craig to his new girlfriend. Danny had also mentioned that she worked north of Wrigley, which made Santori's a good midpoint. *Emma was her name, wasn't it?* Craig thought.

By the time the cab dropped him in front of the restaurant, it was just past seven and there was barely anything remaining of the sunset that had illuminated the horizon. An older restaurant, Santori's was appointed in authentic Italian style. Craig knew that, with Arturo in charge, Danny wouldn't be waiting for a table.

Arturo's eyes lit up when he saw Craig. "Ah, it's you after all. I'd have thought for sure that Daniel was playing with me if I weren't seeing you now."

"Artie. Hi. How have you been?"

Arturo made his way from behind the host podium to embrace Craig. "Oh, I have so many aches and pains at my age that it would bore you to death to hear, and it might distract you from the wonderful food I have for you tonight."

Artie was in his seventies but spry and alert, even as he seemed to have gotten smaller and more stooped over the years. He pulled back from his embrace and held Craig by the shoulders to look at him. "So, why on earth would I do that to you, eh?"

"Exactly," Craig replied and smiled.

"I see your cousin and this beautiful young lady in here a lot lately. But you"—Artie teasingly wagged a finger at him—"you need to come in to see me more."

"You're right, Artie. I do. So, is he here already? I don't see him."

"Oh yes, of course. They've been here for some time. I have them seated in the back at one of the more private booths." Artie leaned in to Craig. "Daniel requested it. I don't think this delicate new flower of his is yet used to your cousin's—how do I say it—gregarious ways."

Artie marched Craig purposefully to the back of the busy restaurant, showed Craig to the table, and then quickly bowed away. Danny was snuggled up next to a small, gentle-looking woman. He noticed Craig at once.

"And speak of the devil, there he is!" Danny said. "Craig Henriksen, meet Emma Holt."

Craig was relieved when Danny introduced her by name so he could be sure he had remembered it correctly. Emma rose, leaving Danny seated as she embraced Craig.

"I've heard so much about you, Craig. It's wonderful to meet you in person!"

As she hugged him, Craig looked over her shoulder at Danny, whose eyebrows rose in a so-what-do-you-think? expression.

Emma was petite, with straight dark-brown hair that fell midway down her back and was drawn back with hair clips on each side. Craig's first impression was that she was nice, very pretty, and well spoken. This was definitely a change from the bawdy, more vivacious women Danny usually dated.

"You too. I'm glad we got the chance to get together. I've heard a lot about you as well," Craig lied.

Danny spoke up as Craig settled in. "Don't let him fool you, Em. I've kinda kept you under wraps with the family 'till now. This is your big debut."

Emma nudged him with her elbow, and Danny playfully feigned discomfort. Craig registered Danny's mention of "family," which gave him pause. He'd never heard Danny refer to him in that way in front of someone.

"Craig, you can't imagine how I've looked forward to meeting some of Danny's family these past months."

Now it was Craig's eyebrows that rose. He hadn't realized the two had been seeing each other for so long. *Why has Danny kept her away from me and his parents until now?* he wondered.

"Every time Danny and I talked about getting the three of us together, something was always going on. Danny's told me how busy you are with work."

Craig maintained a polite smile as he cocked his head in Danny's direction with a "what's up, pal?" look.

"Well come on, we're finally all together now. Let's order," Danny offered with a sheepish grin.

As the wine and courses of fine Italian food flowed, Craig found himself easily engaging in enjoyable conversation with Emma. She was originally from St. Louis and an elementary school teacher a few years younger than Craig. She spoke idealistically about teaching children and the positive impact she hoped to have on their lives. Her quick wit and intelligence made it easy to keep the conversation moving from topic to topic. As they made their way through one bottle of red wine and part of another, Craig noticed that Danny sometimes seemed uncomfortable and left out of the more intellectual discussions where he either didn't know the topic well or didn't care. Craig almost felt sorry that he seemed to be struggling to keep up. Still, Danny intermittently found a way to interject some law enforcement angle into the conversation.

"I couldn't believe that my landlord actually tried to cheat me out of the deposit." Emma was describing an issue she'd had with the apartment she'd just left.

"And you can bet there was no way I was gonna let him get away with that stuff," Danny weighed in.

Craig took note that Danny didn't curse at all in front of Emma, something he might normally be prone to do. Several times during dinner, Danny would wrap his burly arm around her petite shoulder, and Emma would melt into his embrace. Craig could also see that Danny provided comfort and protection that Emma seemed to soak up.

At one point, Emma surprised Craig by making a reference to him having an influence on Danny's career. "I just think it's great that you're able to help Danny with his police work."

The comment pulled Craig out of what had been a light conversation. "Oh? How's that?" He glanced over quickly at his cousin.

"I mean, he always talks about this great intuition you have," she continued.

"Does he?" Craig noticed Danny taking a full drink from his wine glass. "I guess I don't mind being someone that our crime fighter here can bounce his different theories off of."

Craig was curious to see if Emma would go any deeper into what Danny may have shared with her. Clearly, Danny had intimated something to her about Craig's role in his investigations.

"I just think it's so nice that you two kept close as you grew up together after, well, what happened to your father. Oh, I'm sorry . . . " Her voice trailed off in a whisper, as if she realized too late that it was something he probably didn't want to address. There was an uncomfortable silence as she reached for her wine glass.

Craig could clearly see how genuinely smitten with each other the two of them were, and that Emma lived up to the billing Danny had given her. Considering this, and still feeling in a positive mood from his lunch with Lauren, he decided to let both of them off this uncomfortable hook. "Well, you're right. A kid couldn't ask for anyone better than Danny to help him through difficult times. Heck, any little thing that I can help him with now, well, it's just the right thing to do."

"I completely agree!" Emma seemed all too happy to steer away from the subject of Craig's dad's death. "I could only wish that my family looked after each other the way I've heard the Walshes do."

They'd been at the table for close to two hours now, but to Craig it hadn't seemed long at all. They were debating the pros and cons of the various desserts Artie had shown them when Danny's phone rang, and he began fumbling inside his jacket pocket to get it. As Emma asked if he really needed to answer it, Craig thought about what Danny may have told her about how "close" they'd always been. Certainly, they'd relied on one another in different ways. Craig had his strange supernatural ability that benefited Danny and the work he did. For Craig, Danny was a way to stay connected to the outside world—keeping him from being too much of a recluse.

Danny ended the phone call and seemed to think aloud as he said, "Hmm. That's odd. Hammond is swinging by in a few minutes. He must want to keep something off the grid." He turned to Emma. "I'm sorry, baby, but I'm gonna need to step out in a few minutes and see what's going on. Go ahead and order dessert."

"Sure," Craig agreed.

"Can't he just come in here to talk, Danny?" asked Emma.

"He said he had some confidential stuff to talk about, so probably not. Besides, Hammond hates Italian. Craig knows."

Craig didn't know, but nodded, taking a bite of what remained of his rotini. Given Danny's reaction to the call, he wondered what the real reason was for Danny slipping out for a few minutes.

Ten minutes later, and the better part of a tiramisu they were sharing, Danny stepped out.

"So, what about your folks, Emma? Do you get back to St. Louis to see them much?" Craig asked.

She appeared instantly uncomfortable. For whatever reason, Craig felt like he had inadvertently hit a nerve.

"Um, well, sometimes. I don't know. I just think it's better that I've established a good circle of friends here in Chicago. I love my school and the kids. And now I've also got Danny. I guess it makes me less homesick, so I don't feel like I have to go back and visit too often."

Craig rambled on about how it must have been tough for her when she first moved to the city. Unknowingly, and probably confused from the slight buzz he felt from the red wine, he inadvertently reached for Emma's wine glass, thinking it was his. Before she could politely indicate his mistake, Craig raised the glass, but as it touched his lips, he froze. His vision was instantly blurred and fuzzy, a myriad of images began flashing through his mind's eye. At first he saw Emma, just as she looked to him now. Then, an image of a face much younger, as a child. Different images where her face flashed of fear, dread, all while tears gathered in her eyes. Craig heard the echoes of the deep voice of a man. The man's face flashed though Craig's mind. It was hard, with narrowing eyes and a clenched jaw. His hands grabbed at Emma, forcefully, inappropriately. Emma pleaded, "No, Daddy. Please, don't!" The words reverberated through Craig's mind. Craig strained to see what was happening to the child, tried to decipher what the man was doing to her. But just as instantly as the flood of the images had appeared in his mind, they receded just as quickly, ebbing away until all that was left was the wine glass, held against his lips.

As his vision cleared, Emma's face came into focus. She looked panicked, mortified. Her eyes began to well with tears as she looked back at Craig. He couldn't tell how long he'd been lost inside his own head. It felt like several minutes, but he was sure it was probably only a matter of moments. Either way, those eyes that returned his gaze somehow could sense that he knew of what had happened to her, as if he had peered directly into her memory.

Free of the spell that had momentarily woven their minds together, he raced to try to comfort her. "Emma. Hey, is everything all right?"

He placed the wine glass back on the table and desperately tried to arrest her tears. "What's wrong?" he asked.

"You know, don't you?" she whispered. "You were able to sense it or something. But you *know*, don't you, Craig? I didn't really believe Danny when he told me how you had some kind of . . . ability to see what's hidden to others."

Before Craig could answer, fear flashed in her eyes. "Oh, Craig, please. *Please.* You can't tell Danny. He mustn't know. Oh my goodness, it will kill me if he finds out."

Craig leaned across the table and grabbed her gently but firmly by the shoulder. "Emma, look at me. Just hang on. I don't know what Danny's told you, but I can't do anything special. I just . . . I don't know. I sensed that things were rough for you growing up. Like me. Right?"

His attempt to distract her and bring the conversation back to his own past experiences didn't work. She looked scared and desperate.

"Craig, do you promise? I mean, really promise? Danny told me how good you are inside, so I know you won't lie. Do you promise that you'll never tell him? He's the most wonderful thing to ever happen to me. I can't lose him."

How good I am inside? Where does this come from? he wondered. *It doesn't sound like something Danny'd say.* He brushed the thought aside, taking Emma's hand in both of his. "You have my word. I can see how much he cares for you too. I would never want to say anything to him that would make you feel ashamed or uncomfortable. But you know, Danny would understand if you've been through some tough times."

He could see that Emma believed him, but her eyes had grown wide when he'd said the word *ashamed*.

She shook her head as if to protest. "No. I always hear from Danny that he doesn't like to have to be around people who have had . . . unpleasant things happen to them in his line of work. I can't let him see me like that," she said with a finality that made Craig understand the conversation was over.

Over the next several minutes, they tried to force small talk as she composed herself. When Danny reappeared at the table, Craig and Emma were all smiles, but Danny gave Emma a questioning look. "What's wrong, baby? What happened?"

"Oh, nothing. It's just, well, Craig was telling me about how hard it was when he was younger, and I guess I got a little emotional."

Danny looked relieved, even if it might have been at the expense of Craig's discomfort.

"You see, Craig? Is this girl awesome or what?"

"She's truly special, no doubt about that—so what did Hammond want?"

"Nothing. I mean, it's nothing. Just a few messages coming in to the department aimed at me. Just some crackpot." Danny turned to Emma as he sat back down at the table. "Don't you worry about a thing." He smiled boastfully. "You know I can take care of myself."

As Danny and Emma resumed their playful banter, Craig found himself wondering how his simple contact with

Emma's glass could have ignited his "ability." This had never happened before. He didn't dare bring it up with his cousin, lest he betray the delicate confidence that Emma had just placed in him. Plus, they looked genuinely happy and well suited to one another: Danny was the strong protector, but also a little less cerebral and more one-dimensional. Emma was clearly very sensitive, sweet, and delicate. But complex. She no doubt needed someone like Danny in order to feel safe, considering all she had apparently been through.

Dinner had been so engaging and the episode with Emma so intense that Craig was surprised to see that it was already ten fifteen when he checked his watch. "Jeez, guys. I have to get going. I didn't know how late it was. I've got to be at work a little early tomorrow. Danny, any chance we can do Monk's?"

"No can do, sorry. I need to get with Hammond in the a.m. and see who or from where these little love notes are coming. I'll be in touch in a day or two." He turned to Emma, whose hand he was holding. "Plus, you said I could stop in to see you during your class tomorrow, right?"

Craig stood up. "I understand. No big deal. I'll leave the two of you to finish your evening." Craig patted his back pocket where his wallet was, a way to offer to help pay for the meal. Danny wrinkled his nose and gently shook his head, indicating he intended to pick up the check.

"Emma, it has been an absolute pleasure to meet you tonight." Craig turned and smiled at Danny as he finished the sentence.

"Very nice, bro. We'll talk soon," replied Danny.

"You too, Craig," Emma added. "I'm so glad we met and so happy you're a part of my guy's life."

Craig smiled and turned to make his way toward the front

of the restaurant. As he walked past the host stand, he must have looked puzzled. Artie inquired as he passed, "Craig, are you okay there? Come back and see us again soon, yes?"

Craig was too preoccupied to notice or hear him. It was late as he made his way home. But he wasn't tired at all. His mind raced. He had come to grips with his ability to re-create the crime scenes for Danny. But what just happened with Emma was different, and something he had never been able to do before.

7

NEW ARRIVALS

Danny still couldn't shake the troubling information that Hammond had shared with him.

He walked briskly down Randolph street, his tan trench coat flapping around his legs. It had only been a few days since Hammond had interrupted his dinner at Santori's. Danny had met Hammond the following morning to review messages that someone had sent to the precinct. They weren't much different than other angry notes or letters that he'd received before. They were anonymous, usually sent by someone with an axe to grind against the police. Or, it was someone with a warped intention to goad the police. Danny thought that would be all there was to it.

Until this morning.

It was Friday, and Hammond had directed him to arrive at headquarters to review something new that had come in. This in itself was unusual. While he wouldn't elaborate on an early morning call he placed to Danny, he sounded concerned.

It was nearing 8:30 a.m. Since Danny was told to arrive before nine and had a few minutes to spare, he chose to duck into a shop to grab a cup of coffee.

As he held the door for a lady that was exiting, he felt the buzz of his phone in his breast pocket. He pulled it out to notice it was a reminder that he had missed voice messages. He recognized the most recent ones having been from Craig that he had yet to retrieve. *I don't have time for this*, he thought. Still, noticing Craig's number reminded him of the dinner they shared with Emma. He was pleased with how it had gone. He wasn't sure why, but feeling as if Craig approved of her meant something to him. He felt like Craig had a depth and introspection about things, and he valued that. Even if he wasn't always willing to acknowledge it in his actions.

Settling into a short line to order, Danny noticed a television behind the counter tuned to a local early-morning news program. He did a double take as he noticed Hammond in dress uniform speaking to the press.

"What the . . . " Danny started.

While I understand that there have been reports last evening of specific investigators within the department being targets of intimidation, I can assure you that this is just not the case, Hammond was saying.

The barista began to point at Danny to solicit his order. He waved her off and left the line and the shop. In a few moments he was back on the sidewalk, making his way toward headquarters as quickly as he could.

By the time he got through the lobby, up to the floor, and into the conference room where Hammond asked him to meet, it was about ten minutes before nine. He entered the conference room and found it empty except for several large, plastic evidence bags already in the middle of the table. Danny glanced out at a gloomy sky for a moment before the pull of curiosity drew him toward the evidence bags.

As he reached for one of them, the door to the room opened and Hammond spoke.

"Just leave those alone for a second, all right?"

Danny drew his hand back and countered. "What the hell was that dog and pony show with the press just now?"

"The chief didn't like it that things got leaked to the media. I would've given you a heads-up if I had the time."

Hammond let out a relieved sigh and unsnapped the top button of his dress jacket to breathe easier.

"Hate doing those damned things," he muttered.

Appearing frustrated, Danny began. "Let's rewind. Wasn't it just a few days ago that we were at our precinct? You showed me the notes from some crackpot with my name on them but all crossed out? Saying 'it's only a matter of time' and stupid shit like that? Why go public now with any of that? It's just bullshit, and you know it."

"And maybe it's not." Hammond said as he stopped to stare at Danny. "I told you this morning, we've got some new arrivals. Besides, someone in-house must've shot off their mouth last night to the news. And, well, then the top brass tells me to get out there this morning and calm things down. What the hell you expect me to do, Walsh?"

Danny waved off his whining. "What're these arrivals?"

"Body parts," replied Hammond. "Fingers. Five to be exact. One each lovingly addressed to you and a few of your colleagues."

Danny squinted one of his eyes.

"Come again?"

"Oh, but you were actually lucky enough to get two fingers sent to you."

"Why wasn't it just forwarded to me at the precinct?" Danny sifted through several clear evidence bags on the table until he found one labeled "Walsh." He held it up, rotating and twisting it to examine the contents.

"Because it was sent here. And suspicious. That's what we do to protect personnel; we open them up and check things out," Hammond said condescendingly.

Danny held the bag up to the light overhead, squinting his eyes as he scanned it. "I see the note, but only one finger. The note been dusted for prints? What about the fingerprints of the fingers? Can't we send the fingers to the state lab? Run DNA on the blood and ping it against the fed database? Then maybe there's a match to a homicide, or someone missing it." Danny tossed the bag back onto the table as he rattled through the normal forensic steps in his mind.

"Already sent off to check all those on the second finger that was in your bag. A couple of things that'll make that tricky," said Hammond. "No prints on the note. And as for the finger . . . " he paused.

"What about it?" Danny prodded.

"The damn thing didn't have any blood to it at all. Like it was drained out or something. Freaky, right?"

"Really?" said Danny. His mind drifted back to how Craig would use blood traces or residue to channel images at the crime scenes for him.

"So, it might be a little tougher to find the owners of these," continued Hammond.

"The guy sounds different, that's for sure. But are we convinced he's a killer?"

Hammond appeared restless and looked at his watch.

"There's a guy from the bureau that's coming up with the others. He'll give us a profile."

"Others?" Danny wondered.

"The other detectives. It's clear you're not the only sparkle in this guy's eye," Hammond said as he motioned toward the other evidence bags. "Besides, I called you in here early as a courtesy."

"Who are the others?"

"Sullivan. Waggoner. Atkinson." Hammond listed them off.

"All of them are, well . . . "

"Damn good detectives." finished Hammond. "Like you. Focus for a minute. We need to make good use of our time here."

Danny shrugged off the suggestion of urgency. "All right."

"Each of the packages had a photo that was sent too." explained Hammond. "That's what's bothering me." he paused. "A photo of each of you."

"Wait. What?" Danny was genuinely taken aback.

"Yeah, this guy seems to have his stalker act together."

Danny grabbed his evidence bag back off the table.

"Walsh!" Hammond began to protest, before relenting and letting Danny open the bag.

As Danny picked the photo out of the bag by one of its corners, the sergeant explained.

"The photos of the others are pretty grainy. Hard to make out that it's actually them. But yours is different."

Danny held the picture to his eyes and felt anxiety grow in his chest.

"But that one's definitely of you, isn't it?"

There was no mistaking it. Danny saw himself in the picture walking away from a building. He knew exactly where the picture was taken as well. In front of the main door of Emma's apartment complex.

"When was this taken?"

"How am I supposed to know that?" replied Hammond. "You're clearly in this shit, that's for sure. This guy's obviously keeping a close eye on all four of you. But you're the one he got a clear view of."

Danny lowered the picture and turned his head to look out the conference room window. His thoughts swirled.

"Seeing how the four of you got singled, the chief asked that I get out in front of the public narrative. Hence me drawing the short straw for the press conference this morning."

Hammond continued to ramble. Unnerved, Danny was no longer paying attention, until he heard mention of the forensics lab results.

"Wait. The lab work. When did you say it would be back?"

"That's why I asked you to focus. Not until next Friday. Probably the afternoon."

Danny turned away from Hammond and thought about the coming week. *There's something going on then. Oh, wait,* he thought.

He reached into is blazer for a pocket calendar. Thumbing through it, he landed on Friday's date and let out a loud exhale. "Shit."

"What are you looking at?" Hammond started before a rap at the door drew his attention away.

A desk officer appeared to talk with Hammond. Danny seized on the opportunity. He tossed the evidence bag back onto the table, gestured to his boss the need to place a cell phone call, and walked to the other side of the room.

Danny punched in Craig's number and waited for him to answer.

Danny glanced back to see Hammond continue to talk with the officer for a minute or so, appearing to give some type of instruction. The officer left, and Danny could feel Hammond's presence slowly walking up behind him.

"Okay, Craig. Yeah, you're right. The night of her conference is Friday next week. You think there's a hole in your schedule where you could help?" Danny paused for a moment. "Good. I'll leave you a message the first of the week and get you the details. But it's Northburrow Elementary in Ravenswood. She should probably be done around seven."

Danny looked over his shoulder to see that Hammond was waiting to reengage.

"Listen, Craig. I really have a lot on my plate right now. Thanks for agreeing to help Emma, but I kind of have to go. I'm sure you understand."

With that, he snapped his phone closed and turned to face Hammond.

"What was that all about?" asked Hammond.

"Nothing. Just asking my cousin to do a favor for me."

Hammond looked suspiciously at him.

"Why are you giving me that look?" said Danny.

"Are you trying to give him a heads-up on this in case something goes down?"

"No. But if I did, what of it? If something were to go down with this guy, it might make sense for me to pull Craig in. If I thought it would help."

"Don't give me that shit, Danny. I know there's obviously been some benefit that your boy has brought to the work. To the department, with what we need to get done. I don't know how exactly he helps—don't wanna know. But you need to feel more comfortable in the skin you've grown into. Hell, that ceremony the other day should've been validation of that. And this new stuff? It's . . . sensitive. You have to go easy about this. You get me?"

Danny felt a growing need to rely on Craig, in a way he didn't want to acknowledge to Hammond. Or even himself. Regaining his confidence, he responded.

"Eric, we've gone over this before. Trust me. I'd only look to pull Craig in if things were to get complicated. Tricky, just like you described this."

Hammond smiled and nodded but in a way that wasn't convincing.

It grew quiet for a few moments between them.

"Besides," Danny resumed, "this is probably just some crazy dude vying for attention."

"I hope you're right. 'Cause I've got a different feeling about this. And the brass does too."

"Yes. They certainly do, Sergeant," came a voice that entered the room.

An older, balding man had walked in clutching a folder. An FBI shield dangled from a lanyard around his neck.

"You're McCartney, right?" asked Hammond as he extended his hand.

"Yes. John McCartney. Good to meet you, Sergeant."

As Danny strode forward to introduce himself too, three other detectives followed the agent into the room, the last one closing the door behind him.

Each of the detectives had a distinctive look: one in a gray trench coat, short and stout with closely-cropped blonde hair; another was as tall as Danny but rail thin with slicked-back, jet-black hair; and the third had tasseled brown hair and a shaggy, unkempt beard. Despite their differences in appearance, all had an air of self-confidence, a swagger that gave the impression that each of them felt bothered to have been called to headquarters this morning.

As they stood surrounding the oval conference table staring at the evidence bags, one of them finally voiced the sentiment.

"Why pull each of us down here to waste a morning on this typical bullshit. No offense, McCartney."

"No one's trying to waste your time with any of this, Sullivan," explained McCartney. "The department takes it seriously when potential threats display a level of familiarity with investigators. When that happens, they reach out to the bureau for a personality profile."

"I get it," the tall detective interrupted. "Y'all want to tell us what makes a guy tick. But most of us who've seen this before know it's usually bogus." He looked over at Danny. "'Cept maybe Walsh. You're Danny Walsh, right?"

"Yup." Danny replied.

"You just got your merit badge for Senior recently, didn't you? You'll get used to this type of shit that comes with the exposure."

The FBI agent began to share the process that had begun to learn more about the forensic evidence and how it might point to whoever had sent the packages. The other three detectives appeared to listen skeptically.

Eventually, Sullivan jumped in again. "Did I hear it right about these packages? That this guy tried to take pictures of us?"

"That's right," said McCartney.

"See, Walsh?" Sullivan went on, "You know you've made the big time if this guy's trying to get your glamour shot. You gonna be ready if this guy shows up with his camera in your face?"

A couple of them chuckled at the comment.

Danny gritted his jaw as he replied, "Damn right."

The detectives were cocky. Self-assured. Playing off each other's barbs.

"How about we cut the smack for a minute and let our man here tell us what he came here for?" Hammond interjected. "Command has asked that I coordinate with you and your precincts to get the benefit of a profile and share information as it becomes available. So that we can all be a little more vigilant. A little more on alert."

The tall detective took up the argument.

"Like Sully said, no offense, McCartney. But we're always waiting for some big reveal when we get you guys involved and go over this stuff. You say you can pull together all this data, all this psychological mumbo jumbo. You come up with a persona on these guys. Their personality. Whatever. But what I notice is that you usually get it wrong. Or it turns out to be a dud."

McCartney drew in a breath and suddenly looked more authoritative.

"Gentlemen, you need to hang with me on this for a few minutes. I'll tell you why I think this personality is different." He paused to ensure he had their attention. "Whoever this guy is, he has invested a significant amount of time trying to understand your routine. Your rhythms. He's been able to send messages and information into your precincts, and also this city's headquarters that have been devoid—thus far—of physical clues. He seems to have gotten physically close enough to each of you to take your picture. And the body parts he's sent have come from persons believed to be harmed and perhaps dead. Each of those fingers in the bags is addressed with your names on them and appear to lack any blood or physical residue. Now, I don't pretend to have your everyday experience in dealing with things on the street. But to me, that's . . . different."

The self-assuredness that each of the detectives carried seemed to wane.

As the FBI agent continued to review the criminal profile of whoever was sending the messages, Danny narrowed his eyes and listened to the description. He could see a change in the demeanor and attentiveness of the other detectives as well.

Danny felt anxious. He looked over at Hammond, but Hammond was locked on to every word that McCartney was saying.

"I've been doing this work for a long time, gentlemen. And what I can tell you is, there's something to this one. My experience says he'll act. And when he does, it won't be pretty."

As he paused, it was so quiet that the white noise could be heard coming from the ceiling tile.

"You need to be careful," continued McCartney. "Not only for yourself, but also for your family and really anyone in your circle."

Danny was taking it all in. His thoughts went to Craig, then Emma, and his parents. Then, one by one, Danny looked into the face of each of the other detectives. He remembered what Hammond had told him at his promotion ceremony: this type of work makes you a target. Both inside and out.

8

FIELD

For the next several days after the dinner with Danny and
Emma, Craig felt in limbo. What he had glimpsed of Emma's
past, and her reaction to him knowing it, weighed on him
heavily, as did the surprisingly new manifestation of his
ability. Although he couldn't—and wouldn't—explore this
turn in his abilities with Danny after promising Emma he
wouldn't say anything, he'd still felt the need to talk to him.
He'd called several times and left a number of messages,
but Danny hadn't returned a single one. Danny had always
reliably called Craig, either to catch up or pull him into one
of his cases. Knowing this and given how well dinner had
gone, Craig thought Danny's silence was all the more baffling.
He kept wondering if Hammond's unexpected visit to the
restaurant had anything to do with it.

Despite his uneasiness and the familiar angst that came
when his abilities emerged, he felt more alive than he had in a
long time. He knew it had to do with looking forward to seeing
Lauren over the coming weekend. He'd left her a message with
the time they should meet at the museum, but on Friday he
found himself dropping by Monk's in the morning, hoping she
might be there. After settling in at a table, he noticed a small
television behind the counter. It was tuned to the morning
news, which was showing a press conference with the media
asking questions of a uniformed officer. Gazing at the screen,

he realized that the officer was Sergeant Hammond. He'd never seen Hammond in uniform before, but he remembered from something Danny had said that the sergeant had been assuming more responsibility for media relations.

The volume was turned down low, but Craig tried to follow along. Hammond appeared to be addressing some leaks to the media about threatening messages that had been received at his precinct. He was going to great lengths not to provide details but insisted that the focus of the messages had nothing to do with the public. He described it as typical "hate mail" directed at some of the precinct's well-known investigators. Craig paused and shook his head as if to push back his confusion. *It has to be more than sheer coincidence that these public statements are coming so soon after Hammond spoke with Danny the other night,* he thought.

Intending to call Danny to sate his curiosity, he drew his phone from his pocket, only to shove it back inside. It irritated him that Danny hadn't responded to him all week.

By the time he arrived at work, the sky was overcast, and it looked like it might rain. Craig settled into his cubicle and surveyed his files to take inventory of the reports and analyses that lay ahead for the day. As much as he didn't like to admit it to himself, it was difficult for him to get motivated in his job. The drama and mystery he encountered while helping Danny with crime scenes, his budding interest in Lauren, and the alarming twist of being able to see Emma's past made his job seem all the more mundane. He wasn't sure what his vocation was meant to be, but this clearly didn't seem like it. As he thumbed through some paperwork at his desk, he felt his phone buzz in his pocket. It was Danny. *About time,* he thought. "I'd been wondering where you disappeared to," he said when he picked up.

"Hey. Listen, I need a favor from you next week," Danny said without preamble.

"Wait, hold up there, pal. I've been trying to call you all week, and now that you've finally called back, I'm going to need a little more than 'I need a favor.'"

"Listen, Craig, we've had a lot going on at work. It's kept me from getting back to you, okay?"

This certainly didn't sound like the Danny who usually tried to placate Craig in order to talk him into something.

"Seems like it. What's this stuff I saw this morning on the news with Hammond talking about your precinct and hate mail? Is that why he needed to talk with you at Santori's?"

"You can't believe everything the media puts out there. And besides, I can't discuss what's been going on with a civilian."

"A civilian? Are you serious? Listen, I was just curious about what I saw on the news, and you're like, 'Oh, but I really can't tell you anything.' What about all the crap you've gotten me involved with? Where was the concern about me being a 'civilian' then?"

"Craig, yeah, you've helped with some things. But it takes more than just the . . . stuff you can do. Guys like me have to take those visions, whatever that voodoo shows us, and turn around and actually hunt down some real assholes. Arrest them before they can fuck with anyone else."

Danny had never said anything before to diminish Craig's help—and his tone was so dismissive. Craig could feel his anger simmering.

"I just don't like to be used. I think you know that. I mean, I helped you with that stuff last week and spent an entire evening meeting your new girlfriend. It would just be cool to hear from you occasionally when you don't want something."

This was usually when Danny would back off in fear that Craig might not help him in the future. This time was different.

"Yeah. I know that, Craig. That's why the favor I'm calling you about is for Emma. I thought you wouldn't mind helping me since it would actually be helping *her*."

The mention of Emma's name made Craig relent. He remembered how scared and vulnerable she was during dinner. "What? Is she okay? I mean, what does she need?"

"She's fine," Danny replied brusquely. "I just want you to make sure she gets home all right from her student conferences next week. They run late, and I don't like her having to walk through that neighborhood after dark."

"Can't she take a cab? Why can't you pick her up?"

There was a pause in the conversation before Danny responded. "Two things. First, Emma was mugged on her way from a school meeting last spring. It freaked her out pretty bad."

"Oh, wow," remarked Craig.

"Please don't bring it up with her; she doesn't like to be reminded about it."

"Got it," Craig reassured.

"Now, anytime she has to leave late from the school, I make sure to be there. So, that's the second thing: I can't be there to walk her out next week. There's an investigator from New York coming to Springfield who specializes in some of the things we're seeing at the precinct. I'll need to be down there then. Let's leave it at that."

Craig let a few moments pass as he thought through what Danny was saying. It seemed to raise more questions. Why had he turned so secretive? Looking to push ahead, he tried to learn a little more. "I don't know. Maybe *I* have stuff going on next week. You're not the only one with a life, Danny."

Danny chuckled sarcastically. "Okay, Craig. Yeah, you're right. The night of her conferences is Friday next week. You think there's a hole in your schedule where you could help?"

Craig was still irritated and growing increasingly confused about Danny. But since he knew more of Emma's past than Danny did, he felt for her and resisted sparring any further. "Okay, sure, Danny. I can meet her."

"Good. I'll leave you a message the first of the week and get you the details. But it's Northburrow Elementary in Ravenswood. She should probably be done around seven."

Sensing that Danny was about to end the call, Craig interjected, "Wait, that's it? What's been going on with you since dinner?"

"Listen, Craig. I really have a lot on my plate right now. Thanks for agreeing to help Emma, but I kind of have to go. I'm sure you understand."

"Well—" Craig started, but Danny had hung up. "Wow, seriously?" he said aloud as he tossed his phone onto his desk.

Staring out the doorway of his cubicle at the city buildings, he watched as a sprinkling of rain began to dot the windows.

———◆·◆·◆———

Craig stood on the front steps of the Field Museum on Saturday morning, waiting for Lauren to arrive. The cold front that had passed through the previous night was giving way to a cloudless blue sky. Craig had arrived at the museum earlier than the ten a.m. he had told Lauren in his voicemail so she wouldn't have to wait for him. He began to get nervous when it was pushing 10:15, but then he saw a cab pull up near the entrance turnaround and let her out. With the temperature only in the high fifties, she emerged from the cab in a dark knit skirt with leggings underneath and a jacket with a thin scarf. Her beautiful, thick hair cascaded down her shoulders as she swung the door of the cab closed. She paid the cabbie through the window and started the long walk toward the museum steps.

He thought she looked beautiful and carefree, seeming to take in everything around her with wide-eyed enthusiasm. When she began to ascend the steps and saw Craig near the top waiting for her, her mouth grew into a wide smile.

Without any reference to being late, she said, "What? No paper this morning?" Craig only smiled and tilted his head toward the entrance, and they made their way inside.

They started by exploring the Main Hall and several exhibits, chatting about work, sharing stories from their college years, and talking about how they enjoyed living in Chicago. Things seemed to flow naturally, but Craig couldn't keep from thinking ahead to how their day might end and how he could be sure that they'd make plans to meet again soon. As they ate lunch in the food court, he asked, "So, were you surprised that this is the place I chose for us to meet?"

Lauren thought for a moment. "Probably not. I mean, what's not to like about this place? You always hear about the variety of things they have and so far, I can see why." She went on about how much the exhibits reminded her of the places she had loved to visit in her mind when she was younger, using *National Geographic* and other periodicals to paint the possibilities. "My mom would always joke that I was so voracious about reading up on different places and cultures that hopefully they'd help me 'find myself' and what I'd want to do in the world."

Craig shared his affinity for *National Geographic* as well, which seemed to prompt Lauren to remember something. "Wait just a second there, mister. Wasn't this whole day

designed for me to get a chance to know more about you? But
so far, you've been sneaky again. You've let me rattle on while
you've barely said anything."

"What? Me? No way," Craig responded with his hand to
his chest. "Well, okay then. Let me ask you this: what was it
about me that made you want to spend time together, knowing
as little as you do so far?" His question was meant only partly
to deflect. He really was curious about what had drawn her
interest in him.

"Oh, I guess I've just got a good sense of authenticity. I
appreciate people who are the same no matter where they
are or who they're with—at work, home, around friends,
whatever. It's also usually a sign that a person is willing to
be vulnerable. Otherwise, how can you truly get to know
someone or experience things yourself? It's a quality that I
think is increasingly rare."

"And you think that's something I have?" asked Craig.

Lauren winked. "Maybe. I'm not sure yet, but I'll definitely
let you know."

They finished their lunch and proceeded to the second
level, which overlooked the far end of the Main Hall and the
large dinosaur skeleton that stood on the main floor below. It
was here that they found a comfortable bench off to the side
and away from where the majority of visitors were passing.
The conversation had turned back to Lauren.

"Over the years, I've come to respect the feeling or energy
I get from people. I guess I just have faith that the universe
will be able to show me the way of things."

"The universe?" Craig asked quizzically.

"Or God, or energy, or whatever you want to call it."

"Hmm." Craig furrowed his brow. He wasn't convinced.

"Let me try it a different way," she said. "I guess I believe that things and events are generally made to work out like they're supposed to. Haven't you ever felt that way?" She paused a moment, then continued. "Let's take Sue down there."

Craig smiled. "The dinosaur's name is Sue, huh? Only been here a time or two?" he joked.

"Oh, come on, Craig. She's supposed to be, like, a really famous dinosaur, right? Okay, maybe I did a little research on this place ahead of time." She smiled. "Anyway, Sue and her friends roamed the earth for millions of years until, what? Poof. They all die out and give way for the next natural progression of a divine plan that comes together and eventually unfolds into you and me being able to sit here today."

"Then we totally got the shaft with not being in the history books," he cracked.

They both laughed, then he continued. "So, religion is important to you then?"

Lauren thought and said, "I don't know if I would say religion, just that I believe that everything and everyone is placed and prepared in the way they're supposed to be."

"So, it's like this divine plan you mentioned, one that all of us are just supposed to roll with?" Craig said.

"Well, don't get me wrong. I believe we all have to make choices when the time comes, a fact that my mom was always diligent of reminding me when I spent too much of my time 'finding myself.'" Craig remained silent, looking deep in thought. "You don't buy into that type of thing?" she asked. "I mean, your family, like, wasn't into this stuff that much when you were growing up?"

"I guess not. It's complicated. I don't know if religion has worked very well for me to this point. Or the energy, or whatever you're calling it."

"Don't think of it so much as organized religion. Maybe that came across as too categorical. What were the experiences that bonded you as a family? I mean, you've talked as if you and your cousin are pretty close. How did your families establish bonds in ways that you both maintain even now?"

She was prodding into areas where Craig wasn't sure he was ready to go yet. "Danny and I have more of a reliance-based relationship. I'm good for helping him think through stuff from his job, and he loves to swoop in and play the hero. Or as he puts it, look out for me."

"Ah, so that's the story behind the scene at the coffee shop."

"Yeah, that was one of those times Danny felt the need to jump in and take control."

"Looked to me like whatever you did to that guy was doing the trick, and then you let him go," she said.

"It does do the trick. It's called *aikido*, a Japanese martial art. It's one of those styles that can have some really destructive effects if you have to use it when your life is in danger. But it also can be an effective way to trap or immobilize someone if the situation isn't that extreme. That's kind of what I did at Monk's. But even if you go too far with just that kind of technique, you can really hurt a person."

"And you really didn't want to hurt him, did you?"

"Well, no, of course not. But I guess I did let up a little too quick. That's why Danny felt like he had to handle the rest of it."

"Craig, I get the sense that you can totally take care of yourself. But you knew the guy wasn't worth it."

There was an awkward pause between them. Craig was almost ready to voice agreement with her sentiment. But he also harbored doubts he'd never been able to shake. For all the experience and training in his martial art, it was Danny and the aggressiveness he brought that Craig always seemed to rely on.

Unsure of why this had caused Craig to go quiet, Lauren sought to move on. "So, this is good," she said. "We had a plan to use today for me to get to know you better. So far, so good. Now, what about your family?"

"Well, I spent most of my teen years growing up with Danny. Like, in the same house and everything. Or at least since I was about ten."

"Really?" she said, sounding a bit confused.

For some reason, Craig felt like he could trust her. He forged ahead.

"Yeah, my mom died of cancer when I was little. I know that she was a really special person. It's just that I don't remember too much about her. So, early on, it was just my dad—he was a minister—and me." Craig noticed that Lauren hung on to his every word. There didn't seem to be anywhere for him to hide or any way to avoid talking about the past.

"Look," Lauren said gently, "I understand if it might be too uncomfortable to share. I hope, if anything, I've shown you by now that it's safe to open up to me."

Being with Lauren was like immersing himself in a warm pool. It was almost as though he couldn't help but open up to her. He'd never felt so comfortable.

"Then, well, my dad died too. When I was ten. I mean he . . . uh . . . "

"What is it, Craig?" She touched his hand reassuringly.

"My dad was killed."

Craig didn't like to talk about the particulars of how his dad had died. People always seemed to listen to it as if it were a sideshow oddity rather than the tragedy it had been.

"What do you mean?" asked Lauren.

Craig stared straight out across the museum's Main Hall. "He was murdered."

He described to her as ordinarily as possible what he knew and what he'd been told about that fateful day. As he spoke, he avoided eye contact, fearing that it might draw more emotion out of him than he was prepared to share with her just yet. "Then, really, my first memory after it happened was when I tried to overhear my aunt and uncle talking about it. That was the night they brought me here to Chicago."

When he finally finished and looked into Lauren's eyes, she was gazing at him with the deepest empathy he had ever seen. This wasn't the voyeuristic stare of others he had told about his past, whose reactions were always a combination of shock and morbid curiosity about the physical details. Lauren kept looking deep into his eyes as she reached out and cupped his single hand with both of hers. "Craig . . . I . . . I am so, so sorry."

Her tone was genuine and pure. He sensed no trace of her wanting to ask about particulars. She seemed to be reacting with only pure feeling.

This was one of the rare times when Craig let himself feel it too. Her emotional reaction was drawing one from him as well. His eyes welled with tears, and it felt amazingly cathartic.

They sat in silence, gazing at each other as the buzz of visitors moving through the exhibit halls surrounded them in a welcome cocoon of anonymity.

Having composed himself, finally, Craig muttered, "Thank you."

He couldn't remember anyone seeming to *feel* so strongly about what had happened to his father. It validated the sense of loss and disillusionment he had always felt.

He withdrew his hand from hers, wiped his eyes, and

taking a deep breath, broke the silence that had built between them. "So, with my dad being a minister, the whole religion thing has never really hit the mark with me."

"Craig, I realize I can't even imagine how terrible it must have been, but don't you believe it has played a part in making you who you are? The past might be painful, but it's also your origin. It's what has led you and developed you into the person sitting next to me. Are there certain things that you have or remember that help keep your dad's memory alive?"

Craig looked down at the floor. "I don't know," he said.

"Like any mementos or anything?"

"Well, I mean, maybe. But I haven't gone there in my mind in a while."

"I get that—I really do. It's also important to know yourself, know your garden, and know where your water is."

"Know your garden and know where your water is," he repeated. "You say some really interesting things. Where do you get this stuff?"

"I don't know. I guess I just pay attention to what I need, be it body, mind, or spirit. You have to take care of yourself. If you don't, no one else in the world is obligated to."

While Lauren made sense, he had always avoided going deep about how he dealt with things when he was a kid. Growing up with the Walshes seemed to, at least in everyday terms, move him past it. And particularly after the incident in the barn, he found he rarely thought about that time in his past. Craig wasn't even sure where his father was buried. Right or wrong, Jim and Judy Walsh had shielded him almost completely, avoiding sharing details with him.

After a few minutes, Craig said, "I don't want to be a science fair project for you. Am I?"

"You're not asking just because we're so close to science

exhibits, are you?" she said, trying to infuse humor into a question that truly made Craig feel the vulnerability she had mentioned earlier. She quickly changed tone. "You are a real, deep, and caring person. That's what you are to me."

"For real?" he asked again.

"I think there's so much more you have inside to offer the world that, once you come to grips with it, it's going to blow you away too." Then she clasped his hand and said, "Let's check out what else is in here." With that, they rose from the bench and continued on through the museum.

Never had any of the few conversations Craig had with others about his past gone like this or ended so upbeat. He had finally connected with someone who understood him, understood what had happened in his life, and wasn't ignoring, sensationalizing, or avoiding it.

They explored the exhibits until closing time, then walked over to Michigan Avenue in the early evening chill. Craig was feeling lighter for having shared with Lauren. They spent the rest of the evening strolling along Michigan Avenue, stopping for a drink or two along the way.

As darkness fell, they made their way to Craig's L stop. Lauren insisted that she needed to take a cab and stop by her parents' house on the way home. As they parted ways, Craig started by saying, "I really appreciated you listening to me earlier. Sorry if—"

"Please don't say you're sorry." Lauren interrupted. "You get to experience things. You get to be yourself. You get to"—she smiled—"enjoy life with fun people."

"It's a deal." Craig agreed.

Almost before he could finish his sentence, she leaned in for a quick kiss. They looked into each other's eyes for a moment and came together for a longer kiss.

"I had a great time," he said.

"I know you did," she answered, and turned to hail an oncoming cab. He watched as she got in, looked back at him a final time, and rode away.

Once she was gone, Craig realized he hadn't thought to make plans to ensure that they would go out again. But he felt good. He was confident he hadn't needed to.

9

LETTER FROM THE PAST

Over the ensuing week, Craig heard nothing from Danny. Normally, it would be a relief to not be summoned to a crime scene, but this time was different. Craig felt isolated, left to wonder what was going on with Danny's work and with Emma. The thought of her made him ponder the unexpected turn concerning his abilities. Nonetheless, his budding relationship with Lauren was going well. They'd been seeing each other at work, either over a break or at lunch. A few evenings, they grabbed a quick bite of dinner near the office before Craig dropped her off at her apartment. Craig had shared his address, but they hadn't yet spent time there; each night they both went back to their respective apartments. Craig didn't want to push for more at this point, worrying that it might be too soon. He was also trying to keep his relationship with her and his periodic involvement in Danny's world separate. It was just as well; Lauren often needed to stop by to check on her parents. She'd recently shared with Craig that they were having marital problems, and Lauren saw her role as a bit of a buffer to lighten the mood of the household.

On Thursday morning, Lauren stopped by Craig's cubicle. Resealing a dark red bottle of fluid, she wished him good morning.

"What's with the potion you've got there?" he said playfully.

"Oh, this? Just vegetable juice. It's really good for you. Care to try?" she offered, extending it to him.

He started to reach for it but caught himself. Remembering the experience he had when he inadvertently drank from Emma's glass at dinner, he lowered his hand and sought to wave it off more superficially.

"Ah, no thanks. I'm good. I don't want you making me *too* healthy this soon out of the gate."

Not giving it another thought, she went on. "So, I know we haven't talked about the weekend yet. But tomorrow actually looks pretty good if you want to meet up. I just need to swing by my parents' place for a little bit. And, well, you're welcome to come along. I mean, it might be nice for them to meet you. Especially Dad since, you know, you like work for him and all?" She smiled as she finished the sentence.

Craig certainly hadn't been expecting to meet her parents so soon, and Lauren must have seen the surprise in his eyes. "Unless you think it would be weird, because I'm totally not meaning for it to be."

Remembering the commitment he'd made to Danny to meet Emma, he replied, "Oh no, I think it would be fine and all. But Danny asked me to check in on his girlfriend tonight."

Lauren narrowed her eyes in a half-jealous expression.

"Maybe I should explain," he quickly added. "I'm not exactly sure what's up with Danny lately. He's been a bit self-absorbed, even for him. He told me he had some special work thing he had to do tonight, and he was concerned about her having to stay late at her school's conferences. I guess the neighborhood she has to walk through is supposed to be a little rough. So, I probably should've said something to you about it. But honestly, I'm kinda annoyed with Danny right now, and . . . "

Lauren stopped him with a gentle wave of her hand. "Craig, you don't owe me any explanation. You're always free to do whatever you want, or need, to do."

"But maybe I want you to want an explanation?"

"There's absolutely no need for it. I want you to always do what you need to do and feel right about it. I think you know that I'm here for you when you're ready."

There were so many layers to her comment that Craig wanted to explore. Instead, he just accepted it for the time being.

"Thanks. Really. I mean that. Not sure how you come by this outlook you have, but I have to admit, it's pretty cool."

Lauren smiled. "Besides, it sounds like Danny needs your help. You should probably be there for him if that's the case."

"I don't know. I think Danny needs Danny. It's the way he deals with people. If he sees a way that you might be able to help him, then he's gonna expect something from you," Craig said, his cynicism obvious.

Lauren raised an eyebrow.

"Too judgmental, right?" Craig guessed.

"Only you can tell if that's a fair assessment. I just like the hopeful and optimistic Craig. And that didn't sound like you." She looked at her watch. "Listen, I have to run. But I'll call you this weekend, okay?"

She glanced quickly around the office, then leaned down to give Craig a brief, surreptitious kiss on his cheek. She then spun on her heel, her skirt twirling as she did, and left his cubicle.

When she was gone, Craig lingered in his thoughts for a while, thinking about the "hopeful and optimistic" version of himself. He'd never viewed himself that way. Feeling pessimistic and a little bit at odds with things was a place he'd settled into for a good portion of his life. Even if his growing relationship with Lauren was making him happy, he also wondered if it was bringing some new, anxious feelings he had never dealt with before.

———◆—◆—◆———

On Friday evening, he took the L from downtown, then a cab to the Ravenswood neighborhood. Daylight saving time had recently ended, and it was getting dark earlier. He arrived at Northburrow Elementary earlier than he needed to. Danny had never called with further details, so Craig had erred on the side of caution.

Parents were coming and going as Craig entered the school. He wandered about the halls until he located Emma's classroom. A couple was waiting at a table nearby to talk with her. He could see through the window of the classroom door that Emma was in conference with another set of parents.

Craig kept his distance across the hall, watching Emma though the window as she interacted with the family in the classroom. He was struck by how slight and frail she looked. Perhaps she had looked the same when they met for dinner, but Craig wondered if the way he saw her now was being influenced by what he had learned of her past, making her seem even more vulnerable. In that moment, he was glad to have come to see her out this evening.

After about fifteen minutes, the parents left the room, and Emma was ushering in the others when she noticed Craig. Her eyes lit up when she saw him. "Craig! Oh, wonderful. You're here. The Johnsons and I have about fifteen or twenty minutes, and then I'll be ready. Okay?"

"Oh, sure. No problem. Take your time."

It was after seven when Craig and Emma made their way out of the school and walked several blocks toward her bus stop.

"Craig, I can't thank you enough for coming to meet up with me tonight. Danny was really sorry that he couldn't come, but he's got so much going on at work, and he's under so much pressure."

"Emma, please. It's no problem at all." Craig thought this might be a good opportunity to try to understand what was going on with his cousin. "You know, Danny and I haven't spoken much this week. Is he doing all right with everything?"

"You know how he is, Craig. He really doesn't let others in on work things."

Craig felt the irony of being deeply immersed in parts of Danny's job as she continued. "But I know he's probably told you. He says he hadn't told me because he doesn't want me to worry, but I overheard a call he had with his sergeant. Apparently, someone's been sending severed fingers to the police with Danny's name on the bag. It's really freaked me out."

Learning first of this from Emma irritated Craig. Given the unwelcome familiarity Craig had with Danny's world, not hearing this from Danny himself, even with their recent limited interaction, seemed rude. He needed to learn more. "Pretty deranged stuff. Especially now that someone's been leaking to the media that something's going on," he said.

"I know," she replied. "But I can tell it's been bothering him a lot. He said that's why they had to call the press conference, to 'control the message,' or whatever." She seemed deep in thought. "It just seems like whoever is doing this has it out for him. He thinks it's because he's getting so much publicity for closing cases, and someone out there is trying to taunt him. I asked him, where could the fingers be coming from? And what happened to those poor people?"

As Craig took in this new information, he was careful to play along so Emma would continue and not think that she was sharing too much.

"Right. I know he's working with some specialist to try to find clues. He's probably head down trying to figure this out. I'd just like to be able to help him if he needs it, you know?"

"I said the same thing to him about getting your help," she said. "I mean, I know that you've got some type of"—she hesitated—"special ways about you. Like the stuff you were able to know about me." As she said this, she stared down at the darkened sidewalk.

Craig noticed her chagrined tone and said quietly, "It's okay."

Clearly, Emma had decided to trust Craig, freely asking for his thoughts. He wasn't sure if this was driven by the secret he knew she kept, or if her personality was naturally one that latched on to others she felt she could trust.

"But Danny told me that you can't help him with anything on this. At least not yet." She looked curiously at Craig as they continued to walk. "What does that mean, Craig?"

"I'm really not sure, to be honest with you. Like I said, it's been tough for me to connect with him lately."

"It's been the same way for me too. I'm . . . I'm worried about him. I know how tough he is, and all that he can handle. But there just seems to be something about what's going on that's changing him a little." They were approaching her bus stop, and she took the opportunity to press Craig. "Can you please look after him and let me know that he's truly all right, even if he won't come out and tell me that directly?"

"Emma, I know how good you are for Danny. I mean, I can see it. Let me try to connect with him and help if I can. I'll definitely let you know what I'm able to learn, especially if he remains distant with you about this."

She seemed relieved and appreciative of Craig's offer. She stood on her tiptoes to hug him as the bus approached.

"You're so nice. I suspected it from the way Danny talked about you. Now I know it." She glanced at the bus. "Well, this is me. Thanks again for coming all the way up here to see me out."

"It was nothing. Are you sure you don't need me to ride the rest of the way with you?"

"No, I'll be fine from here," she said as she boarded the bus and acknowledged the driver. "Chuck will make sure I get home okay."

Watching as the bus pulled away, Craig cinched his jacket tight against the night's chill. He thought about the discussion with Emma, how she was feeling, and the lack of contact from Danny. He found himself bothered again that he hadn't heard more from his cousin, and he pulled his phone from his pocket and dialed his number. It rolled immediately to voice mail. Craig let out a long sigh, replaced the phone in his pocket, and made his way down the street.

◆—◆—◆

It was after nine when Craig reached his apartment and microwaved something for dinner. His mind wandered as he became more melancholy thinking about Emma, and Danny's silence. The fresh feeling of clarity he had begun to experience with Lauren became muddied by issues related to Danny and his own strange abilities.

As he was cleaning up, he heard a knock over the background noise of the television. He was pleasantly surprised to see Lauren when he answered the door, and his mood lightened immediately.

"Sorry. Is it a bad idea to drop in on you so late?"

"No, of course not! But I had hoped to make this place more presentable for your first visit, so look past anything that's messy," he said smiling. He guided her in and took her coat. "So, you just weren't sure that my story about Emma was on the up-and-up, huh?"

Lauren beamed a little less than usual. "No, it's not that. I wasn't even sure you'd be back yet. I've been playing referee between my parents for the past few hours and just needed to see someone I knew would lift my mood."

"Wait, and you chose *this* guy?" He pointed at himself self-deprecatingly.

She smiled at him as she sank into the sofa. "I don't know, Craig. My parents are a little jaded. A little fake, I guess. I don't feel like I'm anything like either of them. Just further proof that I'm adopted, I guess."

He chuckled nervously, her last statement having caught him off guard. He wasn't sure if she was joking or not, but he knew now wasn't the right time to ask.

She tilted her head in a kind way and looked at Craig. "I just need a little more authenticity than they can provide."

"Any time," he said, smiling back.

"Plus, if only I knew some of that judo stuff or whatever you mentioned you do. There were a couple of times I was worried I might need to use it!" she joked.

"Well, let's hope it never comes to that. It can be pretty effective when needed."

"Did you learn martial arts from your dad? How did that come about?"

He was slightly taken aback by the question. "No, it was more of a way to . . . get a little more empowered when I was young after he died. Danny's dad knew someone on the police force who taught it. They thought it might be a good way to make me feel, I don't know, a little more in control?"

"That makes sense. I guess I was just thinking back to when we were at the museum. It'd be great if there was something that sticks in your memory about your dad, or something of his that would help you remember him more."

He wasn't sure how her words made him feel.

Most people, once they learned of his father's death, avoided the subject like the plague. She seemed to think of it as something Craig should anchor to, or honor in some way.

"I've got a box or two of stuff. The Walshes gave it to me after college, when I moved in here. But it's been several years. The trouble now would be finding it." Craig was being deliberately evasive—he didn't want to go through those mementos and have to relive the memories.

"Come on, Craig." She eyed him with a playfully suspecting look. "You've got a one-bedroom apartment. And, from what I can see, you keep it super tidy in here. You've seen my desk at work and know my apartment is no better. Seriously, there's a place where things go to get lost!"

Craig went along with her humor to move them on to a different topic. Soon they were laughing as he joined her on the couch and they started watching an old movie. Neither of them seemed to care much about its content, enjoying their closeness and each other's company more.

Craig awoke with a start. A quick inhale of oxygen, and he found himself wide awake, having emerged from a dream. He glanced at the television. The movie was no longer on, having been replaced by an infomercial. Lauren was still asleep with

her head resting on his shoulder. Determined to explore the
dream before it vanished in his mind's ether, Craig slid gently
away from Lauren, leaving her comfortable and still asleep,
nearly horizontal on the couch. He was up and pacing around
the apartment. Then stopped and closed his eyes—the dream
was coming back to him.

He had been running. He wasn't sure if it was *from*
something, but he felt overcome with dread. One foot kept
dragging as he ran, slowing his progress. Then his foot caught
on some object and he tumbled to the ground, scraping his
cheek and chin. As he sat there in the dream, holding the side
of his face, he saw that his father had caught up with him.
Looking down at him, his father smiled broadly. *You'll be all
right. Things like this happen, but you'll be okay.* Then he
stooped down to brush Craig off, and as he did, he held Craig's
chin and looked at him lovingly. As his father leaned over, a
silver necklace fell through the top of his shirt. Craig reached
for it. It looked like an old-fashioned silver cross.

His father intercepted his hand gently and said, *No, that's
not for you now. Maybe someday, though.* There was a blur in
the dream as his father squatted down to scoop Craig up, and
then he was gone.

—————◆·◆·◆—————

Craig opened his eyes and looked around the apartment. The
television and lights were still on. Lauren was still sleeping
peacefully on the couch, but Craig was now wide awake and
alert. He had forgotten about the cross his father wore until
that dream. Careful to be quiet and let Lauren sleep, he began
searching the apartment's closets and storage places. He knew
the boxes the Walshes had packed for him were somewhere.
He found a large banker's box underneath a box of trophies

and old coats in his closet. Sliding the box out, he sat down on the floor of his bedroom and sifted through old report cards and school projects, looking for the necklace. It wasn't there, but an old packet, taped shut and resting near the bottom of the box, caught his eye.

The tape was old and brittle. As he undid the packet, he found that it contained a folder, and in the folder were two very old and weathered pages. He pulled them out and noticed the holes where the two pages had been stapled together. The letter was so old that the metal staple had long ago disintegrated, leaving only a rusted tint on the yellowed paper.

The pages were typewritten and dated December 17, 1917.

"What's this?" he said to himself softly. He didn't recall having seen it before.

The letter was from a civic-sounding group Craig had never heard of. It appeared to be a letter of condolence written out of respect for someone named Robert Henriksen. Craig didn't recognize the name. *Is this my grandfather's father?* he wondered. At the top of the page were three letters whose typeface looked ornate for the period, a printed calligraphic style: *c-o-i.*

He began reading the letter. The tone was respectful throughout, but it seemed to Craig that it was worded rather oddly, even for a letter as old as it was. There was one passage he found particularly peculiar:

> We grievously deplore his taking away and the great loss we sustain, as well as the loss to the state, to his church and local society, of so valued a member. And our most sincere sympathy, collectively and individually, go out to the family of the deceased in the irreparable loss

to them of a dutiful, kind, and affectionate husband and father, whose anguish can be assuaged only in the assurance of a reunion in the great beyond. This Council ventures to call to the attention of the individual members of this group that this is the first instance of death, in all his hideousness, having approached our portals since our organization in December 1909, and is only a reminder that we, and each of us, may soon be called by the same relentless enemy to follow our deceased associate. Let us beware, he may come when least expected.

It was signed, *Amos Bright and A.L. Morrison.*

Craig lowered the letter, lost in thought. *What could this mean?* He suddenly regretted that he'd never learned more about his family history. He had pushed that curiosity away long ago, after his dad passed.

He heard a sharp knock at the apartment door. He looked over at the clock on his nightstand. It read: 12:31 a.m.

Craig wondered for a moment who it could be at this hour. He hastily put the letter back in the folder and into the box and dashed into the other room, where Lauren was stirring awake. He went to the peephole as Lauren sat up on the couch and wiped the sleepiness from her eyes. Danny was standing on the other side of the door, dressed in his long trench coat and looking very serious.

"Danny, what the hell's going on? It's nearly one in the morning," he said as he opened the door. Danny pushed his way in, glanced at Lauren, and shook his head in confusion at her presence. He then turned to Craig. "Come on, let's go. I need your help. It's important." He wasn't asking so much as telling.

"Seriously, Danny? You ignore me for, like, two weeks and then barge into my apartment in the middle of the night?"

"Listen, it's been different lately. I know that. And I wouldn't be here if it weren't serious. Now, grab your coat 'cause we've gotta go."

Fully awake now, Lauren interjected herself into the discussion. "Craig, is everything all right?"

"Who the hell is this, by the way?" Danny said, turning his head in her direction.

"She's a friend from work. That's all you need to know," he said defensively. "And I need to stay here and make sure she gets home okay."

"No, you don't," said Danny. "She'll be fine here until you get back. Right now, I need you to get a move on and come help me."

Craig stared at Danny incredulously, shaking his head. The tension in the room was palpable.

"Craig, it'll be fine," Lauren broke in. "I can hang around here. You should go and help your cousin if he needs you."

"So, you know we're related?" Danny commented.

Not wanting to invite any more scrutiny about Lauren, Craig reached for his jacket that was draped on a chair. "Fine. Let's go, then. Lauren, I'm sorry. I'll be back as soon as I can. Or I'll call you to let you know what's up. Are you sure that's okay?"

"Of course. Don't worry."

Craig didn't even look at Danny before walking out of the apartment. Danny gave Lauren another puzzled look, and she returned his stare dispassionately. He then turned and quickly followed Craig out the door.

10

THE TOURIST

He had barely slammed the car door shut when Craig spoke. "You've got a lot of nerve, you know that?"

"Hey, sorry for dropping in like that. And for being out of touch recently." Danny's mood seemed to be softening. "But there's been some heavy stuff going on. Since I haven't had anything that you could help me with, I thought it'd be better if you and I kept a lower profile."

"You've been keeping the same low profile with Emma?" Craig noted sourly.

"What? Oh, she's fine. And yeah, I appreciate you looking after her tonight."

"Why couldn't you look after her yourself? You're obviously back from wherever you were."

"Dude, I just got back a little while ago. Then I find out we've got a scene that I'm gonna need your help with. That's why I came by."

"I told you I wanted out of your investigations. And what happens? You totally ignore me for two weeks, and *then* you pull me in again in the middle of the night. What gives?"

"So, who was that girl anyway?" Danny replied, bluntly ignoring Craig's question.

"I can have a personal life, remember? What exactly is going on?"

"Well . . . " Danny hesitated. "That night you and I had dinner with Emma, Hammond tells me about my name being in the media so much it was drawing some unwanted attention. Occasional notes have started coming in to the precinct. They're brief but definitely from someone trying to poke at me. There was a specialist from the Bureau down in Springfield earlier today. Had him and the crime lab guys use some new tools, scan the notes for traces of anything that might tell us where they came from."

"Let me guess," Craig interrupted. "Nothing, right? And now you need me to see if I can channel anything off the paper for you?"

Craig worried that Emma might have said something about the wine glass to Danny. If she had, now Danny would think he could use Craig's abilities in a new way.

Danny ignored him and continued. "Then, in the last several days, we found a couple of small paper bags at the station with my name scribbled on them. Inside each bag was a severed finger."

Craig decided to throw out an idea. "Could it be the Mob? Their way of sending you guys a message or something?"

"What? Mob stuff? Nah, this is way too subtle for them. Believe me, I've dealt with them. This is way different from anything I've ever come across."

Craig was not completely shocked, given his cousin's line of work and what he had already learned from his conversation with Emma. "Okay, well, couldn't you just match it to someone who died and got their fingers cut off?"

"Craig, do you know how many murders there are in the city of Chicago each year?"

Craig stared blankly out the window as they drove on. After a pause, Danny provided the answer. "Like, seven hundred or so. And those are the ones we *know* about. Who knows whose fingers they are—and even whether the people they came from are dead?"

"How many fingers are we talking?" asked Craig. He was starting to think the conversation was bordering on the absurd. He hated that he found himself so interested. Here he was, being drawn back into Danny's world just when his own looked promising.

"Four so far."

"So, just have the DNA stuff on them run, or whatever, and see who they match to. Right?"

Danny answered, "Dude, we've done that. Crime lab. Bureau specialists. Remember? We couldn't get a match to anything, anywhere."

Craig commented, "Well, that's weird, I guess."

"It's not only that. There's not even any blood to work with. They'd been completely drained." He glanced over dramatically at Craig. "Now there's this grisly murder, and I think it's linked to the guy who's been sending this stuff."

"Have you been to the scene yet?"

"No. When I heard from Hammond earlier, I wanted to swing by and get you first."

Craig hadn't been watching where they were going, but they seemed to be on the south side of the city. Just as they were getting close to the projects, Danny pulled up to the curb and stopped behind what looked to be a ten-story building. There was only one police car out front and no sign of the buzz that Craig typically noticed at these scenes.

"That's why I need you now," Danny started. "The victim in this building was found on the same floor as an older lady I know really well. You're gonna help me figure out who's doing this."

"Dammit, Danny! I don't want to be part of this anymore."

"Hammond told me that the guy who got killed here had four of his fingers ripped off," Danny quickly countered.

"The fingers aren't going to be from this guy, unless you're telling me he was killed days ago, around the same time you found those bags at your precinct."

Danny turned off the engine. "Still, it's a pattern. You see what I mean? This one is different. Are you going to come in and help me, or not?"

Grudgingly, without answering, Craig opened the car door, got out, and began walking toward the building.

The air had gotten even colder, and Craig was in need of a heavier jacket. As they walked up to the back of the building, Craig saw Hammond, who was apparently waiting for them to arrive. Before they were within earshot, Craig asked his cousin, "You want me to just walk in with you?"

Danny shushed him as they approached Hammond and said, "Okay, I got him. Still quiet up there?"

"Yeah. Sixth floor. Our two uniforms are just outside the door. Get up there and do what you need to do so we can get the official process started. All right?"

Danny nodded as Craig stood silently behind him, wondering about the arrangement that Danny had established with Hammond. The sergeant shot him a suspicious look as Craig passed him and headed toward a service elevator with Danny.

The building was aging and in disrepair. It seemed to Craig like the type of apartments that housed lower income people, older adults, and young families. They rode the elevator to the sixth floor, where they got off and spotted the two uniform patrol officers down at the end of the hall. Danny and Craig were making their way toward the officer when Danny motioned for Craig to wait. "Hold on . . . this will only take a second."

It looked to Craig as though Danny was counting the doorways from the service elevator. He then walked up to one and casually tapped at the door. An older woman opened it. Although Craig kept his distance from them, he could still make out snippets of their conversation.

"Maggie, I've got to get someone down to his apartment and start processing the scene. But in a few minutes, I'll be back up to talk with you about what you think might've happened. You know there's hardly anyone left on this floor, so I'll need to get your thoughts on this. Sound good?"

"Well, 'good' isn't any word I'd used to describe what happened to Mr. Williams," she answered his cousin as if all too familiar with him. "But you know I'm not shy, Danny. You also know I'm a night owl; I'll be here whenever you make your way back."

"That's great, Maggie. You're a trouper. See you in a few."

Craig didn't quite understand what Danny was doing or why he needed to talk to the woman. But he didn't really care either. He was nervous and tried to stay several paces behind his cousin as they approached the doorway where the officers stood.

"Hey, thanks, guys. I'm going to pop in for a few minutes alone."

"Walsh, what about this guy?" one of the officers asked.

"Oh, he's from Narcotics. Thought a set of fresh eyes could help."

The officers looked dubious, but Danny had grabbed Craig by the arm and ducked under the police tape and into the apartment with him before they could question him further.

Once inside and having closed the door, Danny quietly slid a chair up to brace it shut in case anyone tried to open it.

"Okay, let's be really quick and quiet, and get you going here," he said to Craig.

With their recent argument in the car behind them, and with the strange news of the fingers providing a ghoulish curiosity, Craig seemed to forget for a moment how much he hated being involved in these episodes. But as he stood looking at the dimly lit living area of the apartment, his shoulders slumped forward, and he felt like a heavy weight had been lowered upon him once again.

"Over there." Danny pointed.

Craig's eyes followed. Lying there was the body of an older gentleman who looked like he had been trying to crawl into a back bedroom but was cut down before he got there. Craig had only seen victims after they'd been decently covered by the first responders. This was the first time they'd arrived early enough that this hadn't been done yet. The victim was definitely older, maybe in his mid-seventies. But his frame looked like one of a healthy man.

The victim was facedown, his left hand outstretched and missing four fingers. His other arm had been twisted and contorted badly behind his back. It was hard to see clearly, but Craig thought he saw lash marks around the sides and back of his neck. The carpet underneath the man's head was reddened from his spilled blood.

"Craig, we have to work fast and quiet. So, let's roll, huh?"

Craig opened his mouth to complain. But given that the officers outside the door were so close by, he decided not to protest but instead find a spatter of the victim's blood, avoiding what was pooled beneath the victim's body.

He found the blood spatter near the base of the wall near

where the man had collapsed. The sight of it sent Craig's heart racing. He stooped down and began to slowly circulate his bare fingers against the grim bloodstain. Immediately, the misty, reddish veil descended over the apartment, making it look brighter than it had just a moment earlier. Everything vanished from sight except Craig, and Danny, who was standing near the door with his back to it. Again, a faint pulsating sound could be heard.

"I don't see anything," Danny whispered. "Oh, wait. There."

They both saw the victim's silhouette backing into the middle of the living area. Its movements reflected those of someone in good health moving quickly but clearly frightened. One hand clutched at his chest while the other waved in a pleading motion at something out of view. The killer appeared from the side of the veil nearest to Danny, then walked toward Craig as he pursued his victim. The killer looked hunched, thin, and wiry. The dark silhouette wore what looked to be a hood that hung low against its forehead, adding a menacing quality to the shadowy outline.

As soon as it had appeared, Craig's sense of unease prickled—something that felt distinctly different from previous re-creations. Although he was accustomed to the jarring emotions that the sight of these crime scenes with their violent images produced, this time Craig felt his face grow hot, and he became physically nauseated.

"Danny, this . . . this isn't right," he said, trying to keep his tone level.

"Shh!" Danny shot back quickly.

With an almost unnatural quickness, the killer closed the distance between himself and his victim and grabbed him by the left arm. He raised it up and, using his other arm, slashed the victim across the face. Although it seemed as though the attacker had used only the open palm of his hand to strike the blow, black spurts of blood erupted from the victim's head at the point of impact.

"Wait. What did he hit him with?" Danny whispered as though to himself.

Craig didn't know. He wasn't watching closely—he was feeling increasingly worse. "Danny . . . too much. I . . . I can't."

"Craig, shut the hell up and let this play out!" Danny said in a harsh whisper.

Trying to push through now, Craig took a deep breath. He watched where the attacker had grabbed the victim's arm, slashing at him again, this time at the man's hand, sending four of his fingers flying. It looked as though the man may have cried out, but the attacker swiftly used the same hand with which he'd slashed the victim's fingers and muffled his face with it.

Incredibly, the dark silhouette of the killer looked like he was lifting the old man off the floor by his face before suddenly, and brutally, slashing the victim's neck with his other hand.

"What the hell . . . " Danny said.

The killer then lowered the victim back down, released his face, and grabbed at the older man's uninjured arm. In one swift move, he twisted the victim's arm awkwardly behind his back, shattering bones as he did so. While holding the mangled arm up against the victim's back, the killer pushed the man to the floor in the direction of where Craig was now crouched.

Gravely injured as he bled from his throat, the victim tried to crawl away. The attacker's silhouette lunged forward and started to lash the man across his back with what looked to be his arms, although they seemed strangely longer than normal, able to extend down toward the victim as he attempted to crawl away.

"Who is this guy?" Danny said, oblivious to Craig's woozy state.

Then the lashing stopped. The victim now lay motionless on the floor. The shadow of the killer stood still for several moments. Then his head turned as though he was scanning the room, and stopped just as his field of vision lined up with Craig.

At that moment, it was as if all of the heat and nausea Craig had been feeling burst forth. He lifted his hand from the bloodstain, and the veil rapidly faded.

"Craig! Wait! What the hell? We need to see what he does!"

But Craig had suddenly slumped forward, vomiting on the carpet.

"What the fuck are you doing?" Danny bellowed.

His raised voice must have alarmed the officers stationed in the hallway. It sounded like they were trying to push open the door, but it was wedged shut by the chair.

"Walsh? Walsh! What's going on in there? Open the damn door!" one of the officers shouted.

The veil and shadowy figures having vanished, and most of the contents of his stomach now on the carpet, Craig felt instantly better. He watched as Danny ran over and removed the chair, allowing the officers to enter.

"Walsh, what's up in here?" one of them said.

Looking over at Craig, still hunched over near the victim, the other officer said, "Is that guy even on the force?"

Craig started to explain the situation, but Danny cut him off.

"Shut up, Craig. We just need to get you outta here. Guys, he wasn't feeling well to begin with. Let me get him some air and have Hammond get things started."

Danny grabbed Craig and was pushing him out of the apartment when one of the officers began to protest. "Walsh, this ain't right, man. We gotta go ahead and call in the rest."

But Danny was already out the door and down the hall, stopping a few paces shy of the old lady's door. He turned to Craig. "Dude, what the hell happened back there? Seriously! I've got issues now, man."

Not even sure himself what had affected him, Craig opened his mouth with the intention to somehow explain. It was then that the elevator doors opened, revealing Hammond, who had come to check their progress.

"Shit!" Danny said, as he tapped on Maggie's door.

When she opened it, Danny whispered quickly, "Maggie, listen. Mind taking my friend here and letting him clean up? He got a little sick. I'll be right back. Okay?"

The word "sure," wasn't even past her lips before Danny pushed Craig through her door and quickly closed it.

Once inside the apartment, Craig could hear animated whispers between the two men followed by their footsteps receding down the hall.

Margaret turned to look at Craig. He was disheveled and red-faced, his hair dampened near the ears from feeling sick.

"You all right there, boy?"

"Yeah, just, I don't know. Maybe something I ate." He felt at a loss and embarrassed to be standing in a stranger's apartment.

"Rule number one for visiting a murder scene would be to hold the onions," Margaret said as though this were an everyday occurrence. She chuckled to herself as she offered Craig her hand in greeting. Craig hurriedly wiped his palm on his pants for fear it might still have some blood on it. "I'm Margaret. But people call me Maggie. Looks like you're a friend of Danny's. You're not a cop, though, are you?"

Still reeling from the re-creation and his violent reaction to it, Craig rubbed his temples with his palms, trying to reorient himself. "Not exactly. I mean, no. That detective—"

"You mean Danny."

"Yeah, Danny. He's actually my cousin, and he has a way of dragging me into this crap."

Maggie had moved over to her modest kitchenette and was dampening a hand towel for Craig. "Well, any help you can provide Danny Walsh is time well spent in my book. What's your name, son?"

"It's Craig," he answered as he accepted the towel and started wiping his brow. "And how, exactly, do you know my cousin?"

To Craig, she looked to be about the same age as the victim whose apartment he'd just been in. Her plain housecoat probably doubled as sleepwear. "Oh, he's picked my brain a time or two about people and the criminal element."

Craig was puzzled. "What?"

"Well, let's just say I wasn't always as refined and sophisticated as I am now," she said self-mockingly.

When Craig didn't react, she laughed a hoarse, smoke-tinged cough. "My past has a few twists and turns. Let's just say I know how bad people work."

"So, you were a criminal?" he asked, his filter momentarily gone.

"I was a lot of things." she said, slightly offended. "But along the way, after hitting rock bottom and nearly dying, I learned the value of doing things the right way." Her joking tone had turned serious. "I learned to be someone who accepts people and understands that pain and suffering are just part of a process. Over time, my faith in people was restored, I guess. People like ole Detective Walsh down the hall."

Still shaking off the ill effects of the crime scene, Craig seemed to have lost his usual circumspection. "Wait, for real? Are we talking about the same Danny Walsh? Maybe you just don't know him as well as I do."

"Well, you're a little bit grumpy, aren't you?" she replied.

"I just know my cousin. He's only interested in himself." For Craig, this was the wrong time for anyone to be singing Danny's praises. "Some people just want to be left alone— they don't want any part of this stuff. It's disgusting and vile. He drags me out here in the middle of the night and gets me involved in this, and for what?"

"Probably because he thought you could help," she said coolly. "Or he likes having you around. Listen, son, what you saw down there was probably rough, for sure. But there ain't a one of us who's clean, you know? I probably don't know Danny Walsh that well. I know you even less. What I do know is that he gives a damn about bad things happening to good people.

"Mr. Williams down the hall? He was a good man. People think he was good 'cause they know how he'd run youth programs around here to keep kids outta trouble. But I know his balls were way bigger than that. He was in World War II, part of the Sixth Armored Division. One of the first vets that liberated Buchenwald. He's way too humble to openly share that type of stuff, but we talked a time or two about it. He told me how it showed him, without a doubt, what's right and wrong in the world." She leveled her stare at Craig, as if lecturing him.

She became more intense as she continued. "It takes guts to put yourself out there. From what you know of Danny, you might say he's mouthy, or selfish, or even reckless. Hell, maybe he is. But he busts his ass out there every day trying to set things right, regardless of what *you* think his motivation is."

Craig couldn't understand why this woman, whom he didn't even know, was taking him to task. Defensively, he replied, "A person doesn't have to sign up for this to make a difference. There are other ways that they can put themselves out there."

"That's true—you're right. So, you probably have your own version of putting it on the line."

Craig didn't answer her.

"No?" Margaret said. "Let me give you a little analogy. Life is kinda like football. You see, you can choose to keep yourself on the sidelines and not be in the game. That's fine. But if that's what you do, you really can't bitch and moan about what's going on."

Tired, Craig just wanted the conversation to end. "I really don't want to argue. The stuff back there was just a little intense. I'm just not sure I'm made for it, is all."

Margaret shrugged nonchalantly. "He obviously thinks you are, or that you can make some kinda difference. Everyone can, whether they know it or not." Finally, she smiled, breaking the tension. "It's just like the lottery, son. You can't win the big game if you ain't gonna play."

Although he disliked her folksy metaphors, their meaning was getting through to him even if he didn't want to acknowledge that to her. It made him think more about what

Danny did for a living. Regardless of how Craig felt his cousin was wired, he did have an uncanny bravery, always plunging head first into trying to do the right thing.

The silence grew between them, to the point of becoming uncomfortable. Craig heard footsteps approaching Maggie's door. There was a light tapping, but as Maggie opened it, Craig saw it was Sergeant Hammond, not Danny.

"Ma'am. Detective Walsh will be down to see you in just a few more minutes. I'm sorry you've had to wait."

"Oh, please. It's fine. Does it look like I'm going anywhere already?"

Hammond's politeness turned cold as he turned to Craig. "Walsh has his hands full working the scene. So I'll take you back. You need to follow me, got it?"

Craig nodded. He understood that he had contaminated the crime scene, and that Hammond was looking to ease him out of the situation before the forensics team arrived.

"Ma'am, I appreciate how helpful you're always willing to be."

She waved her hand dismissively as Craig and Hammond started to the door.

"Um, thanks." Craig said, looking back at Margaret.

"Don't thank me yet," she replied as he walked out the door.

The drive back to Craig's apartment seemed longer than it had been to get there.

After several minutes, Hammond finally broke the silence. "This shit is damn weird."

For a moment, Craig worried that Hammond somehow knew about the re-creations that he conjured with Danny.

"This sick bastard likes to call himself a Tourist, like he's going off collecting souvenirs or something."

Craig remained silent, momentarily relieved that the focus wasn't on the images he created. He was unsure what to say or what Danny may have told Hammond.

"He's baiting us," said Hammond. "Trying to see if Danny has what it takes to bring him down. And now with it getting out in the news? We need to contain this. Gotta figure it out."

Craig realized that Hammond wasn't really talking to him, but just thinking out loud about what had been happening. He seemed to be so involved in his thoughts that he was oblivious to Craig's presence.

As they neared the apartment, Craig decided to speak up. "Eric? It's Eric, right?"

Hammond furrowed his brow at the use of his first name.

"Danny's the cop. I'm not. I don't need to be part of any of this. Can you convince him of that too? I've no interest in being involved. Heck, it's probably illegal for me to be back there anyway."

"Hold up," Hammond cut him off. "I don't know exactly how you help Walsh, and I really don't wanna know. But I need you to man up about this. This Tourist is one sick bastard, and now we know he's a murderer too. You got me?"

Seriously? Craig thought. *Now it's somehow expected that I continue with this?*

When they arrived in front of Craig's apartment building, Hammond rolled the car window down as Craig headed toward the front door. "You're gonna remember what I said, right?"

Craig didn't look back; he just waved his hand over his shoulder in Hammond's direction.

It was nearing three a.m. as he approached his apartment door. He was anxious to see Lauren and find a way to make everything that had been racing through his mind disappear.

Once inside, he announced himself. "Hello? Lauren? Where are you?"

There was no reply.

"Are you kidding me?" Craig shouted to the empty room as exhaustion and anger came flooding out.

He was angry at Danny for barging in earlier and possibly scaring Lauren off. He was angry that Lauren hadn't waited for him to come back. Now, there was no one around to share with. Feeling physically and emotionally drained, Craig lay down on the same couch he and Lauren had been on hours earlier and promptly fell asleep.

11

NOT ENOUGH ROOM

In his dream, Craig was floating on his back, staring up at the ceiling of an indoor swimming pool, trying to remain calm as he felt the two supports under his torso fall away.

Arching his back to stay afloat, he felt his heartbeat quicken. While he tried to remain calm, the lapping pool water was inching closer and closer to his nose and eyes. He started to panic and splashed his arms, which he held out at his sides, forming a cross. His heart was racing as his father appeared at the corner of his eye, walking through the water toward him.

The water was a little more than chest high on his father as he drew close to Craig.

You've got this. Relax, Craig. I'm right here.

Craig felt calmer for a moment, but he felt the water rise against his face again. His father stepped closer and positioned his arms under Craig's shoulders and lower back.

That's good, Craig. You're getting better each time.

Craig didn't speak as he looked up, supported by his dad.

I'm right here. I always will be. You shouldn't worry.

Craig noticed that his father was bare-chested and that the silver necklace hung against his wet skin. Craig lifted his hand to grab at it, but his father moved back until it was just out of Craig's reach.

No, little buddy. Not just yet. You concentrate on this right now.

Lifting his arm out of the water had pulled Craig off balance for a moment, and in that brief instant, the water covered his face and eyes completely. He closed his eyes.

◆ ◆ ◆

When he reopened them, he found that he was no longer dreaming but waking up in his apartment, lying on the couch where he had collapsed.

He felt as if he had slept forever. Glancing across the living room, he saw the digital clock on an end table. It read 11:40 a.m.

"What the—?"

It was nearly noon, and he had slept right through hours of work. Sitting up, he swung his legs to the floor and sat for a few moments. He tried to rub the sleep from his eyes. His vision was becoming less blurred, but his body felt like it had been through a wringer. Glancing down at the coffee table, he noticed his phone and saw that he had a missed call.

Hoping it was Lauren, he dialed his voice mail. It was Emma saying that Danny hadn't returned from the call he had tended to late last night. She was worried because he usually checked in with her in the morning when she was getting ready for school. She ended by asking Craig to call her if he heard from Danny.

Craig felt sorry for Emma. While she might be well suited to Danny's personality, it didn't mean she wasn't coming off as needy. But Craig felt more and more the need to stand for what was important to him. It was neither his responsibility to manage Emma's angst nor to always be on call wherever and whenever Danny needed him.

The toll from the re-creation the previous night was lingering like none other Craig had performed. Whatever the source and reason for his supernatural ability, it felt like an increasing drain on him.

Nevertheless, he did feel chagrined that his presence at the scene and the manner in which he had contaminated it had caused legitimate problems both for Danny and the police force. Maybe he ought to call Danny to ensure that everything had ended all right. But the call rolled to voice mail, as it had so often recently.

He glanced around his apartment, finally thinking about work and how late he was. Usually, he'd feel nervous and guilty for missing work, let alone for not calling in ahead of time to let them know he was going to be late. But his exhaustion, coupled with his irritation that Lauren hadn't stayed last night or called this morning, made him feel indifferent. He decided to take the remainder of the day off and use the time to try to sort through things in his head. It was mid-afternoon by the time he had eaten something and showered. As he finished dressing, he noticed the old file box that he had been combing through the previous evening. Moving closer, he saw that its contents had been neatly replaced. He could only conclude that this had been Lauren's doing, and that she had probably looked through the box as she did. He wasn't sure at that moment how this made him feel. If she had known nothing of his past, he would have felt like she had invaded his privacy. But part of him didn't mind her looking through the files—it might save him from having to describe them to her.

Unwilling to look through the box any further, Craig slid it back into the closet and out of view again. He was tired and in deep thought about how quickly the optimism he had felt in recent weeks was being edged out by this latest drama. He turned on the radio, lay back on his bed, and stared blankly at the ceiling.

There was news about an older man having been murdered last night on the South Side. Craig realized the reporter was referring to the crime scene where he had been and paid close attention to the details. The elderly victim was a gentleman, active in programs for at-risk youth; the police were at a loss to identify a motive for the killing, especially since they had noted that nothing had been stolen; sources within the police department were drawing a link between the killing and the recent anonymous messages the police had been receiving. Most notably, Craig zeroed in on a reference to an unidentified civilian who had been at the scene just following the murder.

He remained for a while in a half-meditative state, his eyes fixed on the ceiling, until he heard a light tapping at the front door. He got up slowly, ran his hand through his hair several times to smooth it out, and made his way to the door. He had taken so much time getting there that the visitor was knocking a second time.

Craig opened the door just as Lauren was raising her hand to rap at it again.

"Hey there . . . " she said cautiously.

"Hey, yourself," Craig replied, and turned, leaving the door open as he walked back into the living room. Lauren entered and closed the door behind her.

"I looked for you at work today. How are you doing? Did things work out with your cousin?"

Craig ignored her and jumped right in with what had been bothering him. "Where did you go last night? I mean, I get back here, assuming that you would still be here waiting, but you were gone. I know it was late, but still—"

"I know. I'm sorry. It's just, well, it seemed strange how

you left. I hadn't meant to fall asleep to begin with, and I worried that I may have overstayed a little."

"I just really wanted to be able to come back and talk with you." Both his irritation and disappointment came through as he spoke.

"Like I said, I'm sorry. I guess I didn't know. You and your cousin seem close. I just didn't want to interfere." Her tone was genuine and calming.

But her comment reminded Craig of Maggie's from the night before. "We aren't that close! In fact, a lot of things that he involves me in make me uncomfortable." Craig was surprised by how quickly his emotions had risen to the surface with Lauren, given that they hadn't known each other for that long. He closed his eyes and began rubbing his forehead with his hand.

She stepped closer to him but still respected his space. "Craig, you can talk to me about it."

"Can I? So, *now* you're available for that," he said sarcastically.

She took a step away from him, her palms raised. "Whoa, hold on a minute. Where's all of this coming from? Craig, maybe it's none of my business, but what exactly are you struggling with when it comes to your cousin?"

He took a breath. "I don't know. I just feel like the situations he brings me in to pollute me in some way. It's been so hard for me to get my act together as a whole. Being around his investigations makes me feel like I'm being pulled into two separate halves." Regretting that his earlier comments had come out more harshly than he intended, he softened his tone. "I'm sorry. I mean, it's been great being with you, wonderful even. But I feel like I'm on a roller coaster ride. As my social life with you gets better, everything else in my life starts to unravel: Danny, his girlfriend, my past." He was staring directly in her eyes. "I'm having these dreams about my childhood that I've never had before. And I actually did find an old box in my closet with some family stuff in it." He pointed toward the closet. "But you knew I found it, didn't you?"

Lauren nodded. "Yes, and I did look through it some. I'm sorry if you feel like that was out of line."

"Then you probably saw that old letter in there, right?"

She nodded.

He went on. "That's what I mean. More and more fragments of information keep coming into my brain, and it makes my head hurt!" His voice was rising again.

"You definitely seem upset since you went away with Danny last night. Is this the effect being around him has on you? Why did he need to pick you up, anyway?"

Craig turned his head away, avoiding her gaze. "I . . . I can't. It's something between me and him, and I can't share. Not now. Maybe not ever."

Lauren nodded. "Okay. I guess I'll have to try to respect that."

"You can? What the hell?" Craig said, half surprised, half angry. "I wouldn't be able to respect it. It would drive me nuts if you said that to me."

"Honestly, Craig, maybe you're right. About this two halves thing. You just did a total one-eighty there. Could you just listen to what I'm saying? I trust you. And if you believe that it's the right thing not to share, then I know there must be a good reason."

He was incredulous. "Wow. Okay. Sometimes it's hard to believe you're for real. You're sweet. I mean, really. But seriously? I haven't met too many people like you."

"Maybe you've kept yourself closed off for too long?" she offered as he looked upward at nothing, feeling beaten down. "Craig, have you ever listened to Deepak Chopra? Like when he talks about getting in touch with your soul?"

"The self-help guy? You're kidding me, right?" The way she'd brought it up, he thought she might be joking.

"Wait. No, I'm not. He has a unique perspective on this. He describes what it's like to expand your mind on things. Follow me on this for a second, will you?"

Craig could sense her energy and passion as she continued.

"You start out with only limited awareness of things. Think of it like you're walking out somewhere at night. It's dark, and all you have is this flickering candle to provide light and guide you. You're just trying to make your way along, but you're stumbling over things. The light really isn't enough for you to see the difference between things that are helpful and the shadows of things that might be problems. So everything seems like an obstacle. And you encounter nothing but problems, and you can't see them until you're right there upon them." She was becoming more animated as she spoke, and Craig felt the positive glow she was exuding.

"Once you can relax and accept things as they come to you, then you can start expanding your awareness. Instead of that little candle, now you have a torch you're carrying to light the way. You can see the obstacles, but you can also see some of the way forward. So while there are problems, they can also produce opportunities. Kind of like they're problems with a purpose."

She paused, looking at Craig as if trying to gauge whether she was getting through to him.

"Then there's purity of mind. That's the original state in which you were born. When you're walking through that dark night, there's a full moon that shines light down. Almost bright enough to cast a shadow. You can clearly see everything that's around you and in front of you. That's when you're centered . . . that's your *soul*." She smiled. "It was there when you were a child, it was there when you were with your father, and it's still here now. Maybe now all of these things are flooding at you because you're opening your mind to things."

Despite understanding what she was saying, Craig also felt exasperated with her for the first time. "You say these things and, I mean, they make sense. But it makes my head swirl even more. I'm not like you. I feel like I've been dragged down over time. You obviously have your shit together with this awareness thing, and I don't, okay? I've *always* felt like I've been in the dark, about things you can't even imagine!"

"Sometimes faith sees best in the dark."

"Is that this Chopra guy too?"

"No, Kierkegaard." she said.

"What the—" he interrupted himself. "Oh, come on." Craig felt thrown off balance and at a disadvantage as she was able to rattle off another line from someone to support her points.

"Craig, I think you're stronger than you can possibly imagine." She wasn't backing down, but he just shook his head in disbelief.

"Not buying it?" she asked.

"All I know is that I was nervous and awkward as a kid. After my mom died, it was just me and my dad. And . . . and he had a way of connecting with me. Then that whole goddamn thing was ripped away from me, and I didn't even know it was happening. Every day"—his eyes were tearing up now— "every goddamn day, I feel like more stuff is piled on top of me. Whether it's fear or apathy, or just trying to hide and survive."

"And maybe sacrificing a little bit of what makes you, *you* along the way?" she added tentatively.

"Yes!" he exclaimed. "That's why it's always been easier to sacrifice part of me. Because being reminded of all I've lost is too painful."

She kept pressing him. "You don't know how to deal with the pain and where to put it?"

"Put it? Are you kidding me?" He was so worked up that he was shaking, his fists clenched. "There's not enough room in the whole world for my pain, Lauren!" Stunned at his own outburst, he fell silent. A stray tear rolled down his cheek.

She moved toward him, tears in her own eyes, and embraced him as he placed his head on her shoulder. Standing there, holding her, he felt the strain and weight of all his years ebb away just a little.

"I can't imagine how you feel. But Craig, I'm here for you."

He believed her with his whole heart.

They spent the rest of the afternoon quietly relaxing, letting all the emotions that had been stirred up subside. Craig felt like they were starting to get back to the easygoing way they went about things when they first met. Then Craig felt his phone buzz in his pocket. Even before he answered, he could guess that it was Emma.

"Craig, I'm sorry to bother you. I was just hoping you had heard from Danny, or maybe know where he is. He called me briefly late last night, and he sounded upset. And even though I tried, I couldn't do anything to improve his mood."

"Emma, I don't know if I can help you with Danny right now." He hadn't meant to sound gruff— it just came out that way.

"But Craig, he's said more than once that he thinks this killer has it in for him. He won't let on, but I know he's concerned. And I'm concerned for him. And . . . and I'm a little worried myself. You probably know how much I rely on him."

"Listen, I'm kind of in the middle of something right now. I feel for what you're dealing with, but Danny hasn't exactly been responsive to me lately, either. At some point, we all have to be able to look after ourselves."

"Craig, I know how close the two of you are—" He felt the struggle of feeling pulled apart again.

He jumped in: "Are you kidding? My cousin only comes around if he needs something, or to take center stage." There were several moments of silence as he thought better of what he'd just said. "Okay, that probably came out a little rough. I'm sorry. Look, I promise to reach out tomorrow, but I really do need to go now."

After a few other parting words, Craig hung up. Having listened to the full conversation, Lauren asked, "What you said about Danny—do you really feel that way?"

Craig sighed. "I don't know. I'm not sure who the real Danny Walsh is: the friend who was there for me when I was young, or the self-centered person I know today. He only seems to have time when he needs me to do that stuff." The words came out before he could stop them. "Wait, I mean—"

"Craig, you don't owe me any more information. Only you know what you have to do, and only you can choose to be there for Danny. Whatever you can and cannot help him with, I'm no one to judge. Let's just let it go, shall we?"

He was surprised but grateful she didn't want to delve further into his comment.

Later, while Craig was making sandwiches for a light

dinner, he asked, "So, I wonder if I'm in trouble with Miller. You know, for not making it into work today."

Lauren looked confused for a second. "Oh, Miller, right. Your boss. Well, I guess lucky for you that you have an *in* with someone in HR."

Craig smiled. "Really? You covered for me?" "Let's just say I sent him an email letting him know that you'd tried to call but when he didn't answer, you made sure to call HR to let us know you weren't feeling well." She smiled mischievously.

"Well, I guess I'm glad I took the time to make that call."

As the evening progressed, Craig was more relaxed, finally having shaken the ill feelings from the night before, and beginning to feel more and more like himself. They agreed to see if there were any movies on TV that might be good to watch together. It had been tuned to the late local news as Craig went searching in the kitchen for a TV guide. Lauren had nestled herself onto the couch.

Glancing over the listings, Craig became more and more aware of the newscast. The murder from last night had remained a lead story throughout the day.

And Chicago police continue to be at a loss as to the motive behind a brutal slaying overnight on the South Side. Those who knew him describe Mark Williams as a kind and gentle man, someone who'd been active in the community for years.

Craig released the movie guide and walked toward the couch. The news anchor continued:

But as sources at our station are learning, there may be more ominous overtones to this particular killing. We

*go now to David Jordan, who is live on the South Side
near Cicero. David?*

The newscast shifted to a field reporter bundled in a coat,
standing just outside the same building Craig and Danny had
been in the previous evening.

*That's right, Mary. Sources have told us that there
were representatives from the eleventh precinct here
for several hours before the Forensic Services division
was called. Speculation is that the killing could have
something to do with the recent messages the police
have been receiving from an unknown individual.*

*David, do your sources believe that the killer could
be the same person who has been corresponding with
the police?*

*No one will say just that, Mary. They also won't
confirm that there was a civilian at the crime scene
along with the first responders, well before the arrival
of the crime scene unit. Theories have circulated this
afternoon about whether this individual might have
been an expert who deals with the occult or ritual
killings.*

*Whoa, David. This is definitely a new turn in this
case. Have you been able to learn who was helping them
at the scene last night, and whether or not this killing
could be related to the earlier messages?*

*Not yet, Mary. But the precinct has a news conference
scheduled in the morning to provide an update. If there
is any connection to the messages, or if the police believe
that a threat exists to the community, the public has*

a right to know. And we'll be there to ask the tough questions . . .

———◆◆◆———

As the broadcast pivoted to another story, Lauren looked up at Craig, who had brought his palms together over his nose and mouth and sighed deeply. Abruptly, Lauren announced, "Craig, I think I need to go. I've got recruiting visits for the next several days, and I have to be up early tomorrow."

"Lauren, wait. This doesn't look or sound good. I get that. But please, believe me that—"

"Craig, I understand there are things that you can't share. I respect that. I think I've made that clear. And I know that you've been struggling with things. But there are times when I need to think things through too." She paused for a moment as she stood up. "And this would be one of those times."

She grabbed her coat and moved toward the door, not looking in Craig's direction.

"I want you to know how much it meant to me that you came back here and spent time with me today. I'm sorry that I can . . . that I can't . . . "

She stopped him by raising her hand. "I just need to go so I can get ready for the rest of the week."

As she opened the door to leave, Craig felt powerless to stop her, or to gather the courage to be completely honest about how he felt and the secrets he and Danny shared. As she walked out the door and down the hallway, Craig called out, "Lauren, can we talk soon?"

But she was already at the stairwell and quickly moving down to the lobby.

12

BETTER THOUGHTS

It was getting colder outside with each passing day. Craig sat on the L during his ride to work, noticing that most of the leaves had already fallen off the surrounding trees. He reflected on the past month and a half, and how quickly things had changed. It hadn't been long ago that he'd felt like he was stumbling through his life, lacking any real passion about anything. He had his job, but he knew in his core that the business world probably wasn't for him. He had his relationship with Danny, but he constantly questioned whether the person he'd spent so much time with growing up really knew him at all, let alone cared about him. It seemed that Danny didn't mind taking Craig out of his comfort zone so he could use him to advance his own career.

Craig's love life had been relatively nonexistent for several years. The last time he'd had a girlfriend of any consequence was when he graduated from community college, about five years ago. The more time went by, the more difficult it was for him to cultivate friendships or love interests.

All this was against a constant backdrop of worrying and wondering about the bizarre ability he had that Danny exploited.

It had all seemed to change after he struck up a relationship with Lauren. He even viewed Danny as having more substance after seeing him with Emma; it had helped Craig understand that his cousin could be interested in someone other than himself. But just as the circle of people in his life grew and he felt like he might be emerging from the shell he'd been locked inside for so long, everything was getting more complex.

He felt as though he was losing his grip on each of the issues that were emerging. One catalyst for this was the bizarre messages Danny and his precinct were dealing with that caused Danny to pull Craig in even deeper and strained Danny's time and attention for Emma. Craig was troubled that while his relationship with Lauren seemed to be progressing, there were clearly things he couldn't share with her. The way she'd reacted before leaving his apartment the last time made him worry that she might be questioning whether they should stay together. Craig also wondered if he unwittingly used his secret as a crutch to keep others from getting too close, subconsciously choosing to remain isolated in a place where he had always taken strange comfort. Maybe it wasn't really a choice for him at all. Perhaps he was meant to continue along his path alone.

As the train approached Craig's downtown station, he wished Lauren would be at the office when he got there; he wanted to talk with her. But he knew she'd be on a college recruiting visit just across the border in Wisconsin for most of the week. He'd left her two voicemail messages, but she hadn't returned his calls. He didn't see how leaving any more would help.

He had heard from Danny though, albeit briefly. Craig understood from the newscast he'd seen the other night that his presence at the crime scene had created a stir among the police, and now with the media. He had called Danny to apologize, even though the problem would never have occurred had Danny not pulled him into the scene in the first place. Danny had indicated during the brief call that they were still at a loss in getting something, anything, in terms of leads from the crime scene. He'd also suggested that the two of them not see each other for a while in hopes that the media questions would die down, or until Danny caught a break in finding the killer. Craig entered the lobby of his work building, feeling alone and depressed.

By the time he retrieved a bottle of water from the cafeteria and made his way to his desk, it was already after nine. As he settled in, the administrative assistant for his department hurried over to him. "Craig? You're finally here," Stephanie said.

"Yeah, just got in. What's up?"

"Jeff Miller, that's what's up," she said, referring to their boss.

"What does Jeff need—oh, wait . . . " His voice trailed off.

Stephanie was nodding at him, a look of reproach in her eyes. "Right. The conference call with Minneapolis started at eight. Jeff came down here asking where you were and if you had the numbers for the proposal."

Recalling the deliverable that he needed to have for his boss and their sister team in Minneapolis, Craig closed his eyes and sank into his chair.

"Yes, definitely cringeworthy," Stephanie said, as if to reinforce the gravity of the situation. "Miller's not a happy guy right now. He canceled the call and said for you to come straight up to his office once you got in."

Craig stood up, his jacket not even off yet.

"Is there anything I can do?" she offered.

Craig stared off through the doorway to his cubicle and out toward the lake. "No, this one's on me. I'd better get up there."

Preparing to deliver his *mea culpa* to his boss, Craig thought about work being another aspect of his life that used to be normal, even if it was boring. Now it was coming unraveled too. All the recent drama had pulled his attention away from things he needed to get done at work. And his blossoming relationship with Lauren was taking its toll on the attention he paid at the office, even before this morning's *snafu*.

As he walked away from his cubicle, he paused for a moment. It dawned on him that Jeff Miller reported directly to Jeffrey Harris. *Great,* he thought. *I couldn't be screwing this up any better.*

Miller motioned Craig in right away. "Close the door and have a seat, Craig."

Jeff was in his mid-thirties, and Craig thought he resembled what he himself might look like in about ten years. He was a good person to work for: always fair and forthright in discussions. You would know if your work was at an *A* or *B* level; you would also know if your grade was closer to a *D*. Craig had the feeling that this would be a *D*-type conversation.

Once Craig was seated, Jeff let out a sharp, quick sigh. "Craig, what the heck's been going on?"

"Jeff, I'm not sure how I could've forgotten about the call this morning. I'm pretty sure I've got most of the analysis done. Is there any way to reschedule it for this afternoon?"

Waving off Craig's words, Jeff continued, "Forget about today. I turned it over to Ankit to finish. No, what I'm more interested in is what's driving these ups and downs with you."

"What do you mean?"

"Craig, you've always been a solid member of our team. Only a couple of months ago, you were locked in, man. I mean, I definitely noticed that you were cranking out good work." He paused, looking Craig in the eye. "Now, it seems like not only has that intensity fallen away, but you're missing deadlines. You've *never* missed a deadline like you did today. What gives?"

Craig wasn't sure how to explain it. So, he chose not to explain it at all. "I'm really not sure. I've been trying to figure it out, myself. I promise you that nothing like this will happen again."

Jeff's expression showed he sensed that Craig wasn't planning on trying to diagnose the issue with him. He appeared to let it go for now, but not before giving Craig something to think about. "Craig, I realize your background has been a little . . . I don't know, hard. You should really try to figure out what it is you want to do. I appreciate the past few years you've put in with us, but maybe you need to reevaluate whether you're committed to us or you need help figuring out your next step."

Craig wasn't sure if Jeff's words were a warning or a legitimate offer of help, but he didn't care to indulge Jeff in trying to figure him out—especially since he had made reference to Craig's past. He had shared some of it with Jeff a year or so ago, and he never liked it when people used things he'd shared with them to make a point.

"I follow you. Sure, I'll definitely give some thought to that and see if there's somewhere I land in my head. How about I check back in with you then?"

Jeff looked disappointed, like his genuine offer to help had been rejected. It also seemed to Craig that Jeff had seen through his lip service.

Their discussion having ended, Craig returned to his desk and sincerely tried to focus on his work for the balance of the day. He hoped that it would serve as its own distraction from the things that had dominated his thoughts during the morning commute.

It was late in the afternoon when he felt his phone buzz in his pocket. Hurriedly, he drew it out, hoping it was Lauren. The number on the display told him it was Danny instead.

"Danny . . . what's up? I hadn't expected to hear from you yet."

"I know. Hammond's been working double time to smooth things over within the department and the media. I think we're getting past it. You and I are overdue for a face-to-face to catch up on what happened in that apartment."

"I know. Listen, Danny—"

"Not now. Not on the phone. How about meeting for a meal with that Italian friend of ours?"

Now Danny was almost talking in code—that was odd. But he understood the reference to Santori's and agreed to meet him there later that evening.

He was actually looking forward to meeting up with his cousin. Having had no contact with Lauren for days now, he was craving interaction with others.

He stopped by his apartment briefly to change, not wanting to show up at Santori's in his work clothes. He got there early, but when Artie greeted him at the front of the restaurant, he told Craig that Danny was already waiting for him at the most secluded table in the back.

"Hey, Craig. Sit down," Danny said when Craig arrived at the table.

Craig sat hesitantly. "You think it's okay for us to meet now?"

"Yeah. Artie let me in the back, so no one even knows I'm

here. I asked him not to seat anyone back this far. Plus it's a Tuesday night, so we should be good."

A bottle of red wine and some bread were already on the table, and Danny looked as if he'd already had half a glass. He poured one for Craig. "I just got some wine. I assumed you'd probably already eaten."

Craig hadn't, having worked later than normal to try to make up for letting Jeff down earlier in the day. Danny took a deep breath. The look on his face made Craig concerned. "Things have you stressed out?"

Danny nodded. "Yeah. This has definitely been bizarre. Even for the shit I do.

"How so?" Craig asked. "What makes this different?"

Danny clearly didn't want to engage and instead deflected Craig's inquiry back at him. "So, tell me, just what the hell happened to you that night with the whole woozy, sick thing? I mean, I know you've never gotten used to seeing that stuff, but what made it so bad?"

Shrugging his shoulders, Craig said, "Honestly, I don't know. It was different. As different as something that crazy can be."

"What do you mean? Different how?"

Craig took a sip of his wine. "It wasn't like any of the times before. It was like I felt hot and sick all of a sudden. Whoever the killer was who did that, he just seemed . . . different—don't you think?"

"There's something to him, all right. So far, we haven't been able to turn up any clues about this guy."

"And he's calling himself the Tourist, right?"

"Wait. How do you know that?"

"Hammond mentioned it when he drove me home that night."

"Hmm. I wouldn't expect him to have let that slip," Danny said, then waved his hand dismissively. "Let's go easy with saying that aloud right now, eh? We've worked pretty hard to keep any sensationalism out of the media. But, yeah. We've received a few notes before and now after the murder where he called himself that. It's obvious it's the same guy who has the preoccupation with cutting people's fingers off."

"Did you ever find them?" Craig asked.

Danny looked puzzled. "The fingers or the killer?" He didn't wait for Craig to clarify. "No, to both. I'm actually going to go back over and talk it through with Maggie a little more. See if she's seen anyone new around."

"The older lady whose room you shoved me in."

Danny nodded.

"Like, what's her deal? She's quite the—

"Smart ass?" Danny finished Craig's sentence. "Maybe. That's probably about right. She's tough as nails though. Glad she and I connected years back."

"I'm not sure I follow."

Danny took a few minutes to explain Maggie's background. She'd been mixed up with the Irish Mafia when she was younger, spent time in jail for several different things. After she got out, the Mob beat her nearly to death to send a message that she should keep the things she knew a secret. Then she was apparently befriended by someone who introduced her to religion. Supposedly, that person had stood up for her and saved her life, which convinced her that she could trust and believe in people again. When this new friend was subsequently killed, it had the effect of cementing her resolve to stand up for what she believed was right.

"So, she's probably seen way more hell in her life than we

have through those shadows you create. She's a badass, that's for sure."

"Just how well does she know you? I mean, does she know anything about what I do? What we do?"

"Not at all. Why?"

"She didn't waste any time that night giving me the business about how I don't like helping you."

"Doesn't surprise me at all," said Danny, his facial expression resolute. "She's fearless. With all she's seen, I'm not surprised if she was pushing you. She knows it's important to be strong when no one else will."

"Danny, I get that. But you know I've always thought that, whatever this thing is that I can do, we probably shouldn't mess with it." Craig's palms were open as he spoke, as if he was imploring Danny to understand. "After whatever the heck happened last time, well, I believe it even more. Just look at the problems I caused you, coming out of it."

"C'mon, Craig. We've done it enough that there was bound to be a time when things would cut a little close."

"It's not just that, man. I feel like it affects me in my core." Craig said, tapping his chest. "*Especially* last time."

"Did you really feel like last time was different? Like *he* was different? Because I'm telling you, this guy isn't right. If you pick up on anything else about him, I'm gonna need that."

Now Craig was feeling used. Again. Why couldn't Danny see, let alone understand, that the re-creations affected him viscerally? How could he not see past his own need for clues and details? Craig had come to Santori's genuinely looking forward to seeing his cousin. He enjoyed it when their conversations didn't have to veer into Danny wanting to exploit him. Craig wondered why he couldn't just back off and stop asking him to delve into what he'd felt that night.

His simmering anger reflected in his words: "Right, because that's all I wanna be focused on. You have any idea what this is like? The twisted irony of it all? I'm able to see glimpses into what really happened to complete strangers only to be reminded that I've got no goddamn idea what really happened to my own dad!"

Danny made a gesture for Craig to lower his voice. "Calm down, calm down. I'm not trying to stir up old stuff for you."

"It's not just that. It causes problems for me in the here and now. With people I care about. That girl I was with when you barged in? When Hammond finally dropped me back off at home, *poof*, she was gone. The way that whole scene went down freaked her out."

"So, who was that girl, anyway?" Danny asked, ignoring Craig's rising anger.

"Her name's Lauren. We work at the same firm, and she's special. She's been helping me realize that I don't need to hide from my past. That there's nothing wrong with me as a result of what happened. I have my *own* family that I should remember."

Danny looked surprisingly hurt.

"I mean . . . listen, Danny. Being involved in these things with you messes with my head. Subconsciously, maybe it reminds me too much of all I've lost over time. My mom. My dad. My youth. Hell, even my optimism." He paused and took a sip of wine before continuing. "I feel like I'm starting to get a better sense of myself from being with Lauren—and being away from those crime scenes."

"Craig, I get it. I always hoped you could use whatever that thing is that you can do to help me—I mean, to help figure out the truth. I know you have your own stuff going on. But doesn't it kinda make sense to use what you can do to help people? To help families get closure when their world gets shit on?"

"I don't know," Craig said reluctantly. He pondered the wrinkle in what Danny had just said. Craig had never heard him sound this encouraging—or altruistic. It made him wonder, for the first time, if Danny actually cared more deeply about the effects his work had on the families that had lost someone.

Danny seemed to weigh something in his mind before saying, "I do know how much you've lost. I'm not trying to twist the knife on any of that. That's why I've always meant it when I said that I've got your back. I know that you had your own family. But you've been part of mine for a long time. That means something to me."

He looked serious and genuine—and rarely did Danny surprise Craig with something that actually seemed heartfelt. Craig swirled the wine in his glass, thinking of how to reply, but in the end, it seemed easier to change the subject. "So, how's Emma?"

Danny seemed almost relieved. "She's a great lady. I see a lot of things, I don't know, differently when I'm with her. I like her, and I like looking out for her."

"I think she likes that too."

"What do you mean?"

"She mentioned to me how busy you are right now. I get the feeling she needs to see you a little more, you know?"

"Believe me, I know. She really relies on me being around. But this latest case is pretty damn important too. I'm still trying to see her as much as I can. Hell, I'm headed over to her place after we're done."

"Good, that's good. You should go on over there. I was going to call Lauren to see if she wanted to meet me afterward too." It wasn't true, but Craig felt more comfortable on this footing.

"All right, sure. I'm glad we could talk through what went down the other night. Seriously, Craig." He paused as he stood up. "I mean it when I say you're part of us. I know how much you help me, and I've never taken it for granted. We cool?"

"Sure. We're cool," Craig nodded. "Now go check on your girl before she gets tired of waiting on your ass."

Danny smiled and slapped Craig on the shoulder as he moved by him, a sign that, in his mind, everything between them was back to normal. Then he turned toward the kitchen and went out through the back of the restaurant.

With Danny gone and the bottle of wine sitting on the table in front of him, Craig looked across to the empty seat his cousin had occupied. He wondered how he would feel if Lauren were sitting in it right now.

The waiter stopped by the table and asked, "Just yourself for dinner, sir?"

Swirling his wine again, Craig answered, "Yeah, just me for tonight."

13

SYMBIOSIS

For once, Craig wasn't feeling so used by Danny. As he navigated the rest of the week, he kept analyzing why it felt different now. Maybe it was because, even though Craig's re-creation hadn't yet yielded any clues, Danny wasn't pressuring him to do more. Or maybe it was the effect Emma seemed to be having on Danny, helping him understand that there was more to life than just chasing down criminals.

Whatever it was, Craig knew he had finally been heard, and it was enough to let him move past the tension he'd been feeling. Since the chance to smooth things over with Lauren probably wouldn't present itself until early the following week, Craig thought it best to immerse himself in work and try to build back some of the equity he'd lost with Jeff. He got into a rhythm throughout the rest of the week, being productive and really focusing on being better prepared for the meetings he had with a couple of the managers. This also kept him from wondering how things would play out with Lauren. Perhaps most importantly, it gave him a sense of purpose instead of feeling sorry for himself.

On Friday, he arrived at work a little later than usual, tired from having pushed himself so hard all week. Stephanie greeted him as he walked toward his cubicle.

"Good morning, Craig. Jeff wants to make sure you can be in the team conference call with the Minneapolis group next

Tuesday. I looked at your calendar, and it seems like it works for you."

Caught by surprise, Craig responded, "Really? He's okay with that?"

"Yeah. I thought you would see that as good news." she said.

He nodded. "Definitely. A little surprised, though. But after what happened earlier this week, I'll take it."

"Oh, one more thing," Stephanie said as she was turning to leave. "That lady from HR was down early this morning, right as I arrived. She left something for you. Here." She handed Craig an envelope, which he assumed—and hoped—would be from Lauren.

"Thanks!" he said as he snatched it from Stephanie's hand.

He swung his work bag onto his desk and sat down quickly to open the letter. His heart quickened when he recognized Lauren's handwriting:

Craig:
I'm sorry I've been absent from work and been a little distant since we last saw each other. I've been working though some things in my head.

He looked away for a moment, hoping that the rest of the note would be positive and not deliver any unwelcome news.

I think I've been able to get my mind in a better spot, if you're open to chatting about this. I'm only in for a little while this morning, but I wanted to drop this off for you. I have to go to Loyola, recruiting all day. Would you be up for meeting at Navy Pier on Sunday? I heard it's supposed to be warmer. By the Ferris wheel at noon. See you there?

Yours, Lauren

Craig's mood was elevated way beyond the feeling he had about being invited to the Minneapolis meeting. Knowing all might not be lost with Lauren after all, he pushed through the rest of his Friday workday and mentally committed to exercising and keeping busy through Saturday as he looked forward to seeing Lauren on Sunday.

On Saturday, he kept his word to himself and got up earlier than normal to go for a jog before breakfast. Then he showered, got dressed, and prepared to go out and get a haircut. He snatched his keys off the table and, just as he was leaving, there was a knock at the apartment door. For a moment, he hoped it might be Lauren, but when he opened the door, he found Emma standing there. "Emma. Hey, how are you? How did you know where I lived?"

"I know, right? I'd asked Danny for your address because I wanted to send a thank-you note for meeting me at school. But then I thought I might stop by instead." She paused for a moment, looking slightly embarrassed. "I know that it's really poor manners to just stop over unannounced, but is it okay if we talk for a minute?"

Puzzled, Craig motioned her inside, and as they exchanged pleasantries he couldn't help but realize how his view of her was evolving. He felt for her after learning of her past, and he saw that the support and safety she received from Danny were important to her. But he was also beginning to see a neediness in her that was part of her personality, no doubt exacerbated by what she had been through. Regardless, he was curious to get a sense of how she and Danny were doing. He hadn't heard from him since their last meeting at Santori's.

Craig offered her a seat at the kitchen table. "So, how is Senior Detective Daniel Walsh doing?"

She smiled hesitantly. "Oh, you know Danny. As intense as ever."

Even though she was smiling, Craig could see she was tense.

"Craig, have . . . have you been able to talk with him much?"

"Only the other night, briefly at Santori's. We were just catching up."

Lowering her voice, she said, "But you know about that case from last week and the new suspect that's been antagonizing him, right?"

"Yeah, a little bit." Craig was interested in hearing Emma's perspective. "Tell me, how's he handling it? Do you know if they're making any headway?"

"I'm not sure there's much 'they' to it," she said. "Danny's been talking like he thinks this is something personal. That everyone else in the department either doesn't understand or see how to help him." She paused. "I guess he's feeling like he's alone in figuring it out. Which, well, has left me alone too. Because he's at work so much.

"Craig, I figure he's always relied on you to support him through things. I just wanted to see if he was reaching out to you for help, or just to talk"—she lowered her head—"because I'm really not getting too much from him these days."

Craig fiddled with his keys as he sat across from Emma. "I'm sorry to hear that. I know that being in a relationship with a cop can be hard. Especially with someone like Danny who's really driven. He's probably just working extra hard to solve this one. I've heard from him and on the news that this suspect is pretty ruthless."

Emma began kneading her petite hands as she spoke. "That's what's worrying me. I've been around your cousin long enough to see that there's not much that intimidates him. This . . . this seems different. He's really been on edge and short-tempered, in ways I haven't seen from him before."

Emma's description was certainly at odds with how Craig had always seen Danny: stoic and fearless, but also collaborative and by the book. Even the secret he and Craig shared was the epitome of him wanting to work closely with others.

"Emma, when I saw him just the other day, he seemed to accept that this one would take some time. Not every case is going to crack open as easily for him as some have in the past."

Emma nodded and seemed to take some comfort in Craig's words. The two moved toward lighter conversation, including when they might get together again at Santori's.

"Yeah, and this time I can bring Lauren along, so I won't be such a third wheel."

"Oh? Who's Lauren?" Emma asked.

Craig wasn't too surprised that Danny hadn't mentioned Lauren to Emma. It seemed to further underscore that Danny was laser-focused on the case and not sharing much of anything with her.

"Oh, nobody really. Just someone I promised to treat to some really good Italian food. We'll figure something out. But yeah, we should definitely try to get together again soon."

They talked a little more about how her teaching was going and whether or not she had made it home to St. Louis recently (she hadn't) before she got up to leave. Craig assured her that he'd look in on Danny and encourage him to keep her in the loop. Seeming to feel a little better, she thanked him for allowing her to drop in. As he watched her leave, Craig noticed that, despite what he'd said, he didn't feel compelled to check in on Danny or let him know that Emma had reached out again with her concerns. He was intent on maintaining his resolve on the points he'd made to Danny in their conversation at Santori's. He felt like he had already done enough by talking with Emma.

———◆◆◆——

Sunday finally came, and Craig took the bus to Navy Pier. It was cold, and he'd worn his heavy coat, but he was hoping the bright sunshine would warm things up as Lauren had predicted in her note. He walked nearly the length of the pier to the Ferris wheel before seeing, to his delight, that Lauren was already there waiting for him. She was bundled up against the winter chill and had gloves on, but to Craig she seemed to have a glow that was unaffected by the unseasonably cold air.

She closed the distance between them and greeted him with a warm embrace.

"I'm so glad you asked to meet up," he said as they separated from their hug.

"Of course. I've missed you this past week. I just had some things I needed to think about."

"I know, and I probably gave you a lot to think about. Listen, about the stuff with Danny, I'm sorry I've been vague about why he wants my help. I'm not trying to keep anything from you, it's just . . . I don't know. Complicated. It's probably for the best that you not know. It's nothing, like, terrible. But it is something." He felt like he was rambling and started to worry that he might be blowing his chance to make amends.

Lauren was looking more serious as the cold lake wind blew in her auburn hair. "I have to be okay with being in the dark, huh? I guess it bothers me because it makes me think about how my own parents are."

Craig's eyes grew wide.

She smiled softly. "Don't worry. I'm not looking to fast-forward anything between us. But when I look at how they are, it's like there are whole parts of each other's lives they hardly know about. Honestly, by now it seems like they don't even care anymore." She paused for a moment, looking out in the distance. "It's sad to watch how it's playing out."

Craig stared at Lauren cautiously, trying to acknowledge her concerns. "I understand, and I get where that would hit you. But Lauren, I really like you a lot. I'd never want to hurt you. I hate that my relationship with Danny has thrown us off."

"Craig, I trust what you're saying. At the end of the day, I really do. I'm an only child, and I guess that I need to come to grips with the fact that the two of you are maybe even more interconnected than you realize."

"Oh, really?" he asked, wondering what she meant, especially since he and Danny weren't siblings.

"There seems to be some kind of symbiosis with the two of you."

"Okay, Ms. Psychologist, what does that even mean?" he asked with a smile.

She didn't return the smile. "I'm a big believer that we all know what we need, and that we're all interconnected the way we're supposed to be. Maybe you're supposed to be that way with Danny? More so because of what happened to your parents when you were so young?"

Even though the mention of his parents made Craig uncomfortable, he appreciated Lauren's trying to think through things that he sometimes wondered about himself.

But he didn't have much to offer in return. "Yeah, maybe," he said noncommittally.

"I'd only caution you to not let yourself get too stuck in negativity without knowing that you can always pick a different path or a better place. Remember what we talked about: you have to know your garden—"

"And know where my water is," Craig jumped in. "There you are, making me think through things again."

Lauren still didn't seem ready to let humor into the conversation. "But really, maybe subconsciously you just haven't embraced some things in your life, like learning things that you needed to know, or ignoring signs of what your heart has needed."

"Maybe you're right. I'll be honest with you on one point—I think about you constantly. I just seem more positive when I'm around you. Isn't that an example of me following what you're saying about choosing a better path . . . or a better person?"

Finally, she smiled. "I've got you coming around, don't I?" She placed her gloved hands gently on the sides of his face and leaned in for a kiss, then withdrew and looked directly into his eyes. "I'm going to try to stay patient as you deal with all that's going on in there"—she tapped his forehead gently—"at least until you're ready to completely let me in. I understand where your past has made that hard for you to do."

Grateful but still leery, Craig asked, "But why are you okay with doing that?"

"I don't know. I guess I just believe in you." She winked at him. "And I think you're meant for big things. Even if you don't yet think you are."

"Well, I'm glad you have faith in me, because I'm not sure I do."

"Of course you should have faith in yourself. Don't you feel it?"

Craig just looked at her, slightly dumbfounded.

She smiled again, shaking her head. "You have trouble with this whole faith part, don't you?"

She had an uncanny way of drawing him out, despite his tendency to avoid introspection. "I'm not sure. Like you said with my past, maybe things that were important to me or close to me are things that I eventually lose. Maybe that's why I end up keeping my emotions, and other people, at a distance. So I don't let them get too close and then risk losing them."

"Well, you've been honest with me about the fact that I mean something to you. I haven't gone anywhere. So, maybe it's time to let that thinking go? Did you ever try to talk with Danny or his family about how you struggled with this?"

Craig shrugged. "The Walshes never really wanted to go too deeply into a discussion about what happened to my dad. I get that. I think they believed they were doing the right thing by trying to shield me from those memories. But at the same time, I really wasn't honest with them about what was going on in the back of my mind. I believed that if I let them in, something bad would happen to them."

Lauren remained silent, as if leaving an opportunity for Craig to continue to work things through.

There were a few moments of silence. Craig looked out at the water as he thought. He then looked up at the sunny sky as a gust of wind buffeted them. Forcing a shudder, he joked, "I'm not sure you read the full weather report there, Harris."

"Okay, well, maybe I didn't even read it at all." She laughed. "Come on. Let's go back into the city and find someplace warm for lunch. Then maybe we can hang out at my place—if you want to."

"Are you sure you're up for all that?" Craig felt good about how things were going and relieved that she seemed to be ready to move past where they'd been stuck.

"Absolutely."

They locked arms and made the long walk back toward the city.

◆◆◆

The sun had set an hour or more before they arrived at Lauren's apartment in Wicker Park. Craig had enjoyed the few times he had visited with her there. Her apartment was definitely nicer than his and located in a trendier neighborhood.

Sitting on the couch, they sipped white wine and chatted while the television played in the background. Lauren toyed with Craig's newly cut hair and whispered softly, "Would you want to stay tonight?"

"Sure. If you're really okay with me staying over."

As they snuggled closer, Craig let his worries go—about Danny, the re-creations, and his reticence about telling Lauren more. There was something magical about being in this moment, embracing and kissing this wonderful woman. But the faint and familiar sound of the phone vibrating inside his coat pocket broke the spell. Trying to ignore it, he thought back to the conversation he'd had with Emma the day before. He apologized profusely as he separated from Lauren's embrace and quickly retrieved his phone. It was Danny.

"Dude. You're not at your apartment. Where are you?"

Looking over at Lauren, Craig said, "Uh, I'm at Lauren's. Why? What's going on?"

Danny's voice was monotone, more serious than Craig had ever heard. "Hammond was just at your apartment to get you. I'll radio him to tell him to pick you up there. What's the address?"

"Danny, wait. What's going on? Why would you have Hammond come here?"

Lauren's curiosity piqued at the mention of Danny.

"Remember Maggie?" Danny asked. "She's been killed. Just like the other one was. I need you over here with me ASAP."

Craig closed his eyes as dread swept through his chest. "All right," he said and gave Danny the address.

Lauren's face dissolved into a look of irritation as Craig finished the call.

14

MAGGIE

Craig and Lauren sat in tense silence as they waited for Hammond to arrive. Lauren didn't seem angry so much as surprised, and perhaps confused that something like this had come up again so soon, Craig being whisked away just as they were getting close. The timing couldn't have been worse. Craig opened his mouth to say something several times, but each time found himself at a loss for words. What could he say?

He was genuinely shocked to hear about Maggie. His work with Danny had never involved anyone he or Danny knew personally before. Granted, Craig had only had a brief encounter with Maggie, but Danny seemed to have known her well. Craig was suddenly worried that the images he would channel this time might hit a little too close to home.

It was after nine when Hammond knocked on Lauren's door. Craig grabbed his coat and walked over to Lauren and leaned in to gently kiss her cheek. "I'm sorry," he whispered in her ear.

She pursed her lips and nodded, a resigned look on her face as he left.

Hammond wasn't very talkative on the way to the crime scene, but he did instruct Craig on how they would be arriving. "You see that hat and jacket at your feet? I'm gonna need you to put those on before we get there. You follow?"

"Yeah, I get it."

"There's also a pair of glasses down there. Put those on too."

"But I don't wear glasses—"

Hammond irritably cut him off. "They're just for show."

As Craig donned his "disguise," Hammond seemed to be thinking aloud. "So, we just have to get him up there, and then get him back out as quick as we can. Dammit, we're cutting this one close."

Puzzled, Craig asked, "Are you talking about me?"

Aware that his thoughts had made their way into words, Hammond looked to cover. "Of course I'm talking about you. Who the hell else would it be? Pay attention now. I know that you and Walsh can only do . . . " He seemed to struggle with the right words. "Whatever it is you all do. Since the responding officers are already there, we've told them that you're someone we brought in from the outside. Someone who has experience with this type of stuff."

"What kind of stuff?"

"They're gonna think you're from another forensics team, but someone who looks into ritual violence, cult shit, things like that. That's the cover we're gonna use to get you in there and alone for a while." Hammond shook his head. "Because believe me, once this hits the scanner, every news crew in the damn city will be down here."

"Why?" Craig inquired.

Irked, Hammond said, "Where you been, exactly? It's a goddamn serial killer. Nothing stirs everyone up like this kinda shit getting out there." He turned to look at Craig briefly. "That's why, however you can help Walsh, you need to come through. This is my precinct, my name that's out there, and we're gonna catch this bastard. You hear me?"

Craig well understood.

"Yeah. Yeah. I got it. I'll do whatever I can."

"No, you'll do *everything* you can," Hammond corrected.

When they pulled up to the apartment building, Craig noticed there was already a larger police presence than there had been the first time, barely a week and a half earlier.

Hammond seemed satisfied that Craig looked whatever part he thought Craig should play to get him to the scene. They didn't speak after they entered through the back of the building and rode the same service elevator to the same floor.

They walked down the hall to Maggie's apartment door, which had already been roped off. Two patrol officers stood guard.

Hammond addressed them. "Listen up, boys. This guy's from another precinct. I need him to start poking around with Walsh while the other team gets their shit together and gets out here."

Craig looked at the floor, pretending to be deep in thought while one of the officers went into the apartment to retrieve Danny. Thankfully, Craig thought, he didn't recognize either of the officers as having been there when Craig had gotten ill.

Danny emerged, acting as if he might only know Craig casually. "Oh, hey, Jim. Glad you were willing to come down here. Let's have a look and get any thoughts you might have." He ushered Craig inside and the two patrol officers started to follow. Hammond blocked their path.

"Walsh is gonna take a little bit of time with, um, Jim here so they can check things over without distraction. I can't have a ton of people tromping about just yet. You two just hang out here in the hallway. Keep anyone who wants in out of there. I'm gonna go back downstairs, and I'll get the other team up here just as soon as they arrive. Walsh and this guy are to be left alone unless I say to disturb them. Are we clear?"

As Hammond set the ground rules, Danny and Craig continued into Maggie's apartment. Unlike the crime scene farther down the hall, her apartment was well lit. Craig remembered where she had been standing when she offered him a towel to clean up. Now he was looking down at the edge of the kitchen where Maggie's body lay, uncovered.

She was wearing a housecoat similar to the one she'd worn the night he had met her. She had suffered significant trauma to her hand and arms. Like the other victim, her body was face down. A large pool of blood had spread on the linoleum under her neck.

Danny broke the silence first. "I know we talked at Santori's about you pulling back from these. But you gotta see why I brought you here. This is a pattern, Craig. Clearly, this guy is some type of serial killer."

"It still doesn't make my being here right," Craig countered, but his cousin acted as if they were using up valuable time arguing.

"Craig. Come on! Even you have to see the difference. I know this lady was busting your balls, but she was a good woman. And she was a real, *living* person you met, if only for a few minutes. Don't tell me you don't wanna find who the hell did this!"

Of course, Craig was interested in knowing. It *was* different, and not just because he had met Maggie. The sensational way this killer had been goading the police made it seem like a constant threat. While it felt like there was a better rationale for Danny wanting his help this time, Craig was afraid that trying to unravel this mystery would close the door that had been opening in his talks with Lauren. Craig worried that the door might stay closed if leaving Lauren again pushed her away.

Out of the blue, Craig asked, "Does Emma know where you're at? I mean, are you keeping her up to speed on what's going on with this?"

"Craig . . . what? Of course. Where the hell is this coming from?"

Craig wasn't sure why, but he deflected his concern about his relationship with Lauren toward Emma's with Danny.

"I just think she's a bit frayed."

"Wait, how do you know this?"

"She's talked with me some. Confided in me, I guess."

"What?" Danny sounded offended.

"She's just lonely for you. Concerned about how deep you are into all of this lately. And she's a little scared herself."

Danny looked pained. "Just how are you getting—oh, wait. I get it. For real? You're giving me shit for asking you to help find out how someone was fucking killed? But you're completely okay somehow with channeling how my girlfriend's feeling?"

Craig realized that he shouldn't have said anything, and he was thankful Danny seemed to let it go when he continued: "Listen, we don't have unlimited time here, so let's get rolling."

Feeling relieved not to have to talk anymore about his connection with Emma, Craig looked for a spatter of blood somewhere against a wall or cabinet in Maggie's kitchen. On the wall, he spotted a bloody handprint where she had reached for a light switch. Craig touched the tacky dampness of the stain and began to slowly knead it with his first two fingers. The misty red veil descended on the room, once again leaving just Danny and Craig alone in its ether as they heard the muffled pulsating sound begin again.

Then they saw Maggie's silhouette thrown back against the wall near Craig's hand. The suddenness of the action in the re-creation took both of them by surprise. The shadow of Maggie's arm reached over toward the light switch. *Was she trying to turn the light on or off, and why?* Craig wondered.

"Okay, where's our guy?" Danny now appeared to be fully engaged and sounded impatient.

As if on cue, the same thin, wiry shadow appeared from outside of the veil, slowly approaching Maggie. Instantly, Craig once again felt the wave of nausea and warm clamminess he had experienced in the last re-creation. Shaking his head, he said: "Feels exactly like last time—not good."

"You're gonna have to hang in there. I need to be able to see what happened."

"I got it, I got it," Craig reassured him.

The shadow slammed Maggie into the wall again and then backed up. She straightened and seemed to walk defiantly in the direction of her attacker. Unfazed as well, the attacker walked toward her until the two of them were separated by barely a few feet. It looked like the killer was talking to her. Unwavering, Maggie proudly held her head higher.

"Damn!" Danny said aloud, acknowledging her bravery.

Then, with unnatural speed, the killer snatched Maggie's left arm and seemed to hold it tightly in place. She tried to resist, and in a flash, the killer slashed at her, severing her hand from her arm. Doubling over, Maggie could be seen cradling her injured arm.

"What the hell is he using to cut her?" Danny sounded anguished.

Craig watched, enduring the warm, queasy feeling. Maggie's pain was obvious as she crumpled at the waist.

The killer then lifted her mutilated arm and seemed to wipe Maggie's face with its bloody stump.

"Goddamn sick bastard!" Danny shuddered with anger.

The killer flung her arm down, grabbed her by her hair, and lifted her entire body off the floor with a strength that belied his thin, wiry frame. He used his other arm to slash through her neck, creating the fatal wound. He lowered her back to the floor and cocked her neck where the wound was spilling blood. He seemed to be looking in her eyes as he said something to her. She shuddered, and then Maggie's body went limp. As he had done with the victim who lived down the hall, the killer flung Maggie face down to the floor, where her dead body now lay.

Then something peculiar began to happen, not unlike what Craig had seen hints of in the other re-creation of this killer. He heard Danny announce with frustration, "Seriously? That's it? He's just gone?" Craig didn't understand. He'd kept his hand in touch with the bloodstain, and the misty veil remained. He could see that the killer's shadow hadn't left the scene. Why couldn't Danny see the killer while Craig still could?

"What are you talking about? He's right there."

Danny glanced toward the floor where Craig had indicated, but announced with annoyance, "Go ahead and dial it back, Craig. I need to start looking around the room without all the gray. We're gonna run out of time!"

Something isn't right, Craig thought. He was still looking closely at the killer's silhouette, which had been staring down at Maggie. But now its head looked up, appearing to turn its gaze in Craig's direction. His nausea grew in waves, and he felt panic building inside him—this wasn't the way these re-creations had ever worked before. The killer seemed to be looking directly at Craig in real time. Trying to get his cousin's attention, Craig said, "Uh, Danny. Something's really not right here."

But Danny wasn't paying attention to him, rather muttering to himself as he kept glancing around.

It was then that Craig noticed the killer's shadow tilt its head to one side, as if looking to where Craig still maintained his touch against the bloodstain. The shadow raised its chin and nodded slightly, as if confirming something to itself, then turned around and appeared to stare directly at Danny.

"Danny, seriously. Don't you see him? He's right there. Something's definitely not right. How does he know?"

"Knock it off and shut it down already. We're running out of time, and I don't know what the hell you're talking about!" Danny's anger was palpable. Craig cringed as he saw the menacing shadow approaching Danny. "Danny! He sees you. For real—he sees you, like, right now. And he's coming toward you!" Craig was close to yelling.

"What the hell are you talking about?" Danny said as he looked in Craig's direction, oblivious of the silhouette in front of him.

Shaking his head and forgetting for a moment that he controlled the veil, Craig was breathing hard, sweat pouring from his forehead. The killer's shadow had nearly reached the spot where Danny stood. "Oh my God! What's going on?" And it finally hit him—he yanked his hand away from the bloodstain. The reddish mist quickly evaporated, and the shadow with it. But even as everything disappeared, Craig could have sworn that the silhouette turned back and looked right at him.

"Craig, what the hell? What do you mean he was coming for me?"

Craig felt on the verge of hyperventilating. Shaky and covered in sweat, he began to peel off the forensics coat and hat. He bent at the waist, hands on hips, trying to gather himself and comprehend what he thought he'd just witnessed.

Danny strode over to him. "Talk to me! What do you mean he was coming for me?"

"I don't know. It's what I was seeing there at the end."

"Are you sure? 'Cause I didn't see anything like that. Are you positive that this woozy stuff isn't just getting to you?"

Craig finally found the strength to stand upright. "Danny, I swear. I'm absolutely sure. The shadow of this guy seemed to, I don't know, understand, at the end, who you were. Even though this was supposed to only be a replay of what happened in the past. It was like he sensed you in the here and now. Jesus, I don't know."

A loud knock at the apartment door made them both jump. Hammond entered, leading the forensics team with him. "Walsh? You guys wrapped up and all?"

Hammond's question didn't seem to register with Danny, who stared incredulously at Craig.

As the real team started its work, the lead examiner took note of Craig. "Wait, Sergeant. Who is this guy?" Craig clearly looked drawn and haggard from enduring the nausea and alarm.

Hammond didn't seem ready with an explanation. "Well, we, uh, brought him in to see if he recognized any gang signs or cult paraphernalia."

The lead examiner didn't seem satisfied and pushed Hammond harder. "Sergeant, I'm not sure what you're talking about, or who this person is, exactly"—he pointed sharply at Craig—"but in no way should he be at this scene right now."

"Now, wait. Hold on there." Hammond seemed to regain his authority. "Let's talk this through." He turned to Craig and Danny. "Walsh, maybe it's best you take our specialist downstairs. Now."

Needing no further prodding, Danny grabbed Craig by the arm, and they made their way out of the apartment. In the hallway, Craig could still hear the examiner taking Hammond to task about who exactly Craig was and why he was at the scene ahead of those officially responsible.

As they walked to the service elevator, Danny pressed him again. "Craig, you really saw this guy coming after me?"

But Craig had had enough. What he'd seen only confirmed to him that he wanted out for good. "Danny, let it go. I'm done with this stuff. Out!"

They were riding down the elevator when Craig continued: "I've got to get back to Lauren and try to do some damage control with her." He looked squarely at his cousin. "I'm sorry about your friend Maggie. I really am. But this stuff we do? There are things that we just don't understand. And these last two times have just gotten too bizarre."

They had reached the back door of the building. "Craig, if what you saw is what happened, that means this guy is trying to dial me in. This is my ass that's on the line now. All the shit he's sent to the precinct. And now this! I'm gonna need you even more until we figure him out."

Craig argued, "You'll only be in danger if you *choose* to stay in this stuff, Danny."

"What are you talking about? This is my goddamn job, Craig! I need you shoulder to shoulder with us trying to figure it out."

Craig shook his head vigorously. "Are you nuts? No, Danny. Not anymore. Like I said, I'm out. We're in way over our heads with this, and I get to choose if I want to be involved."

Danny stepped aggressively toward Craig. "I don't think so. You're coming back up there, because I'll be damned if I'll have a friggin' serial killer toying with me while my family isn't willing to try to help me bring him down."

Craig pushed through the door of the building, but Danny caught up with him quickly, grabbing his arm firmly, trying to pull him back in. For Craig—angered, confused, and shocked by what had transpired in Maggie's apartment, sickened of being surrounded by death and defilement, it was the final straw. Just as Danny grabbed him, Craig used Danny's momentum to pull his grasping arm down. In a flash to try to compensate, Danny tried to retract his arm. Craig pinned Danny's arm with his free hand and flowed back with Danny as he withdrew his hand. Craig then used Danny's retreating momentum to torque Danny's arm almost up behind his shoulder, which upended him. Danny fell backward, off his feet and onto his back.

Danny sat up, stunned that Craig had reacted so swiftly. Then they both became aware of their surroundings. The sidewalk was peopled with news teams waiting to question the police about the murder. They raced forward with a barrage of questions, asking Danny what had happened—why he was on the ground.

As Danny got to his feet, he tried to take the lead and get control of the situation. Some of the reporters turned their attention toward Craig, who tried to fade back against the building. But the reporters had seen the altercation and were peppering Danny with questions, which he wasn't handling very well, as evidenced by his boiling anger. Thankfully, just then Sergeant Hammond exited the building, accompanied by another officer, and began immediately barking out orders. "Walsh, you're needed back upstairs with the team—now!" He turned to the reporters. "Listen, everyone. We will get to your questions shortly. We need to process the scene first, and then I'll be back to talk to you. Until then, Officer Gibson here can take a few of your general questions."

When Gibson stepped toward them, Hammond quickly turned to Craig and pointed in the direction of his car. "You and I are outta here. Come on!" As they walked away from the building, they could hear Danny shouting angrily. "You and I need to be together on this!"

Shaking his head, Hammond let out an, "Oh, Jesus," looked at Craig, and said, "Let's hustle." As the two approached Hammond's unmarked car, they could hear a couple of stray questions being posed to Officer Gibson.

"Who, exactly, is the sergeant taking away?"

"Is that individual linked to this new slaying?"

On the drive back, Hammond seemed flustered, clearly worried about the public drama Danny and Craig had created. It was late, and Craig wasn't sure that going back to Lauren's was a good idea, so he asked Hammond to take him back to his own apartment. Neither of them spoke during the drive, and it was pushing midnight by the time Hammond stopped at the curb in front of Craig's apartment building. As he was getting out of the car, he felt Hammond's firm hand on his shoulder. "Henriksen, I don't know exactly what happened back there, but this train has gone off the rails. I'm beginning to see how bad an idea it was to ever let Walsh talk me into letting you be involved. I've got another dead victim. And, all of a sudden, my best detective is losing his shit. Now I got the media whipped into a goddamn frenzy."

"And what do you want me to do about it?" Craig said, trying not to sound confrontational.

"Here's what you can do—lay low on this and keep your distance from your cousin until I can figure something out."

Craig nodded, and as he shut the door behind him, Hammond made one more thing clear. "Oh, and keep your damn mouth shut, right?"

There was no need to answer. As he watched Hammond's car speed away, he took in a deep, long breath of cold night air and looked up into an overcast sky. His chin fell to his chest, his shoulders rolled forward into a slouch, and he made his way up to his apartment.

15

THE TUNNEL

It was midmorning when Craig was awakened by the buzzing of his phone. Exhausted, he had collapsed into bed in his clothes right after Hammond dropped him off. He realized he was late for work again, but after the events of last night, he didn't really care.

The re-creations had always been troubling— just the fact that he could do what he did. But last night had been alarming. The killer's shadow had seemed fully aware of his and Danny's presence—in real time. It had looked like the killer was trying to get at Danny through the veil. *How could he sense us during the re-creation?* It puzzled Craig. *Could Danny be in real danger now?*

Sitting up in bed and grabbing his phone, he saw that he had missed several calls and voice messages; one had been from Emma. He'd hoped Lauren had called but realized this was probably wishful thinking.

Emma sounded stressed and had left a long message. She said her nerves were frayed, so she hadn't gone to school today. Danny hadn't stopped by to see her either. When she had reached him by phone early today, he'd yelled at her. He said he was having trouble with the case and that neither Hammond nor Craig would help. She asked Craig to call her back so maybe he could help her understand what was going on. She finished her message by asking why he wouldn't help his cousin.

He inhaled deeply and let out a sigh. Emma's reaction was a little over the top, and at this point, frankly, he was more worried about Danny's state of mind and about his own relationship with Lauren. For the first time after one of the re-creations, he was genuinely concerned by the fact that the killer was still on the loose.

The other two calls he'd missed had both been from Danny: one in the middle of the night, and the other very early this morning. He'd only asked that Craig call him back. But after Hammond's parting admonition, Craig had no intention of reaching out to Danny yet. Nevertheless, he desperately wanted to talk to someone about what had happened. Without Danny, there was no one else to turn to. Craig felt more isolated than ever.

He didn't bother calling in to work, knowing that he had probably sealed his fate by not showing up again. He did, however, call Lauren's office number, assuming she'd be more inclined to answer her work phone. He was right.

"Hi, this is Lauren. How can I help you?"

"Would you like that alphabetically or in order of importance?" he tried some levity. "Hi, Lauren. It's Craig."

"Craig, are you all right?" She didn't sound put out.

"Yeah, I'm fine, thanks. But I need you. I mean, I need to talk to you. I'm ready to try that letting-you-in thing, like you said on the pier."

She paused and then said, "That's good. Does this have anything to do with last night?"

Craig let out an audible sigh. "Maybe. Obviously, I didn't

make it in to work today, but that's kinda the least of my concerns right now."

"I get that. You want me to come over?"

"I definitely want us to meet soon, if we can. Just not here." Hammond's words were still in his head, and he thought it better to go someplace Danny wasn't familiar with. "How about that bakery a block or so from work?"

"Riley's?"

"Exactly. Can we shoot for like an hour from now? That should give me enough time to get ready and get down there."

"Of course," she said, adding, "Please be careful."

Craig felt a wave of relief wash over him as he hung up. Lauren still wanted to see him, and she seemed genuinely concerned about him. If he could really open up to her, maybe the roiling anxiety in his chest would ease.

It was just after noon when he got to Riley's, both a bakery and *delicatessen* with limited seating at a few Formica tables. Craig was surprised to see Lauren had arrived ahead of him— again. This was the woman who, by her own admission and Craig's limited experience, was late to most of her meetings. It meant a lot to him that she saw these past two meetings as important enough to be there waiting for him.

After a quick embrace, they sat at a two-top toward the back. Craig noticed Lauren's eyes darting up to a television on a shelf behind the counter. It was tuned to the local noon news and seemed to be reporting about the activities Craig had been involved in.

. . . another murder on the Southside last night in the same apartment building as last week. Residents there

are alarmed and beginning to wonder whether the two latest slayings are related.

Some footage from last night began to roll while the anchor continued to talk about the case.

Sources have told our station that there is a real possibility that the two murders could, in fact, be the work of a serial killer. Police thus far have refused to comment. But late last night, as our crew arrived on the scene where an elderly woman named Margaret Morrison was killed, they had some drama of their own. Reportedly, a civilian gained access to the crime scene ahead of the investigation unit, causing a confrontation between the unit and noted detective Daniel Walsh. You'll recall Detective Walsh has been a central figure in many recent breakthroughs with homicide cases in the greater Chicago area over the past few years. Police refuse to comment about whether there were non-police personnel at the scene, or whether the two recent murders have any relation at all . . .

Lauren looked back down from the television at Craig. "Are they talking about you?"

Exhaling, Craig nodded.

"So, what goes on, Craig? Why does Danny want you there?"

Suddenly, he rethought his brave talk on the phone. Maybe it was better to backtrack. "Do we have to talk here? I mean, isn't there a more discreet place?" While the bakery wasn't very busy, Craig felt too exposed to go into any detail there.

"Craig, you're the one who picked this place," she said, exasperated.

"I know, I know. I'm sorry. Can we just go someplace where we know it will be quiet."

"Where, then?"

Craig suddenly felt foolish. "I'm sorry. How about this—you tell me where we should go right now. Your complete call. Just somewhere where you think it'll be quiet and no one will be around."

"All right, then. I know a place. Come on."

About twenty minutes later, they found themselves at the Art Institute near the waterfront. Lauren's choice had been appropriate. Because it was early in both the week and the day, hardly anyone was there. After paying admission, they wandered up several floors until it was only the two of them in an exhibit hall. They sat on a cushioned bench in front of an Impressionist painting.

Lauren broke the silence. "So?"

Just as Craig was about to speak, he felt his phone buzz. As he withdrew it to look at the number, Lauren asked who it was.

"Don't worry. I'm not answering it." Looking into Lauren's eyes, he began. "It's like this. Once Danny got on the force and into homicide, we figured that I could help him think through and reenact some of the crime scenes in ways that gave him clues and ideas on how the murders occurred."

She looked at him, uncomprehending.

"It's . . . well. It's a little more complicated than that, I guess. It got to the point where he felt superstitious about needing me with him in order to solve a case." Worried that he might lose her with the flimsy pretense he was offering for his presence at the scenes, Craig tried to push ahead. "Can we please just roll with that rationale for now? It's a huge deal for me to even share this much with you."

"All right. Go on." She didn't sound convinced.

Craig explained that as Danny got more and more successful in his job, he'd come to believe that Craig had some sixth sense or intuition. He had become adamant that Craig sneak into crime scenes with him, against the rules and department procedures.

"And you were okay being around all of that . . . those terrible scenes?" she asked.

Craig shook his head. "No, not at all. That's one of the biggest things. I've hated it. It always seems to dredge up feelings that remind me of my dad being killed." He paused and looked away from her. "But Danny and the Walshes were always good to me, taking me in and all. Danny in particular helped me through some pretty tough times growing up. I don't know . . . it was hard to say no to him."

"But Craig, I can see where being in the midst of those scenes would be torture for you—almost perverse, given your childhood."

"Danny's made the point that I never really saw exactly what happened to my dad. You see, the Walshes never told me how it happened—other than it was really violent. But with that in the back of my mind, I'd go with Danny to these scenes and find myself filling in the blanks of what might have happened to my dad."

"Craig, it's not right for him to use you and put you through all that." Lauren looked pained.

Craig shrugged. "Danny sees it differently. He always thought that's why I would want to try to help him figure out what had happened to others. That it could help bring a killer to justice. Especially since I couldn't do anything about what happened to my dad."

They sat together in silence, each of them thinking through what Craig was sharing.

Finally Lauren said, "I know that the way Danny and his family looked after you means a great deal to you. And I know that Danny in particular has meant a lot in helping you become the person that you are now." She took his hand in hers. "But only you get to decide when enough is enough. You decide when you're available to support him with things that don't have anything to do with his police work. Craig, you get to choose what you think you owe him, but also what makes you happy."

Her words made sense. He felt a little guilty for not being more specific about his abilities, but he was afraid that if he told her everything, he'd risk driving her away. Nonetheless, it was still comforting to hear a perspective other than Danny's or his own, both of which had been rationalized over the years.

Craig looked down at the floor and nodded. "This has been huge. Thank you for hanging in there with me."

"Do you feel like you can separate from this? Everything that's been blasting on the news today is all about this. It sounds as if the police are struggling. And, well, it also sounds like your cousin in particular is pretty deep into it."

Craig felt some guilt creeping back in. "I know. It is different. It's as if—" He stopped short, and changed tack. "I mean, it seems like whoever is doing this is on some kind of mission. Certainly, the person is sick. But it also seems like he's putting some calculation into how he's provoking and engaging the police. Especially Danny."

"You think you can stay out of it?"

"I hope so. Being around you makes me see how much better that sounds."

She smiled softly but looked hurt. Craig thought she could sense that there was more, much more, to the conflict that raged inside him. Like she knew he was unable or unwilling to share more.

"So, what's next?" she asked.

"Well, after last night, Danny's sergeant told me that I need to lay low. The truth is, I just really want to spend time with you. Leave all this behind me."

"Me too," Lauren said. "Why don't you come back to my place tonight?" She smiled in a way that made it easier for Craig to walk away from all the turmoil.

"That would be great," he said.

As they got up to leave, Craig felt a single buzz from his phone, a reminder that he had received a voicemail. "Hmm. I forgot about that call. Can you give me just a sec to check it?"

It was Emma again. Craig rolled his eyes. She sounded scattered and worried, and spoke of her concern for Danny again. She asked if Craig had told anyone about the talk they'd had when they first met at dinner. Then she said something cryptic about a package she'd apparently received, asking why anyone would send her something that was addressed like that. She ended the call almost pleading that Craig call her soon.

As Craig slipped the phone into his pocket, he thought for a moment about whether he wanted to drift back into a drama that involved Emma and Danny. He decided to let it go.

They spent the rest of the afternoon at the Art Institute, then took a cab back to Lauren's apartment, ate a simple dinner, and snuggled on the couch to watch a movie. Thank-

fully, there were no interruptions this time, and the two of
them fell asleep in each other's arms.

———————◆━━◆━━◆———————

He was looking into the dark opening of a tunnel. His heart
felt as if it would beat out of his chest. He was gasping for
air. His lungs burned. Behind him, he could hear his father
speaking. He turned to see him and heard, *"I know the fear
you feel right now, Craig. You grasped for this before when I
told you to wait. But now it's time."*

Andrew Henriksen only looked to be about five feet away
from him but seemed miles away at the same time. Craig
tried to run toward his father but something stopped him. He
turned around again and stared forward toward the entrance
to the tunnel, which felt more intense and darker than it had
just a moment ago. He clenched his hands into tight fists,
trying to withstand the energy he felt coming out of it. He
turned again to look at his father, who seemed even farther
away this time. But Craig heard his words loudly in his ears
as if he were still almost within reach. *Craig, you can do this.
It'll be hard, and you will feel it, but you have to stay strong.
You can do this. You know you can.*

Craig faced the tunnel's entrance again, and it felt as if it
were nearly upon him. The dark emptiness of its void filled
his entire field of vision. He could feel dark energy pouring
out and washing through his very core. It was too much.
He turned back again, looking for his father, but he was
gone. Panicking, Craig realized he was all alone to face the
darkness. He turned back toward the tunnel and saw nothing
but blackness ahead of him. He shook as if he would explode.

———————◆━━◆━━◆———————

He awoke with a start, covered in sweat, his breathing labored as if he had just sprinted a mile. He swung his legs over the side of the couch, trying to get his bearings, and remembered he was at Lauren's.

Lauren sprang up as well and held him from behind. "Craig, what is it? Are you okay? What happened?"

Shuddering as he spoke, he said, "Just a bad dream. It was . . . it was . . . I don't know, Lauren."

"Shh. It's okay. I'm here. You know I am," she said, doing her best to calm him.

They sat in silence, Craig staring off into the darkness of the room. Lauren kept holding him, her head resting on his shoulder. Slowly, his breathing moderated as he began to let go of the terror and dread he had brought with him out of his dream.

They sank back on the couch. Craig glanced over at the digital clock on the end table. It was a few minutes before six a.m.

"What happened in the dream?"

Before he could tell her, they heard a loud knock at the front door. It startled them both, and Craig felt his heart start racing again. They looked questioningly at each other in the dim light. They didn't have to wonder long. "Chicago Police. We need you to answer the door, please."

Craig rolled off the couch and stood up. Lauren got up as well. The knocking came again. "This is the Chicago Police Department. We need to speak to either Lauren Harris or Craig Henriksen. We need you to answer the door."

Lauren grasped Craig's hand, and they made their way to the front door together. Placing Lauren behind him, Craig opened it without unlatching the chain. Through the gap, Craig saw two patrol officers and Eric Hammond just behind them. Once Hammond saw Craig, he moved in front of the officers. "Henriksen. I need you to come with me. It's urgent."

"Why? I don't get it. What's going on?" Craig asked, shaking his head.

Hammond looked down. "Please, not here."

Gathering his courage, Craig said, "No. You tell me what you want with me. What's going on?"

Hammond looked back at Craig. "Emma Holt's been found dead."

16

EMMA

Craig staggered back from the door. "No . . . no . . . " he repeated under his breath.

"Come on, Henriksen. Let me in!" Hammond nearly shouted.

Lauren undid the chain, and Hammond asked the two officers who'd accompanied him to watch the door.

Craig slumped into a living room chair in shock. "What happened? How did she die?" he asked.

"Apparently, it was this goddamn Tourist. Someone called it in after hearing a struggle and screams last night at her apartment. Same way . . . she was killed in the same damn way those others have been."

Lauren covered her mouth with her hand and shook her head in disbelief.

Hammond went on. "But there's at least one thing that was different from the other scenes."

"What do you mean?" asked Craig.

"Well . . . " It was clear to Craig that Hammond was struggling with whether he should share details with him. "When we found her, there was a small package lying on top of her body. It was something that had been mailed to her."

The package Emma mentioned in her voicemail, Craig thought.

"The handwriting on the label looked like the same

scrawl on the packages we've been getting at the precinct. The ones addressed to Walsh. Only this one was addressed to Stepdaddy's Favorite."

Craig was perplexed by this but pushed for more details. "Well, what was in the package?" His mind was spinning with impressions from his first meeting with Emma.

"That's the weird thing," said Hammond. "Nothing, really. Just a bunch of shredded newspaper."

How could the killer have known about the abuse Emma suffered at the hands of her stepfather when she was young? Craig wondered. He rose and paced the room, deep in thought. If he hadn't sensed those things about Emma that night at Santori's, what Hammond was sharing now wouldn't make any sense. But there was obviously an ominous connection here. *What could it possibly be?* he asked himself.

Hammond interrupted his thoughts. "I'm just glad we were able to catch your cousin alone at his apartment last night to let him know before he learned of it on his own."

Craig looked wide-eyed at Hammond. "Danny already knows?"

Hammond nodded. "Yeah. I got him to surrender his gun and phone before we informed him about Ms. Holt. Told him I thought he was getting out of hand with the media and the scene he made with you processing the other crime scene."

Craig collapsed on the sofa. It now made sense that he hadn't heard from Danny.

"What happened then? How did he take it?"

"He's losing his damn mind, as you can well imagine. Said it was all his fault 'cause he hadn't caught this guy. He thought that since the killer was taunting him so much, he should've put Ms. Holt under protection."

Craig closed his eyes and held his head in his hands. "Oh, no . . . " he started.

Lauren sat down by his side and put her arm around him.

"Where is Danny now? I need to see him. I need to try to help him through this," Craig said.

"Just hold on," Hammond said. "This whole mess just got a ton more complicated. I got a lot of questions for Walsh right now. And I've gotta maintain some type of order with how this gets out in the media. They'll have a field day with it. It doesn't look good to start with, and sure as hell's not gonna look good for your cousin."

"What do you mean?" Craig challenged. "Are you saying that you suspect him somehow?"

"Listen, Henriksen. All I know is that your cousin's been getting lots of limelight from solving cases. Then someone starts sending these messages, directed only at him. These latest murders start, and he's got no luck figuring out who the hell this guy is. Then what? He starts coming unhinged. Hell, look at how he reacted at the Morrison crime scene! Shouting some crazy shit at us as I tried to get you outta there. Then his girlfriend ends up dead? I'm not saying he was involved, but this looks damn bad from the outside."

Some of Craig's greatest fears were starting to materialize. He and Danny had always wanted to make sure they were the only ones who knew about Craig's ability. Now, with questions arising about Danny, there was no way Craig could offer any assurances to Hammond without divulging why Danny sought to involve him in the crime scenes.

Before Craig had a chance to insist on seeing Danny, Hammond added, "Besides, I've lost track of where he's at."

"What do you mean?" Lauren interjected.

Now Hammond started to pace as he said, "Danny lost his shit after we told him about Ms. Holt. He got away from us before we could restrain him or get him secured somewhere. We're looking for him everywhere and figured we'd reach out to people he might contact. Like you, or his parents, or others on the force he trusted. I was hoping that Danny might have tried to come by to see you here."

Craig sighed. "So, what's next? I need to be there for Danny. Or help somehow."

Hammond kneaded his forehead roughly. "There's a lot that's next. We're pretty much through processing the Holt crime scene, and we're in the process of notifying next of kin in St. Louis."

Emma's parents, Craig thought.

"But like I said before, not only is this whole situation a mess, it's damn dangerous for Danny and anyone else he might come into contact with."

"You think Danny is dangerous?" Craig asked, puzzled.

"There's still a killer out there. Plus, I've got a detective whose world's been turned upside down. He's scared, confused, and out for vengeance. Finding him is my first priority. To get some questions answered and get him stable. Then we can deal with all the other shit." He stared squarely at Lauren and Craig. "With all the variables I got swirling here, I need to start locking a few of them down. Henriksen, I need you to stay away from your apartment and away from here too. It's only a matter of time until Walsh tracks you down here." He turned his attention to Lauren. "Ms. Harris, I know you have family here in the city. Is there a place where the two of you could go and be safe until I unravel a little of this?"

Craig guessed that Hammond had already connected the dots to Lauren's father being a partner in their firm, which is why he thought there could be options for where they might stay. Going someplace else to hide for now seemed drastic, but he didn't immediately protest the idea. As it was, with all he knew and had seen, he felt like he was in way over his head.

"Sure. Of course. My dad actually has a spare apartment in the city near the office. He stays there sometimes when he works late."

Craig wondered if the apartment had more to do with her parents' troubles than with her dad's work, but he quickly let the thought go. At least they had someplace to stay. Still, he was conflicted. While he understood Hammond's need to control the overall situation, Craig felt like he had to talk to Danny. Soon. He felt responsible, wondering if his role in Danny's police work had placed Danny under suspicion. Everything Danny had worried about recently—that the killer was somehow targeting him, that Maggie, one of his close informants, had been murdered, even his concern about Emma—now seemed valid. Craig was also feeling gut-wrenching guilt for having rebuffed Danny's request for more help, especially since Craig had clearly seen the killer's shadow take notice of Danny and approach him during the last re-creation. He couldn't help but think now that he really should have done more.

Hammond seized on the option of the apartment Lauren mentioned. "Great. That'll work. I'll have one of my guys outside take the two of you over. Like, now."

"Right now?" Lauren asked.

"Yes, Ms. Harris, now!" Hammond said impatiently. "You're two variables I can account for right now. Work with me here. We've got to get to Danny and bring him in first. Then, Craig, we can definitely get you two connected. I get that it's important to you."

Craig nodded. "Okay. I understand. But the moment you hear anything about Danny or bring him in, you promise me you'll let me know?"

"Sure. But for now, let's just get things moving." The sergeant left the apartment. And as Lauren and Craig retrieved their coats, Craig apologized for having dragged her into this.

Placing her hands on his, she said softly, "There's nothing to be sorry for. There's no other place I'd rather be right now than with you."

The officer drove them to a building a few blocks from the Grey, Parker, & Harris office. The apartment was a small efficiency on the tenth floor of a nice, clean building. The furnishings were spartan, and there was no real decoration, no evidence that it was frequently used.

"Do you ever stay here?" Craig asked.

"Only a couple of times," Lauren said. "Mostly it's been my dad's place. Well, it's really been for those times over the past couple of years as my parents grew apart. Sometimes after he and my mom have fought, Dad just stays here rather than go home to face her."

"Any chance he'll be by while we're here? I mean, is this going to be a problem?"

"No," Lauren assured him. "Dad's traveling out west for quarterly meetings through the end of the week. So, we should be in the clear at least until then."

Craig hoped they wouldn't have to stay that long, only until Danny could be located.

They tried to settle in through the afternoon, each of them showering. Then they had to put back on the clothes they'd been wearing the night before, having had no time to grab anything else to wear.

Eventually, Lauren broke the silence that had descended upon them. "So, do you want to talk about all this? I don't mean to pry. I can only imagine what's going through your mind right now. It's terrible what's happened to Emma. And I know you must be worried about Danny."

"Emma was a really nice girl. Kind and sweet. She was definitely what Danny needed. I guess I've always been more focused on what seemed to be Danny's selfish aspects. But when I saw the two of them together, it helped me see a different side of him. He seemed more real, more authentic. It also made me understand how much he really believed his life was about keeping others safe. He liked the idea of keeping Emma safe . . . " his voice trailed off. He stared blankly before resuming. "Danny deserved having her as part of his life. So that everything wasn't just about being a detective and catching the bad guys while trying to live up to some standard in his mind. Now that's been taken from him. It's just not fair. I know what that feels like. I guess I just wish I could be there for him right now. To let him know that I understand."

"You will be soon, Craig. They'll find him and get the two of you connected. Then you can help," Lauren said.

She seemed to understand that, deep down, Craig felt Danny had always helped him through the tough times and tragedies in his own life. Now it was his turn to return the support. He looked out the window. The first snow flurry of the season had started. "It looks like it's getting colder," he said.

Lauren turned the television on to the local news to catch a weather report. There was a brief snippet of a promo for the evening news. One of the newscasters was saying,

Coming up at six, we'll give you the latest on another slaying similar to the recent ones on the South Side.

This time, it occurred on the north side of the city, and the victim looks like she had ties to one of Chicago's lead detectives . . .

So it begins, Craig thought.

———◆•◆•◆———

As it neared five o'clock, they were startled by a loud rap at the door. Craig approached the door cautiously and looked through the peephole. He glanced back at Lauren, looking relieved. "It's Hammond, and he's alone."

Hammond looked overwhelmed. He was carrying a large envelope. He asked how they had been holding up. Craig assured him that they were fine and pressed Hammond for an update.

"Okay, let me start with a few basics," he said. "Ms. Holt's family has been notified, and they're on their way to Chicago. No new leads on our Tourist yet. The forensics team has yet to pull anything useful from the physical evidence, which unfortunately is consistent with what we found at the other two scenes as well."

"What about Danny?" Craig interrupted impatiently. "Have you seen him or gotten ahold of him?"

"I'm getting there. That one's trickier. The short answer is no. We haven't been able to bring him in yet. He's obviously very interested in finding you, though. My guys went by your apartment and could see that someone had been there. No real forced entry, but they could tell that someone had gained access. We ran the security video from your building and confirmed that it was Danny who entered." Hammond's gaze grew puzzled. "He kinda turned your place upside down, Craig. Like he was looking for something. He tore through some of your cabinets and drawers. Emptied out a few file boxes. Stuff like that. You have any idea why he would do that or what he's looking for?"

"No, I don't."

"Anyway," Hammond went on, "we circled back to his apartment looking to place a uniformed presence there in the hope that we might catch him if he returned. Apparently, we were a little late there too. Once inside, my guys found a gun case on a table and evidence that he'd loaded a personal firearm. They also found a note that must have gotten him pretty worked up."

From the envelope he'd been holding, Hammond pulled out a sheet of paper in a clear evidence sleeve.

"Apparently, our Tourist left this for Danny inside his apartment. Whatever it's referring to, it seems to have gotten his attention. Like he now knows where he can find this guy. And it looks like he's gone off locked and loaded."

"What does the note say?" asked Craig.

Hammond whipped a pair of reading glasses out of his pocket and peered through the evidence sleeve. "The crude writing generally matches the notes that accompanied the fingers this guy sent to the precinct. Here's what it says: 'Nearly done passing through. If you wish to meet, I'll wait for you at a place of which you have already heard. The place where you first learned from others what I can do.'"

"What does that even mean?" Lauren asked, unnerved.

Hammond looked at Craig and said, "No idea. But I'm hoping you might have one, Craig. This ring any bells based on what Danny may have said in the past?"

Craig's mind was thrown into confusion. Wanting very much to think this through, he also knew he couldn't let on to Hammond that he was interested in doing so. "No, none at all."

Hammond continued looking at him as he dropped the hand holding the note to his side. "Henriksen. I need anything. Anything you can give me here. This serial killer is out there. Now I have our best detective, your cousin, on a mission to go after him by himself."

"I got nothing. Sorry."

"C'mon, Craig. Goddammit, this is for real!"

"Don't you think I know that?" Craig responded, equally agitated.

Hammond pressed on. "This is your damn family we're talking about. Anything you might know about what the hell this guy is talking about, I need it. One of Walsh's neighbors told my guys that she thought she heard him tear out of there an hour or so ago. I need to get an idea of where he might've gone!"

"I'm sorry, Sergeant. I wish I knew something, because I really want to help find him. But I've no idea."

Lauren looked over at Craig but said nothing. Hammond took in a long, deep breath and let it out. "All right, then. I've got things to get back and check on. I need you to keep thinking, though. If anything comes to mind, anything at all, you call me immediately. Got it?"

Craig nodded.

"So, what happens now?" Lauren asked as Hammond started toward the door.

Hammond turned, his hand on the doorknob. "I got units all over the city looking for Walsh. He's not stable, and he's at risk, so that's priority one. You two, I need you to stick around here. One of my officers will be by within the hour. He'll be stationed here to protect you. Then, we'll go from there."

As he left, Hammond called back to Craig. "Henriksen.

You hang in there. We'll find Danny and get him safe. I'll let you know just as soon as that happens."

Craig nodded again but was lost in thought.

After Hammond left, Craig took up pacing by the window. He glanced out occasionally at the now steadily falling snow.

Leaning against the door and watching him, Lauren waited for a minute or two before finally asking, "Craig, do you really have no idea where Danny could've gone?"

"I don't know for sure. Some of the things that come to mind . . . they just don't make any sense." He was unsure whether to fully share his thoughts.

"But if this guy is trying to lure Danny—"

"I know, Lauren. I might have an idea. But I'm sorry. I need to do this on my own. To try to help him on my own."

"Is this the last wall you've got between us that keeps you from letting me all the way in?" Her frustration was clear.

Understanding she might feel hurt, Craig said, "No, not at all. There are certain things that are deep and complex and can only be between me and him right now. Lauren, I won't put you in danger. Remember, even you said that I'm the one who gets to decide what I'll accept and what I won't."

"But Craig. This is so serious. So real!"

"I know that. You said yourself that you could deal with this until I was ready to pull you all the way in. You have no idea how close you are to being there. I care about you so much, but I won't risk you in all of this yet."

His words seemed to catch her by surprise, and a tear began running down her cheek.

Craig didn't seem to notice. "I need to go right now and see if I can find him."

"Are you kidding me?" Lauren said, shocked. Craig walked

over to her, embraced her, and then stepped back. "Please. I don't expect you to understand. This is just something I have to do by myself."

"I don't want you to have to go." She composed herself for a moment, then continued, "But I understand. I know that this is deeply personal for you, and I'm willing to stand by what I said. I'll wait for you."

"This will be over soon, Lauren. Once the danger is lifted, I promise I'll be 100 percent committed to us."

"You know I'll hold you to that." Her tone was serious. "I'm scared to death for you, Craig. But somehow, I also feel like you know what's best here. I'll hold on to that until this is over."

She moved away from him while he gathered his jacket and put it on.

"I need to leave before Hammond's officer gets here. Please tell me your dad leaves a car in the garage."

Lauren had turned away from him but nodded and said, "Yes, it's in the basement garage. Space twenty-seven, I'm pretty sure."

She went to a desk near the kitchen and retrieved a key that hung there. She walked with him toward the door, then lowered the key into his palm. She caressed his arm, tugged at his jacket, and straightened the bottom of it. "You're precious to me, Craig. I want you to be careful. I want this to be over. Will you call me as soon as you can? Please?"

"Yes, I promise."

He kissed the top of her forehead and left quickly.

The door having closed, Lauren placed the palm of her hand against it. With her other hand, she covered her eyes and began to sob.

17

CEDAR TOWNSHIP

His hands were stiff from clutching the steering wheel. He was driving to Cedar Township, and the snow had been falling in large flakes, sweeping toward the windshield like stars in the dark sky of early evening. It had become increasingly difficult for him to focus on the road ahead as his mind continued to race with thoughts that had gathered over the previous three hours.

He'd stopped once for gas, shortly outside Chicago. He was determined to reach his boyhood town as soon as he could, hoping his hunch about Danny's whereabouts was correct. Danny's behavior since Emma's death had seemed so erratic. He'd always been resilient and undeterred. What Craig was hearing from Hammond, however, was anything but the simple, salt-of-the-earth approach he had always known Danny to take. Of course Danny would have been shocked at Emma's terrible fate.

But Craig assumed that he would fall back on his training, involve others, and use whatever resources he needed to flush out the killer. Instead, he was isolating himself. Maybe heeding Hammond's insistence that Craig keep his distance hadn't helped matters, but the only thing he could do now was try to find his cousin, regardless of what Hammond or the police wanted him to do.

It had always been easy for Craig to think of Danny as one-dimensional, predictable, always reliable, and dispassionate in his support for Craig. Now things were different. Danny was in deep pain and in danger, and Craig had to help him in any way he could. *Did Danny feel the same way about me when we were younger? Did he understand everything I'd lost?*

He was seeing his cousin through a new lens now. Danny's family had taken Craig in, cared for him, and loved him as their own. Danny in particular had provided Craig both protection and insulation. Craig had always thought that it was more about Danny building himself up than supporting Craig. Danny seemed different now, and perhaps Craig's exposure to Emma and their relationship had an effect on Craig. He also saw that his own growing feelings and the warmth he felt for Lauren helped him understand the support and sense of family that he now saw more in the Walshes. These feelings galvanized him as he drove into Iowa through the blowing snow.

Craig saw a road sign that read *Cedar Township* and eased up on the accelerator. The buildings and houses he passed in his approach to downtown held a level of familiarity he'd almost forgotten. There was little activity evident as the Saturday evening grew dark.

He drove through downtown, over the railroad tracks, and up a small incline. The sight that came into view stood out clearly in his memory: Holy Redeemer Lutheran Church, an old-style, German Gothic building with large limestone blocks making up the base of its foundation. Night had fallen, but Craig could see that the church had been well maintained. He remembered his father telling him that it had been built sometime in the 1930s.

When Hammond had read aloud the note they'd found in Danny's apartment, Craig immediately thought it referenced the earliest murder scene Danny would have been familiar with, and not necessarily a murder that Danny himself would have investigated. As he'd thought about it since leaving Chicago, he figured that his uncle would have shared the circumstances of his father's slaying with Danny when he was old enough to join the force. There was nothing else Craig could think of that pointed to a different location. Even if he couldn't fathom how it was all linked together, Craig felt in his gut that he was headed to the right spot. He also felt strongly that, given the secrets he and Danny kept, he had no choice but to keep his destination from both Hammond and Lauren, at least until he understood more.

When Craig pulled into a parking space at the side of the church, he saw Danny's car in the parking lot. A sense of relief washed over him, but it was quickly replaced with one of apprehension. Judging by the amount of snow that had accumulated on his car, his cousin had been there for quite some time.

Climbing out of his car, Craig squinted against the snow and a cold that seemed too harsh for this time of year. It was much colder in Iowa than it had been when he'd left Chicago. He wished he had a heavier coat. He wrapped his jacket firmly around his neck and hunched his back to brace against the cold as he stepped through the snow toward the back door of the church. He looked up at the night sky and stopped briefly. The absolute quiet was eerie. The sky, the surroundings, almost everything held a heavy weight of silence. He pulled his eyes back downward and noticed that the back door was slightly ajar.

He opened it cautiously, careful to be as quiet as he could. Without knowing what Danny may have encountered, what he was doing, or whom he might be confronting, Craig didn't want to be a hindrance or risk to the effort.

Once inside, Craig gently brushed the snow from his jacket. He was standing in a stairwell at the base of a set of steps that curved up to a main level. It was dark, but the outside streetlamp reflecting against the white snow shed a little light through a few windows. Craig still couldn't hear any sounds. With great effort not to create any noise of his own, he ascended the stairs on tiptoe before coming into the narthex of the church. He looked briefly at some of the pictures on the bulletin boards, but nothing stirred any memories.

He made his way to where the sanctuary aisle met the narthex, then slowly walked along the wall until he could peer down the aisle toward the altar at the front of the church. His fear and caution momentarily fell away as images flooded back into his memory, and he absentmindedly stepped out from hiding and stood at the end of the aisle.

The church sanctuary was as familiar to him now as if he had seen it only yesterday. It was nearly unchanged despite the passage of time. It was a medium-sized sanctuary with perhaps twenty or so rows of pews. Overhead, dark wooden beams came together in an occasional arch as they spanned toward the front of the church. It was dark in the overhead cage of the church's ceiling, but canned lights that hung down from it every few rows would normally provide full light to the congregation during a service. Only about a third of them were lit now. As his eyes scanned the altar, he saw a few steps leading up to a chancel platform, behind which was a massive wall with a large, ornate cross hanging against its side wall. The cross looked to be of dark wood and was close to ten feet tall. Everything was as beautiful, inspiring, and holy as it had seemed to him when he was a child.

Pulling himself back from his memories and into the present, he glanced around quickly, suddenly feeling naked and vulnerable out in the open. He looked back and forth through the church but saw no one. *Maybe a janitor left the lights on,* he thought. But that wouldn't explain why the back door had been ajar. There had been no footprints leading from Danny's car to the back door—but the snow had fallen enough at this point to obscure them. *Where is Danny? Even if he has left the church and gone elsewhere, where could he have gone without his car?* Craig wondered.

As he kept looking around, a glimmer of light reflecting off something near the altar caught his eye. He wasn't sure what it was, but he felt drawn to it. He stepped forward and began walking cautiously down the aisle. The winter chill he had felt moments earlier seemed to be replaced by thick heat and humidity. He kept walking forward, feeling almost compelled to do so. The air grew heavier with each step he took toward the altar. So warm, in fact, that without thinking, he stripped off his jacket and dropped it onto one of the pews.

He had nearly reached the front of the church when he began to discern the object that attracted him lying on the plain wooden altar. It was a rustic silver cross, polished so well that it reflected the dim light from above. Despite the warmth he'd been feeling, Craig shuddered. "What the . . . ?" he exclaimed. From both his childhood memories and his recent dreams, he recognized it as the cross his father had worn.

Forgetting all caution now, he moved quickly down the remainder of the aisle and stepped up onto the chancel to stand over the large, wooden slab. Feeling his eyes tear up, both from sweat and a surge of emotion, he reached for the cross. The metal was cold and sent a tingling sensation through his whole body.

A misty veil descended across the front of the church. Craig staggered back. But this veil of mist was unlike the ones he had channeled before. A clearer, pale blue light illuminated not only the area at the front of the church but the entire sanctuary. Instead of ghostly black images like those from earlier re-creations, Craig could see everything clearly, and it shocked him.

As he looked across the chancel, he saw his father and himself, as a boy, at the front of the church. Both figures weren't black silhouettes but clear, distinct images. As amazing as it was for Craig to have this visual clarity, he could also *hear* what was being said.

"Why do you always come down to church on Saturday nights, Dad? You don't have to teach church till Sunday, right?"

"Minister, little man." Andrew Henriksen gently corrected his son. "I minister to our friends on Sunday. And we want to make sure we've got everything set up for tomorrow, don't we, little buddy?"

"Sure!" the boy replied, clearly pleased to be spending time with his father and helping him.

"Hey, Craig, how about being my helper and grabbing that box of candles over there?"

"Okeydokey," the boy replied happily and scampered over to a table near the front of the altar. Andrew seemed to watch his son with pure love as he retrieved the candles.

Captivated, Craig watched the scene unfold, becoming lost in this old memory, forgetting the present and why he had come here. It was comforting to see himself interacting with his father and to be reminded of how kind and gentle he was.

He watched as his dad studied his sermon notes on the ledge within the pulpit. While the boyhood Craig gathered up the candles in a box, Andrew's shoulder tensed. He looked up from his notes, pale and alarmed, and slowly scanned the rows of pews, wide-eyed.

Continuing to look back and forth throughout the church, he called out to his son, "Hey, Craig, let Daddy help you with that."

"Okay," answered Craig, still busying himself with the candles.

Andrew moved quickly toward the boy, knelt down beside him, and turned him around to face him.

"You know how much I love you, right?" he said as he softly stroked the boy's hair.

"I love you too, Daddy."

Young Craig then smiled, and Andrew pulled him close, kissing the side of his head. "You will always be the light of my life, and I love you with all my heart."

It looked as though Andrew was blinking away tears. He held his son at arm's length, looking him squarely in the eyes. "Craig, remember this—I love you, your mama loved you, and Jesus loves you. Don't ever forget how powerful that is."

"Dad, I know all this stuff. God holds our family together, even though Mom's gone." He looked at his father, seemingly puzzled by his dad's emotional words.

Andrew focused intently on the boy's forehead, then purposely drew his hand across it. He scooped his son off his feet and began to carry him. "Aren't you getting tired? Don't you want to rest for a little bit while I finish up?"

Almost instantly, young Craig's face looked slacked with fatigue.

"Yeah. Wow, is it getting late or something?"

"It sure is, little man," Andrew answered reassuringly as he carried Craig a few rows back from the altar steps to one of the pews.

As he positioned his son on the pew, he removed the thick sweater he had been wearing, leaving himself in only a T-shirt. He rolled the sweater into a ball and gently slipped it under his son's head.

"Good night, Daddy," the boy said as his eyes succumbed to sleep.

Andrew remained kneeling beside the pew, his hand lovingly placed on his son's forehead. He did this for a minute or more with his eyes closed, then said, "I'm sorry to provide you this gift that you do not yet understand or accept. You'll understand someday. Then you'll know how much you're loved and how important you are." He opened his eyes and stared back at the entry to the sanctuary. "And why this is necessary."

He then took both of his son's hands in his, so that their arms formed a cross over the boy's sleeping body. He held them for a few moments—an absolute stillness and silence between them. As Craig watched through the re-creation, for a moment it looked as if a warm, golden glow surrounded young Craig's hands as Andrew held them.

Andrew then said, "It is done." He gently released Craig's hands and settled them back against his sleeping body. For a moment he remained bent over his son, appearing to breathe heavily as if the moment that had just passed between them had drained him of energy.

Andrew stood up, let out a long, deep exhale, and extended

his arms out over the boy. With his eyes closed and his face lifted toward the heavens, Andrew mumbled something rhythmic and unintelligible. As he finished speaking, young Craig's body shimmered and began fading, becoming more and more transparent and blurred until it was barely visible. Andrew lowered his arms, opened his eyes, and gently reached down to touch the young boy's invisible, unconscious body.

In the present moment, Craig watched with rapt attention, clutching the silver cross within the palm of his hand, holding it close to his chest.

Apparently satisfied that his son was visually concealed, Andrew walked briskly up the altar steps and to the middle of the chancel. Once there, he looked back at where his son rested on one of the pews, now hidden from sight.

As Craig watched these events in the bluish light of the veil, he stood no more than five or six paces from where his father stood. Without his sweater, wearing only a T-shirt and jeans, Andrew Henriksen looked much more muscular and fit than Craig remembered him. He stood looking out at the pews, hands on hips, seeming to be satisfied with the state in which he had left his son.

His stature and countenance suddenly changed. His chest seemed to swell and inflate, looking stronger and thicker underneath the T-shirt. His face looked more angular and hardened. His eyes narrowed. His arms and shoulders also appeared to become more rigid and powerful. His T-shirt began to show the distinct speckling of perspiration, while beads of perspiration appeared on his brow. He remained rooted in place and took several deep breaths.

A shuffling sound from the back of the church broke the silence. Andrew's hands moved off his hips and tightened into fists.

"Did you really think I would have forgotten about you?" a low, raspy voice said.

Craig followed Andrew's gaze and saw a dark figure wrapped in a cloak and hood standing in the narthex. It looked to be a man of medium height, thin and wiry. The cloak and hood that concealed him were dirty and tattered, giving him the appearance of an eerie vagrant.

"You are the Scandinavian I have long sought. I know exactly what you represent," the cloaked man said. "Your kind has its last stop at my hands."

"You may step foot into this house, but you cannot remain here long." Andrew's voice issued forth in a deep and resonant baritone. Craig couldn't remember ever seeing his father appear so serious and powerful.

"I need only stay long enough to see this through. We have long culled the herd to which you belong. You don't have any of the others here to help you, no one to aid in your escape this time."

"I was younger then!" Andrew snapped before quickly regaining the strength and measure of his voice. "I'm much stronger now. You'll see." A small, confident smile flickered on his lips. He seemed almost to taunt the fiendish visitor, who had started advancing down the aisle, but paused following Andrew's comment.

"I'll grant that you have a stench that's different. Much greater than those who have come before you. But each of their charms now resides with me," the visitor said. He then drew forth from inside his tattered coat a long, dark metal chain, the end of which he clutched in his hand. Attached to it were a variety of crosses and other symbols that could have once graced a necklace or bracelet. As the man held out the chain and glared at Andrew, his pale, weathered hand seemed to grip it with ferocity and hatred.

Momentarily, Craig's eyes moved from the chain the stranger gripped to his own hand that held the cross.

Andrew was unintimidated. "You're nothing more than part of a despicable pestilence. I'll stand my ground while I erase the impact you've had on our world."

The creature began a long, rolling laugh that broke into a thick, heavy cough. An evil grin creased his shadowed face. "Your brothers and sisters once spoke as you do now. Until they felt my nails at their neck."

Craig found himself backing away from the altar. As he did so, he couldn't help but notice that his father remained unmoved in the face of this advancing adversary.

Andrew and the stranger appeared, for a moment, to be quiet and motionless. Then, suddenly, the visitor let out a guttural roar and lunged toward Andrew, closing the distance between them in a blink.

Craig was surprised to see his father dive athletically and roll toward the side of the altar that Craig had backed into, avoiding the attacker before coming up on one knee and launching what seemed to be visible ripples from the palms of his hands that slammed into the attacker. Struck by whatever Andrew had unleashed from his hands, the adversary landed in a heap on the far side of the altar.

Andrew stood up, his hands flying like an orchestra conductor's as successive waves of force shot out from his palms toward the attacker. Thrashing about, the adversary dodged some of the blasts while others hit various parts of his body.

After several exchanges, Andrew was able to keep the

attacker at bay. While the force he launched from his hands was skillful and effective, it was clear to Craig that his father's energy was being drained. Between the volleys, Andrew stopped to gather his breath in deep gulps. The time between the blasts was also getting shorter as Andrew's attacks seemed to affect his opponent less.

Squinting into the pale blue veil, Craig noticed that the longer his father's assailant was kept at bay, the skinnier the hooded figure appeared to become. Craig wondered if this was what his father had meant when he told the attacker that he couldn't remain here long.

At one point, Andrew drew his arms to his chest before flinging out both rigidly open palms. A great burst of force blasted out against the attacker, sending him flying back and crashing through several rows of pews opposite where Andrew's son was concealed. In the brief moments this afforded, Andrew turned his attention away from his attacker, directing it to the pew where his son lay. A faint outline of the young boy's body had started to become visible. Andrew quickly closed his eyes and moved his hands rhythmically as he had earlier, and the boy vanished again.

A harrowing yell from his attacker made Andrew turn in his direction, but too late to avoid a direct assault. The attacker's arm slashed at Andrew's chest, knocking him back on the chancel as his momentum carried him past. Knocked on his back, Andrew cradled his chest with one arm as he struggled to get to his feet. The attacker vaulted through the air toward Andrew again, apparently intent on smothering him. Lying on his back, Andrew projected a shielding wave of force that deflected the attacker in midair and sent him crashing through the wooden pulpit and slamming into the opposite wall.

Andrew struggled to his feet as his attacker rose. Craig noticed again how much smaller and thinner the attacker seemed since he had entered the church. Their attacks and counterattacks raged on.

Andrew kept stealing glances in the direction of his son; each time he did, he was a fraction of a second too late to avoid a vicious lash or blow from the cloaked figure's relentless pursuit.

Andrew's chest was heaving, and his T-shirt and jeans were in tatters, sweat-soaked and bloodstained from attacks he could no longer avoid. Animal-like, the attacker roared louder and louder, delivering a blow that forced Andrew to his knees, his hands held up in self-defense.

As Andrew tried desperately to catch his breath, his attacker spoke. "You are alone here! It is only a matter of time. You will succumb."

Andrew tried in vain to launch bolts of force from the palms of his hands to slow the approach. But the attacker, head down, powered through them to reach him. He grabbed Andrew brutally by his shoulder, flinging him end over end until he landed at the front of the chancel facing toward the pews. Flat on his stomach now, Andrew peered out across the rows of pews. Through the re-creation, Craig thought he saw the younger version of himself becoming visible. Several paces behind Andrew, the assailant himself was wheezing, as if he too was half exhausted—and half excited that he was about to close in on his prey.

"There is nowhere for you to go now—no one that can possibly help you," he said.

In what seemed a desperate effort, Andrew flung his arms up from his prone position, launching an array of disjointed waves of force from his palms that shot out toward the rows of pews. The waves forcibly upturned the first two rows into a pile that covered over several others. The upturned pews now covered the pew where his son rested, effectively concealing him from sight.

The attacker had apparently interpreted Andrew's action as one of desperation or despair. "You're flailing!" he bellowed. "Why do you resist when you know this is the end?"

Andrew slumped over the side of the chancel, clutching its edge. As he looked out, his face reflected a sense of relief. He let his head droop down from exhaustion and fatigue, sweat and drops of blood falling from his face.

The fiend let out a wail. "This place burns! I hate it. I hate it!" His now bony fists were drawn up to his temples, while his dark, deep-set eyes were closed as if he was absorbing some hidden pain. Then his black eyes shot open and locked on to Andrew's slumped figure.

"But I will see this through. Now!" he shouted. Andrew lifted his head slightly, still facing away from the visitor and looking out at the sanctuary. His eyes cringed from the streaming sweat that pooled in his eyes. With a deafening roar, the attacker launched himself on Andrew's back. With his bony fingers held rigid and fashioned into a point, he plunged both of his arms through Andrew's back, penetrating through the front of his chest just below the collarbone.

"No!" Craig shouted out into the pale blue mist as he saw his father impaled.

Andrew writhed in silent pain as the creature lifted his body off the ground and threw him. As he was hurled through the air, Andrew's eyes were open wide with agony and fear, his arms grasping forward as if to try to reach his son one last time. His battered body landed flat on its back, his arms moving helplessly as he desperately tried to breathe through his choking throat. The attacker descended on him, using his hands and arms to slash and rip at Andrew's body.

"No, no, no," Craig muttered, until he finally screamed, "No!" In despair, he flung the cross onto the steps of the altar.

Immediately, the blue illumination that had served as a portal to the gruesome past vanished, leaving the quiet, dimly lit front of the church just as it had appeared when Craig first entered.

He fell sobbing to his knees.

18

THE SAME RELENTLESS ENEMY

Transfixed by the intense re-creation, Craig had become oblivious to his present surroundings. The labored breathing he suddenly heard startled him back to reality.

He listened closer and heard a faint voice say, "Craig . . . "

Was that Danny? Frantically, he followed the repeated calls of his name until he discovered Danny wedged in a dark corner of the altar area, behind the organ.

Craig ran over to his cousin, flinging himself down to where Danny lay to get face to face with him.

"Danny, you're here! Thank God I found you. What the heck were you thinking driving all the way out here—"

Craig leaned back and scanned Danny's body. A wave of realization hit him. He'd knelt down so close to his face that he hadn't taken in a full view. Now he saw that Danny was bloody and badly injured. His heart plummeted.

"Oh my God. Danny, what happened?"

Danny wore the grim expression of a man in intense pain. Craig's eyes followed the outline of his body as Danny reached his hand up to him. Craig didn't immediately see Danny's other arm until he realized that it was gruesomely contorted, dangling behind his back—his shoulder was dislocated. Continuing to follow the outline of Danny's body, he shuddered when he saw through the tears in Danny's pants that one of his knees had been bashed in at the side. Just below it, the lower part of his leg was sticking out at an unnatural angle. Craig felt panic rise in him.

"We've got to get you help!" His mind racing, Craig wondered what had done this to him. How had he gotten here, so completely out of view that Craig hadn't noticed him when he'd first arrived? He quickly glanced back to the altar where he had first picked up the cross and now saw several fresh bloodstains.

"Shit! My phone! Where the hell is my phone? I gotta call for help!"

He smacked his pants pockets, but his phone wasn't there. He felt a rush of despair. *I know I put the phone in my jacket in the apartment with Lauren. Where is it?* Craig thought.

With rasping breath, Danny spoke to him. "Craig, you don't understand. I was wrong about everything. It's you, not me. You've gotta get outta here! Now!" Despite his agony, Danny became increasingly frantic. "You're in so much danger, Craig. You have to go!"

"Are you crazy? We've got to get you help. What can I do? How can I stop the bleeding?"

Grimacing through his pain, Danny seemed intent on spurring Craig into action. "Craig, it's always been about you. You don't have time to wrap your head around this. You just gotta go before it starts again."

"Before what starts again? What are you talking about? None of this makes any sense!"

Danny groaned. "Leave me. Please! You just saw what happened to your dad, didn't you?"

Of course, Craig thought. Danny must have witnessed the entire re-creation himself.

"Craig, the same thing is gonna happen to you unless you leave. You've *got* to leave!" His chest was heaving between words, as though he was trying to gather enough breath to steel himself against the next wave of pain. Given the state he was in, Craig was amazed that Danny was still conscious.

Unable to triage his cousin's wounds, Craig held his hands up in front of himself in a panic. It was then that Craig felt them grow warm. Not understanding where the impulse came from, Craig placed one of his hands on the side of Danny's head, the other on his shoulder. Danny appeared to be soothed by this.

Danny took a deep breath. "It's okay for you to leave me," he went on, still intent on convincing him.

Craig looked helplessly at Danny, shaking his head in confusion and disbelief. He suddenly saw fresh droplets of sweat beading around Danny's brow and cheeks. Danny must have seen the same on Craig, since his eyes opened wide with fear. "Oh, no. No, Craig! You have to go. He's almost here again."

Craig too felt the growing heat around his own face. "What do you mean? Is it the—person—who did this to you?"

"He's the same *thing* that's been doing all of this, Craig. Don't you understand now? What happened to your dad, what happened to those people in Chicago. It's all been part of trying to get to *you!*"

Then they both heard a voice coming from the far end of the nave.

"It looks like you will both be staying," it rasped. "I was always sure the Scandinavian had a son. It must be you. Sometimes it takes a while for us to flush your kind out of hiding. You see, unfortunately my brothers and I aren't as omniscient as our father. It takes a bit more effort to find and expose your kind. Once I understood there was a connection with the law enforcer, I knew it would only be a matter of time before I drew you out."

The shape of the man standing at the far end of the aisle was similar to the one in the re-creation, although this one's hooded coat was less bedraggled. The man beneath it was also gaunt and wiry. Craig saw the resemblance to the silhouettes in the recent re-creations he had channeled in Chicago. The man's hands hung outside the cloak, and in the distance Craig saw that they were pale and shriveled—claw-like.

He walked slowly up the aisle, his left hand gliding menacingly just over the top of each pew. His voice turned proud and boastful.

"It took time and proved difficult to arrange our meeting. When I killed the others, I sensed there was a hand of truth touching their lifeblood. And while the brightness from it blinded me from seeing you, it did illuminate quite clearly the man to whom you are presently attending."

Craig stood up and glanced back down at Danny, who only shook his head in response.

"But then, there's the shiny little charm I left for you when you arrived. It was all too familiar and too dear for you to resist, wasn't it?"

"Who the hell are you?" Craig shouted.

The man stopped his advance, his gliding hand hovering over a crucifix that adorned the end of a pew. He withdrew it and concealed both hands inside his cloak.

"I'm known by a variety of names depending on where I happen to be hunting. Among my brothers, I have been the one to search in secret in the large cities for others like you. So, if I was in a cold Russian city, I was *temnyy messendcher*. Or

I was *la minaccia mascherato* in Roma. Or *der ünnaturliche Zerstörer* in the German backstreets."

Craig was confused by the flurry of foreign words that rolled off this dark visitor's tongue.

"But when I got close to finding you, I chose a much more . . . pedestrian moniker. Ah, tourist. Yes, of course. I am the 'Tourist.' Or your pursuer. Or your father's pursuer. Or whatever you choose to call me here at the end."

Craig was riveted to what the man said, trying to make sense of it. Still crouching, he placed a hand on Danny's side to shield him, if only symbolically. As he watched the Tourist resume his advance, Craig tuned out Danny's continued whispered urgings to leave.

Then it happened. Craig experienced everything connecting at once in his mind. The re-creation he had just channeled from the cross confirmed the role of this person, or thing, in so much pain Craig had carried through his life.

"I can feel you thinking it through right now. Curious. You don't know, do you? You really don't understand what you represent? What a shame. The ending should be so much easier than the pursuit has been. There are not as many of your kind left. But since there are only three of my kind now, it still leaves so much left for us to do."

Now the Tourist was only about thirty feet away from the cousins. His hands came back out from under his cloak, and he held his palms upward. "But alas, I truly expected more. Especially considering the fight your father offered me."

The words flipped a switch in Craig's mind, and he felt uncontrollable rage surge through his body. Gone were the fear and reservations he had grown so accustomed to, replaced by a drive to confront whatever this thing was, given all it had taken from him. He stood up.

"Craig, Craig! What're you doing? You don't understand what this thing is!" Danny hissed. He attempted to hold Craig back, but he was too weak to have any effect.

"No more. No more." Craig found himself repeating the words over and over. "You don't belong here, do you? I could see when you attacked my dad that being here leaves you weaker, doesn't it?"

Unfazed, the Tourist replied, "Boy, don't confuse yourself. I can remain in this wretched spot long enough to make sure you and the detective never leave it."

Craig felt an unknown sensation welling up in his neck and chest. He could feel it travel down his arms as he clenched each fist tighter than he ever had before. He was shaking, but not from terror. He felt like a powder keg ready to explode. The images of his father's final moments kept flashing though his mind. And then there were other images: his father when he was young, he and Danny growing up, seeing the painful death of good people re-created as shadows, the fear and shame Emma had felt when she was younger, the broken body of his cousin now on the floor behind him.

Almost as if the killer could sense Craig's building rage, he suddenly sprang forward, running at Craig.

Craig lashed out. "Not anymore!" he roared. He instinctively thrust out his arms, both palms open as if to serve as an outlet for all his rage. Ripples of force shot forward from his open hands, just as they had from his father's. The waves traveled visibly through the air and funneled directly at the Tourist, striking him squarely in the chest, knocking him back a dozen or more feet into a row of pews.

Craig stared at his hands in disbelief.

"Craig, you need to do that shit again. Quick, before he recovers!"

Incredulous, Craig again stretched out his arms and unleashed another blast of force just as the Tourist was rising to his feet. The blast glanced off the side of his cloaked head but still managed to spin him backward, pushing him farther back into the pews.

The Tourist got back up slowly and straightened his garments with a casualness that hadn't been apparent to Craig in his re-creation. In the images of his father's battle, it had seemed that the longer Andrew had drawn out the confrontation, the more the killer was drained of strength and energy. *Is this the only way to defeat this thing? If not, what do I do?* Craig thought.

Eerily, as if he'd read Craig's mind, the Tourist spoke. "You may be starting to understand, but it is too late. This place does indeed pain me, but I need only endure it a short while longer."

Craig turned his back for an instant to look at Danny, whose eyes looked frenzied with horror. "Craig, look out!" he hissed as the killer bounded over several rows of pews, landing at the front of the elevated chancel. Craig tried to move away as the Tourist lunged at him but wasn't quite quick enough. The very tip of the Tourist's hand slashed him across the head and temple, sending him sprawling to the ground.

The attacker's hood had slipped, revealing a bald, gray, sallow head, creased with deep lines and wrinkles. His cold black eyes looked over at Danny still lying helplessly on the floor.

"I haven't forgotten about you—I'll be back again soon," the Tourist said ominously.

Craig hurried to his feet, knowing the Tourist was near

Danny. Acting with new instinct, he thrust forward another wave of force with a quickness and intensity that caught the killer off guard, hitting him square in the chest and hurling him against the wall with such impact that the large wooden cross that hung there jarred loose and fell across the Tourist's body, pinning him to the floor.

For a moment, Craig stared at the killer as he struggled under the cross's weight. The physical contact with it seemed to pain him. His cloak had been blown off by Craig's attack, and its absence highlighted a writhing, sinewy frame.

Craig took advantage of the lull to go to Danny's aid.

"Craig, please! You've gotta leave me. Go!"

"No way!" Craig grabbed Danny by the shoulder and belt and began dragging him away. They moved as quickly as possible, Craig glancing across the room at the killer struggling to free himself.

"There's no time to waste!" Danny said, gasping for air as Craig dragged him toward a side exit at the front of the church. But suddenly, Craig felt a painful grip on both of his shoulders and was ripped away from Danny, thrown into the air, back across the chancel, landing violently near the cross under which the Tourist had just been struggling.

The wind knocked out of him, Craig tried to recover enough to get up. He looked over at the killer, who was hunched over, his hands open and rigid, his black eyes glaring at Craig.

Staggering slightly, the killer advanced toward Craig with steely determination. Craig could see Danny on the floor behind the killer. His cousin was looking directly at him as if to get his attention. Craig realized that, despite Danny's injured arm, he'd been able to use his other arm to grab the shaft of a metal flagpole that had toppled during the struggle. Craig believed he understood what Danny meant to do. Still crouched on the floor, Craig brought his palms together as if he were cupping an invisible ball. He then thrust out a focused wave of force that knocked the killer back in Danny's direction. Danny used all the strength in his one useful arm to violently swing the flagpole like a baseball bat as he rolled to one side. The timing was perfect. As the killer was thrown backward, Danny brought the full force of the flagpole to land a powerful blow to the killer's neck and spine so powerful he could hear the bone cracking. The killer was sent crashing into the back wall behind the altar.

Craig breathed a sigh of relief as the Tourist lay motionless. Craig started to try and gather himself until, shockingly, he heard the rustling of the killer trying to get back up too. The side of his neck where Danny had struck him was bowed in and slackened. Even so, he seemed to be unfazed. *"Damn you! You have intervened enough!"* the killer growled at Danny.

The killer was slowed by his injuries, but Craig still wasn't quick enough in getting to his feet to stop him from lunging within inches of Danny. Standing over him, the killer drew back his arm, formed a dagger-like point with his fingers, and plunged it into the side of Danny's chest.

Danny let out a howl.

Enraged, Craig scrambled toward the killer, colliding with him just as he withdrew his hand from Danny's chest. Craig tackled him, grasping him in a bear hug and pinning the killer against his hip. Jamming his hip deep into the Tourist's side, Craig hoisted him up before spinning and slamming him to the ground. He dove down atop the killer in an effort to choke him. But the Tourist had drawn back his arm and slashed it across Craig's face, catching him diagonally across the cheek, above one eye, and across his forehead. The blow was painful and threw Craig onto his back. He looked over at Danny, who was on his back and shaking uncontrollably. Danny's shirt was ripped where the killer had stabbed him, and Craig could see blood pumping out of his wound.

Craig tried to get to his knees and crawl toward Danny. Blood was running down his face and made it difficult to see. But again, the Tourist grabbed him and flipped him over on his back. "Now I finally have you," he hissed, crouching atop Craig's chest. His hand once again fashioned into a point, aiming to pierce Craig through his heart, and the killer stabbed down. Craig squirmed enough that the killer missed his target, instead plunging his hand into Craig's chest near the collarbone.

Craig wailed in agony. Blinking through the blood gathering near his eyes, he could see the killer readying a fatal blow as he drew back his arm to slash Craig's throat. Craig bobbed his head to the opposite side, leaving the killer's arm to instead strike the floor near Craig's head. In the split second that the killer's arm was across his own body, Craig wrapped both of his arms around the killer's neck, pinning his shoulder against his own neck. Grasping it as tightly as he could, Craig knew that if he arched his back and wrenched both arms to one side, there should be enough force to break his neck.

Desperate to end the conflict, he closed his eyes as he twisted and torqued the killer's neck with all his strength. Craig could hear him gasping and spitting as he felt the sickening crunch of neck vertebrae being crushed. Finally the killer stopped struggling, and Craig slowly released the body and pushed it away.

"Danny? *Danny?*" he called out. But there was no answer. Danny lay motionless, his eyes half open and staring at the ceiling.

Wiping the blood and sweat from his eyes, Craig crawled over to his cousin and saw blood pooling around the wound in his chest.

"Danny! Are you with me? Hang on!" He ripped Danny's shirt open and struggled to think of how to arrest the bleeding of Danny's wound.

Then something came over Craig. He became calm for a moment and felt warmth within his hands again. Turning one palm to his face, he could swear that he saw a faint glow surround it. Visualizing this warmth and energy within it, he placed his palm directly on Danny's wound and held it firmly in place. He closed his eyes and tried to see Danny being kept whole.

But suddenly, a wave of dread engulfed him as he heard rasping and spitting behind him. He turned to see the killer writhing on the floor and, to Craig's shock and horror, begin dragging himself in their direction, gripping at the thin carpet to pull himself along. The blow Danny had delivered with the flagpole was preventing him from walking, and the damage that Craig had done to his head and neck kept him from speaking or controlling his movements. The killer's body was emaciated and broken, appearing more wraithlike by the moment. Nonetheless, he was moving relentlessly toward them, his black eyes locked onto Craig. Letting out a maddened scream, he gnashed his teeth and shook his head like an animal, as if the sight of Craig still alive was driving him mad.

"What the hell are you?" Craig screamed with renewed terror.

Just then, Danny started to make a choking sound. Still keeping his hand pressed firmly against Danny's side, Craig now tried to keep him conscious. "Danny . . . Danny, can you hear me?"

Danny's eyes remained partly open. He tried to mouth words, but Craig couldn't understand them. "I won't leave you, Danny. We'll be all right. No matter what happens. I thank God for every way you've been there for me." Craig coughed, and tasted blood coming from his own mouth. He was also getting dizzier, not sure if from exhaustion or loss of blood. He could see the killer still struggling to pull himself toward them.

Everything seemed to move in slow motion. A surreal feeling came over him, and his fear began to drain away. He felt at peace, despite his heart beating erratically and the blood pooling around him. Ignoring the stabbing pain in his chest and the slow crawl of his inhuman adversary, Craig looked up at Danny's face with a sense of deep gratitude. It was through this lens that Craig knew, no matter what happened next, staying by his cousin's side was the only right thing to do.

He continued to hold his hand firmly against Danny's wound, sealing it and focusing all the energy he had left on it. He felt a warm breeze against his face. Looking back in the direction of the Tourist, he saw a thick plume of whitish dust come thundering down atop the crawling form, violently blasting the body in different directions. This same powerful downpour seemed to end where the Tourist had been crawling toward them, with only a warm wind blowing over Craig and Danny.

Still holding tightly to the wound on Danny's side, Craig felt his own exhaustion. He looked back at the dust and the Tourist's remains. Then he saw the fuzzy outline of a man crouched near him. Trying to open his eyes wider against the white dust that still hung in the air, Craig saw the unmistakable face of his father.

It'll be okay, son.

Craig tried to blink through the blood, sweat, and dust that filled his eyes. "Is this another dream, or is it really you?"

His father's face seemed translucent, his voice peaceful and kind. *It's not a dream, Craig. I'm here with you now. I've always been with you.*

Craig was shuddering from shock and exposure. Mustering just enough energy to speak, Craig said, "I don't understand any of this. Nothing has made sense after you were taken from me. I've missed you so much. Now everyone I care about is being taken too."

Nodding, his father said, *I know how hard it has been for you. I pulled you into this ancient struggle and gifted you with abilities before you could understand what they were and accept them. Leaving you unaware was the best way to keep the truth hidden until you could learn the part you played. Until then, I knew that you'd have no choice but to follow the same lonely path I did. For that, I'm so sorry, Craig.*

Craig felt more and more lightheaded but tried to maintain rapt attention to every word his father spoke.

I've been trying to tell you that this time would come, and now it has. Through all that you endured, you've been able to persevere. And now you've been made pure.

"But Danny . . . he's dying, and I can't stop it!"

You already have. You've offered your own sacrifice in the face of this nemesis so that he could live.

Craig sobbed gently and almost silently.

His father continued, *Your growth and selflessness have brought you pain but have made you strong. They have also brought you help from our Father against this creature.*

"I don't even know what that thing was. Why was it after us? Why was it after you? What do I do now?"

You will need to prepare. There is more that you will face. Let me show you.

Craig squinted as he watched his father's hand come up to his face, and then placed it across Craig's forehead. The warmth of the touch soothed Craig, and he stopped shuddering. Craig closed his eyes, and from the spot where his father rested his hand came an energy that pulsed through Craig's head.

A collection of images started to drift through his mind's eye. A grassy clearing appeared, surrounded by small trees. A man in a robe peered through them. Craig's mind floated toward him, until it was as if Craig looked through the man's eyes and saw what he saw.

A massive, dark figure clutched a smaller man before tossing him to the ground. This foreboding figure then hacked at one of his hands with the other. Fingers were sent flying, landing near the other man. They grew and took the shape of dark, emaciated versions of the man from whose hand they'd been cut. The four attacked the man who was on the ground. He repelled each in a manner similar to how Craig had launched blasts of force against the Tourist. The four scattered, and then were gone. But the large, menacing figure snatched up the other man, holding him aloft by the throat. He was finally released, cast to the ground again. The dark one snapped the edge of his cloak with one hand and vanished, replaced for a moment by thick, dark wisps of smoke.

The man's eyes through which Craig saw was now next to the man who had been attacked. The face he saw was kind. He watched as their hands joined together. A warm glow emanated from them.

Then, the scene that had assembled in Craig's mind began to vanish into gray. He opened his eyes, struggling to make sense of it all. "What was all that? What am I supposed to do?" he asked.

His father assured him, *You've done so much, Craig. Now I think you'll understand better. I'm sorry you've had to go through this. But it is done now. It's time for you to rest. Close your eyes, son. It is done now.*

Craig obeyed his father's instructions and closed his eyes, feeling no more pain.

19

RECOVERY

Craig heard a soft voice speaking to him, and he answered by saying, "Don't leave me yet."

"I will always be close to your heart. Please try not to doubt that," said the voice.

"Dad? Is that you?" Craig asked.

"No, it's me."

Blinking through blurred vision, Craig saw Lauren's face come into view as she leaned over him, holding his hand with both of hers. He was lying in bed in a room that seemed mostly white.

"Lauren? Am I alive? Where am I?"

Smiling broadly, she said, "Yes, you are most definitely alive. You're at the University of Iowa Hospital. You've taken longer to come out of a coma than the doctors thought. They airlifted both of you here from Cedar Township after they found you in that church."

"Both of us?" Craig said, still groggy. Then he lit up. "Danny's alive? Where is he?"

"Please, just try and rest. Yes, Danny's alive. He was pretty badly injured, but he's definitely going to pull through— thanks to you."

Craig was slowly coming into awareness. He glanced around the hospital room, taking in the scene. He lay under blankets. Several monitoring pads were attached to his chest and head with thin wires emerging from them, and thick bandages wrapped his shoulder and covered his collarbone. He felt the oxygen nose clip and the tubing that wrapped around his head. Lauren was on one side of his bed, and monitoring equipment was on the other. His lips felt parched, his throat raw and scratchy.

He tried to sit up but immediately felt pain from the stab wound near his shoulder and was overwhelmed with fatigue and stiffness. He licked his lips in an attempt to moisten them and speak more clearly. "I don't quite follow. Lauren, help me understand."

"You both have been through quite an ordeal. But it's over now, and you're both safe."

"I need to see Danny," Craig said.

"You definitely will. Just take it slow and ease into this right now."

As images from the church flowed into his consciousness, Craig was beginning to realize that it was truly over, and they had survived. "I can't tell you how happy I am to see you right now. All of it seems like such a long, crazy dream."

"Well, you've certainly been out long enough for a dream like that."

"Wait. How long?"

Lauren thought for a second. "About four days."

"What? No way . . . wait . . . how did you find Danny and me?"

Lauren grinned. "Well, let's just say I was able to slip my cell phone into your jacket pocket when you left. I'd heard the newer ones like mine could be tracked. When Sergeant Hammond returned, I gave him the details on it in the hope that they could find where you went. He assumed you probably knew where to find Danny. They were able to see that you made it all the way to Cedar Township. Then the blast cut the phone's signal."

"The blast?" Craig asked.

He tried to reach out to Lauren with his hand but felt a sharp pain in both his chest and hand. "Ow, what the . . . Lauren, how bad of shape am I in?"

She listed off a few things. "Well, you had a pretty deep stab wound in your chest and lost a lot of blood. That nasty gash across your forehead. The concussive force from the blast is what the doctors think sent you into the coma, since you bore the brunt of it when you shielded Danny. Other than that, you seem to being doing great."

She smiled playfully as Craig saw the relief reflected in her eyes.

Still processing her comments, he said, "So, the blast. Shielded Danny from it. I'm trying to remember it all. Did they find the Tourist? Was he captured?"

A little puzzled, Lauren asked, "Craig, just how much do you remember?"

Craig stammered, "Well, I . . . um . . . "

"Remember what you promised me? Once this was over and everyone was out of danger, you said you would give me 100 percent. Do you remember that?"

"Absolutely. There's nothing I want more. So, does that mean the killer's gone and everyone's safe? Because believe me, there's a ton I need to catch you up on."

"That's good," she said. "I can't wait to hear it all."

Craig took a deep breath, ready to unload his thoughts about the events and everything he'd kept from her. But instead she cut him off.

"Wait, honey. It's probably important that you and I talk through a couple of things really quickly. I need *you* to trust *me* now, okay?"

"Of course."

Lauren started a quick update. "They've been coming in each afternoon around this time to check on you, to see if you've come out of the coma. So, they'll probably be here soon."

"Wait. Who?"

"Sergeant Hammond and someone from the Bureau."

"The Bureau, as in the FBI?" asked Craig. "Why?"

"I think because the chase for this killer stretched across state lines, or something like that. But whatever, Craig. Follow me for a moment, okay? They've already interviewed Danny, and he's given them his version of the events. Let me share that with you now."

"How do you know?" asked Craig.

She smiled as if she had deeper knowledge of Craig's past than before. "Danny and I spoke at length yesterday, after he had his interview with them. What he told me was that you had left to find him, remembering that his dad helped investigate the killing of a minister in Cedar Township about twenty years ago. You went after him because you were worried and felt the police would take too long and might not understand how it could all be related."

Craig's eyes widened as Lauren spoke.

Gauging to see if he understood, she said, "Right? So, let me continue. You drove there through the evening because you didn't want him to face danger alone. When you arrived, you found that he had been attacked inside the church. When you saw that Danny was badly injured, you tried to fight the killer off and protect him. Because he was so intent on killing

Danny"—she paused for a moment—"and because he wasn't sure if he could finish the job once you arrived, he detonated some type of explosive vest he was wearing. It killed him, but luckily, it only injured you and your cousin."

"An explosive vest?"

"I guess so," replied Lauren. "It blew out most of the windows of the church, which is how the police knew that both of you were in there. The police arrived about twenty minutes or so after the blast. They worked quickly with the paramedics to stabilize each of you and get you flown here."

"Wow," Craig said, absorbing the story so he could recite it to the FBI investigator.

Lauren smiled slightly as she looked into his eyes and held his unbandaged hand.

"Does that match up with how you remember things?"

Craig could see that Lauren had learned much more, perhaps everything, from her talk with Danny. Pushing aside his desire to hear more about their conversation, however, he prepared to recollect the events at the church for the authorities as she had explained them to him.

More important was the fact that he and Danny had both survived and that the adversary they faced had not. Craig was awash in gratitude. He was grateful for Lauren's presence and her appreciating the need to prep him at this moment. But he was most grateful that his effort to find and save Danny had worked, even if the supernatural manner in which he did it raised more questions in his mind than were answered.

He smiled at her and said, "Yes, I think that's the way I remember it too."

She leaned over the hospital bed and kissed his forehead and whispered in his ear. "Remember your promise, mister. I'm so glad you're okay. We'll talk more later."

Craig felt relief settle over his sore and stiff body. Lauren straightened back up, and just as Craig was about to reciprocate the feeling and his intention to keep the promise, the door to the room opened. Through it entered Hammond and an older-looking police official, followed immediately by a doctor and nurse.

"Craig, you've finally rejoined us!" Hammond exclaimed. "Lauren, how is he? Did he come to recently?"

"He literally just awakened a few moments ago."

The doctor and nurse had pushed past Hammond to attend to Craig, appearing annoyed that Hammond was in the way.

"Mr. Henriksen, I'm Doctor Boardman. It's great to see that you're fully conscious again."

"Fully conscious?" asked Craig.

"Right. We didn't think your injuries alone were severe enough to keep you in the coma as long as it did. You struggled to reach consciousness the past two days. This is the first time you've fully emerged from it. You're a lucky man."

The doctor and nurse busied themselves with reading various monitors and checking Craig's vital signs. Hammond and his companion approached Craig's bedside while Lauren moved off to a corner of the room to allow the two teams to function.

Hammond appeared jovial as he looked at Craig in disbelief. "I don't know how the two of you made it through this. Bound together like always, I guess." The other police official who accompanied Hammond clearly wasn't familiar with the background or history of the relationship between Craig and Danny, or with how Hammond's familiarity with them fit in. Realizing this, Hammond introduced him. "Craig, this is Thom Wilson. He's a special agent with the FBI. He's gonna need a statement from you soon, and then we'll see if we can put this whole business to bed once and for all. Danny's really looking forward to seeing you after we get done. That is, if you're up for it."

"Mr. Henriksen," Dr. Boardman interjected, "are you sure you're in shape to do this right now? I can ask that they come back if you'd like a little more time."

But Hammond wasn't to be deterred. "We try to get statements from witnesses as soon as they're physically able— it's really best to tap their memories while they're fresh."

"No, it's fine. Really," Craig answered. "I'd rather just get it over with."

The nurse assisted Craig in drinking water through a straw as the FBI agent stepped up to his bedside. "Mr. Henriksen, I appreciate you taking the time for us to get this statement from you. It's important that we round out the evidence we've collected, along with your statement and that of Detective Walsh. This shouldn't take long. Is it okay if we go ahead and get started?"

Craig nodded, and for the better part of the next hour, he reviewed with the agent the events leading up to and including the night at the church. He made sure that everything he said was consistent with what he and Lauren had briefly reviewed. At the end of the interview, Special Agent Wilson appeared satisfied with what he had gathered, and left, wishing Craig a speedy recovery.

Hammond remained in the room with Craig and Lauren.

Looking relieved that the FBI agent was gone, Hammond said, "Isn't this just a crazy bunch of shit? I mean, really. Craig, how you feeling, man?"

"Don't think I've ever been this sore over every inch of my body. But I'm grateful to be alive, and I'm really happy Danny pulled through. When can I see him?"

"Oh, soon. Definitely soon." Hammond assured him, "He really wants to see you too. But Craig, I want to make sure you know a couple of things."

He pulled up a chair and sat close to Craig's bed. Lauren sat in a chair and moved it closer as well.

"See, I've already had this conversation with both Danny and Lauren here. And when I have it with you, well, that's all I'll have to say about it."

"I'm not sure I follow you," Craig said.

Hammond leaned in to talk quietly but still loud enough for Lauren to hear.

"My guys worked the scene along with the FBI. And I can tell you with complete confidence that, rather unfortunately, we were unable to collect any specific DNA evidence on the suspect. Now, don't get me wrong—I know that there was an assailant with you two, and that he did detonate an explosive in an effort to kill not only himself but the two of you too. But whatever high explosive he used was some rare hybrid that we couldn't get an exact match on. While that's the bad thing, the good thing is that the blast was so localized and intense that it spared you and Walsh but didn't leave a damn trace of the killer. Given his injuries, Walsh could've easily died even with the blast being contained. But he didn't, thanks in no small part to you shielding him and applying pressure to his wound."

Craig wasn't exactly sure what Hammond was trying to convey. "So, what you're telling me is—?"

"What I'm telling you, like I told Danny and Lauren here, is that whoever that sick bastard was, he's completely gone. With that, and the statements you and Walsh gave the FBI, this case will be closed. Forever. Craig, what I'm saying is"—he smiled—"we don't ever have to talk about it again."

With that, Hammond had made it clear that Craig and Danny were off the hook in terms of having to explain or relive the event any further. Craig appreciated that this might be a relief to Hammond for having the situation resolved. But Hammond had no idea about the malevolent creature they had faced. Or that others like it still existed. "Eric, thank you so much. This will definitely help us move forward."

Hammond smiled before his tone turned serious. "My pleasure. But Walsh, he's . . . he's gonna need you. He got busted up pretty bad. You'll be there for our boy, right?"

"Always," Craig nodded.

Hammond nodded back and said, "Let me give the two of you a little time together. I'll be back, and then you can go over and check on Walsh, all right?"

When Hammond left, Lauren stood and leaned over Craig, holding his free hand again.

"I guess you miss a lot when you sleep for half a week."

She laughed softly.

"So, how much do you know, exactly?" Craig asked.

"I know that I was right when I said to you at the museum that I thought there's so much more that you have inside yourself to offer. And that once you came to grips with it—"

"It'll blow me away, huh?" Craig completed her sentence. He smiled. "Well, almost, I guess. But seriously, Lauren. What do you know?"

She didn't seem willing to play the games they used to when Craig had kept so much from her. She spoke in a larger sense. "I know that there were a lot of times when you had difficulty understanding your role and place in the world. Especially after you lost your father to the same type of senseless violence. I know you've struggled in the way that you were able to help Danny, but didn't really like how it reminded you of your dad." She continued to show signs of having talked to Danny at length. "There was a plan for you to come full circle and save him from that killer, who chose the exact same location where your dad was killed. And if it wasn't for you going to his aid, alone, Danny would've died."

She paused for a second. "Is that a decent start to what all I know? At least until you're willing to fill in the remaining blanks for me?"

Craig nodded. "Yeah, I would say so."

"How do you feel now about what you think your purpose is, or your reason for being?"

Craig welcomed the chance to be reflective. "Well . . . I feel like there are a whole lot of things that give me purpose now. Not the least of which is you. You've been opening my eyes to understanding a lot of things. I knew my dad was a man of God, but I don't think I ever really understood what that meant. All the things I encountered for most of my life didn't do much to establish any faith or belief inside me. To have someone like you here, right now, proves to me that faith was there for me from the very beginning. I just didn't know it early on, and then I denied it as I grew up. I finally understand what my father went through, and why he went through it. That helps me make sense of my place in the world."

His eyes had been welling with tears as he spoke. Her eyes were now tear-filled as well. A single drop ran down the side of her cheek as he went on. "I hope our story is just beginning. But before we go even a step further, I want to thank you for being patient with me. I promised you that I'd let you all the way in, and I will. You're going to see the best that I have to offer."

"I think, knowing all you've done to land yourself in this hospital bed, I already have."

20

FORGED

Craig had underestimated how weak he was, and he fell back to sleep while holding Lauren's hand. Later in the evening, he awoke to find her still at his bedside. "Lauren. You're still here."

"Of course. Are you feeling okay?"

"Yeah. My head's becoming a lot clearer. But I really do want to see Danny, if they'll let me."

Nodding, she said, "He's been asking for you ever since he learned that you'd come out of the coma. I'll get someone to arrange taking you to his floor."

"He's not on the same floor?" asked Craig.

"Craig, I don't know if you remember, but his injuries were . . . pretty extensive. He was in surgery for the better part of a day after you both arrived. Then he was in ICU after that. They've just recently moved him into a regular room."

Noticing Craig's alarm, she assured him, "Oh, he's doing a lot better now. It's just that he's not as mobile as you are. They said that when you're ready, one of the care assistants will take you down to him. Before you go, I want to give you something I've been keeping for you."

"What do you mean?" he asked.

She opened a small handbag and withdrew something from it that she had wrapped in cloth. When she uncovered it, Craig immediately recognized the silver cross he had seen in the church and from which he had channeled the re-creation of his father's death.

"Oh my God. That's the cross my dad always wore. It's some type of Celtic cross. Where'd you find it?"

"You were clutching it in your hand when they found you. They secured it while you were being transported, and since I was the only family or friend around, they let me keep it for you."

She waited for a moment and then said, "And it's actually not Celtic. It's called a Scandinavian rune cross."

"How do you know that?" he asked.

"I looked it up on one of the computers here," she said, smiling. "I've had a few days to pass the time, you know."

She handed him the cross as he looked up at her and said, "Thank you so much."

Bending down, she kissed him gently on the lips.

———————◆◆◆———————

Craig waited for about half an hour before a care assistant arrived to move him from his hospital bed and into a wheelchair to go and see Danny. Craig felt as if every muscle in his body ached, both from his injuries and from being sedentary for the better part of a week. Secured in the wheelchair, he looked over at Lauren, who was still seated next to his bed.

"Aren't you coming?" he asked her.

"That's okay. You go and talk with him first by yourself. I'll be right here when you return. Promise."

After attaching an IV bag to the wheelchair, the care assistant took Craig down several floors to Danny's room, pushing him into the middle of the room before quietly retreating. Jim and Judy Walsh were standing over their son's bedside and hadn't yet taken notice of Craig. Craig's eyes grew wide as he saw the many pieces of equipment that were anchored at different points on and around Danny's bedside. As the assistant left, the spring on the door held it open for a few moments. When it finally clicked shut, Jim and Judy were alerted to Craig's arrival.

"Craig!" Jim Walsh exclaimed. "There you are! How you feeling, son?"

Judy added, "Oh, it's so good to see you awake and about. We've been to your room several times, waiting for you to wake up. Then when we heard you had regained consciousness, we kept our distance until Eric and his friend could talk to you. And we knew you probably wanted to catch up with that pretty girl."

Jim added, "Craig, she's been here pretty much 24 hours a day, 7 days a week waiting for you to come to. She's definitely a keeper."

From just behind them on the bed, Danny's voice added to the assessment.

"She really is, Craig."

Jim and Judy parted to give Danny an unobstructed view of his cousin.

"Danny, are you okay?" Craig asked, concerned by what he was seeing.

Danny winked as he nodded his head to one side. "Eh, I think they've done their best at trying to put me back together."

Danny spoke clearly but in the subdued tone of someone who was trying to downplay how bad he actually felt. Craig looked him up and down. Lauren's cautionary words had hinted that Danny wasn't in great shape but hadn't prepared him for what he was now seeing. Danny had multiple IV lines and tubes attached to his body. Several of the cuts and bruises on his face looked as if they were beginning to heal. But the arm that the Tourist had mangled was stretched out on a platform by his bed with multiple screws drilled through the skin to hold the bones in place. His leg was in a similar state, stabilized above and below the knee. The puncture wound he sustained during the attack was heavily bandaged, with two different drainage tubes exiting it.

As Craig took it all in, Danny said, "It's not as bad as it looks."

Judy jumped in. "Listen here, Daniel. You know that it very much was touch and go for a while. You just need to be thankful for your body being able to withstand it all, and for Craig arriving when he did."

"Ever since the two of you were young," Jim added, "you've always seemed to be a pretty damn good team at watching out for each other. Boy, was that important this time!" Then, looking at his wife, he said, "Judy, let's go down to the cafeteria and get some dinner and let these two catch up."

Jim pushed Craig closer to Danny's bed as Judy bent down to gently hug him. Jim then patted Craig's uninjured shoulder and the side of his head as they left through the door.

After a long pause, Danny was first to talk. "Well?"

"Danny, I had no idea that everything was linked together the way it was. Even from the beginning. I feel responsible for everything." Craig felt all the emotions he'd been holding back surge to the surface. "And Emma! Oh my God, Danny. I'm so, so sorry."

For a moment, Craig felt the joy he had experienced at being alive, and seeing Lauren, give way to guilt for having caused Danny such injury and loss. Craig stared again at his injuries. "You were so badly hurt. Dammit!"

"Craig, don't. It's true that during the past few days since the surgery, it's been hard knowing that she's gone. She was beautiful and wonderful. And I know that can't undo what happened to her."

Craig's chin dropped, and he was silent.

"But whatever it was about her that clicked with me, I feel like a part of it is still there. She just helped me see things differently. I'm never gonna forget that. In any event," he continued, "I guess I'll be needing your help this time, 'cause I know you've been where I am now. I mean, your father, Craig. What the hell? That thing that killed him was the same thing that was after us." He corrected himself: "After *you*, I mean. Don't you feel like this whole thing is so . . . " Danny couldn't finish the sentence as he struggled to find the words to explain what they'd been through. He asked, "Do you understand it at all?"

"You know, I never really learned the details of how my dad was killed. I don't think you did either, except for whatever your dad might've shared. But no, I don't fully understand what that thing was. I do know one thing for sure—it wasn't human. I mean, not in the way you and I might think of it."

"Then what the hell was he? And how did you re-create the scene of him with your dad?"

Craig opened his hand, showing Danny the cross he held.

"What's that?"

Craig explained, "When I was a kid, my dad always wore this on a chain around his neck. It's some type of old Scandinavian cross. I had been seeing it in my dreams in the weeks leading up to when I found you in Cedar Township."

"It was from you touching it that you channeled the re-creation?"

"Yeah," Craig acknowledged.

"Do you think your dad was leading you to it?" Danny asked, his eyes lighting up to the mystery of it all.

"I don't know. Maybe the Tourist wanted me to find it to prove to himself that I was really my dad's son."

"You and your dad were linked, for sure, even if you never really knew it, Craig. I mean, that much was clear from what I heard from him in the re-creation."

"So, you saw the whole thing?" asked Craig.

Danny now had an energy that belied the state he was in. His hands were animated as he talked, causing several of the monitoring wires and tubes to bounce around as he did.

"Yeah, totally. What do you think the Tourist really was? And how was he destroyed? I mean, I like how the suicide vest played so well in what'll be the official version. But what the hell? How did we make it out alive and that thing didn't?"

"I'm not really sure. But . . . " Craig hesitated. "Danny, I think I could hear my dad talking to me at the end. Just after the explosion."

"Seriously? Do you think that it's at all related to how the Tourist got blown up?"

Squinting his eyes as he tried to think back to it, Craig said, "I'm not sure. Just before he started to talk to me, I was looking over at that thing. It was still trying to crawl over and finish us when something that looked—I don't know—like an avalanche of white dust crashed down on it. I'm not sure."

Danny didn't seem interested in dwelling on how their adversary was destroyed, so long as Craig could assure him that it was gone. He rested his hand on his chest for a moment, as if to ensure that he was whole. "So, you did see that he was killed, right? That's good. But what about that thing with your dad's voice? What was he saying?"

"He was trying to comfort me. He told me that you and I would be okay." Craig took a moment to gaze out the window into the distance. He went on. "He also said something about having given me a gift without me yet understanding it. And that he was sorry for pulling me into some—he called it an ancient struggle—without me knowing it."

Lost in thought now too, Danny said, "I wonder if he was talking about how you could do those re-creations. Or whatever you were shooting from your hands. Or all of it?"

Craig thought of delving into the visions that he saw as his father rested his hand on Craig's forehead. The images of someone else, long ago, that could do the things that Craig could do. In that moment, Craig decided to withhold it from Danny. At least for the time being, until he was able to better understand what they meant.

They both sat in stillness for several moments, going through their thoughts and absorbing what Craig had heard from his father.

Danny broke the silence. "Do you think you and your dad are supposed to be part of something—I don't know what, but something bigger than us? Maybe bigger than a lot of things in the world. I don't know, man. It sounds crazy."

Craig didn't shy away from the sentiment. "I know. The gravity of this kind of blows my mind. We always had this secret about the re-creations that we couldn't share. What we're talking about now, and what happened in the church with my dad and that thing . . . it seems like it's all on a whole different level."

Craig turned both of his hands, palms up. "I am glad my father gave me whatever it is about this touch I have. It's like, I don't know, a way to reveal things. Or a way to understand things."

"Or a way to defend against things," Danny offered. "Putting all of that together, the Tourist was hell-bent on stopping you and keeping you from whatever it is that you're supposed to do. Whatever that thing was, he knew you were a threat. But it was like the only way to smoke you out was by killing those people. He was trying to lock in on you, not me. Like I was the way to get you to reveal yourself. That's probably why you saw him make a move toward me at the end of the re-creations, when I didn't see him. It's like he sensed that you were helping me with the crime scenes he created." Danny was growing fatigued from talking so much, but paused to catch his breath. "And don't forget about the kind of people he killed. Those were good people, Craig. Decent people just trying to help others and do the right thing."

Craig looked away as Danny stared directly at him.

"He was willing to do anything to get to you. Like, whatever this gift was your dad gave you, he knew you had the ability to discover the truth about things. And he saw that as a threat, Craig. There's real power in what you can do. Lemme tell you, thank God for that, seeing the way you were able to keep that thing at bay in the church. It's like you've always been part of something bigger . . . " Danny's voice trailed off.

Craig continued the introspection. "I'll be honest with you. All my life I felt like I avoided things. I tried to keep to myself when I was a kid. I didn't want to try to figure out what I should do in life. I didn't want to think too deeply about what happened to my dad, and why it happened. And the re-creations? They were too weird to think about or explain. I guess now, after what we've been through, I feel different. I don't feel like I have to hide anymore. I wanna know who I'm supposed to be and what I'm supposed to do."

As Danny tried to reposition himself in the bed, he grimaced in pain. Craig felt another wave of guilt. "Damn, Danny. I see now how all of this has been about me and my dad. I hate it that you've had to go through so much."

"Craig, don't. Really. We've both been through hell. Literally. But it's like this for a reason. It's forged us together as a family. A family originally torn apart, with all that you went through when you were young. What I'm going through now. But we're gonna come back together, even stronger."

Craig felt his anxiety building. "It's hard to see you this way. To know that I'm responsible for so many people's suffering."

"Craig, listen. Or better yet, look at this . . . " Danny began peeling back the edge of a large bandage on the side of his chest near a drainage tube.

"Danny, no! What are you doing?"

Danny lifted up the bandaging enough to expose a part of his skin that had a deep imprint and the burned outline of several fingers. "See that? That's what you're responsible for. For keeping me whole. For keeping me alive."

Craig gazed in amazement at the scarring where he had held his hand against Danny's chest during the blast. It served as a visual reminder of Craig's resolve to try to save Danny, no matter the threat that existed as the Tourist crawled toward them. Craig looked down at his own bandaged hand and now understood why it had been injured. Having been fused to Danny during the blast, it had kept Danny from bleeding out.

"That's incredible," Craig said.

"I know, right? No doubt part of whatever this gift is." He paused for a minute, then wondered, "What do you think you're supposed to do with it?"

"I'm not sure, but I really want to try to understand it. I feel like, whatever it is and whatever it means, it predates both me and my dad."

"That thing we fought in the church—didn't he say there were others like him?"

Craig nodded. "Yeah. Which is another reason I have to figure this out."

"So, this might not be the end of it. Have you thought about that at all?"

Craig was feeling oddly at peace with what Danny was pointing out. "Not yet. But I think I can be ready for whatever comes along. Kind of like my dad was, I guess."

"I only hope"—Danny looked down at his broken body—"that I can get myself back to where I can help you figure it out. Kinda like you did with me at the crime scenes."

"You were right when you said that I've been exactly where you are. Except I hadn't made an impact on people's lives the way you have. I was young when it all fell apart for me. But I had you and your family to lean on. Know this—I'll always be there for you, just like you've been there for me." Craig nudged himself closer to Danny's bedside. He reached over and placed his uninjured hand on Danny's.

Echoing Craig's gesture, Danny said, "Thanks, man. We're a team in this now. I'll be ready for it when you are."

Craig nodded.

"Now that you understand the type of guy your dad was and exactly what happened, does it make things better?" asked Danny.

"I'm not sure yet. I feel in my heart that I understand things better, even if my mind doesn't yet. It does provide some closure, that's for sure. I feel like I have a purpose. My father gave me a gift that involved the touch of my hands.

To know the truth like you said, I guess. But also to protect people from others like the Tourist. I feel like I'm supposed to be an instrument in some way."

"I think that's right," Danny said. "I really do, Craig."

They both heard the hospital door to Danny's room open, and Jim, Judy, and Lauren entered.

"There they are," said Judy. "Are you boys getting caught up on everything?"

Danny and Craig looked at each other before Craig answered: "Yeah. Something like that."

21

LAUREN

Chicago, Illinois: Eighteen months later

Jim Walsh poked his head into the room where Craig and Danny were waiting.

"I was able to get a smaller Class A jacket. I'm guessing it'll fit better than the one you've got. It'll be showtime soon. You boys ready?"

Craig turned around to see Danny's father holding a dry-cleaner's sleeve that contained a police dress uniform jacket. Danny looked away from the full-length mirror he'd been staring at.

"Okay, good. Thanks for chasing that down, Pops. How much time do you think we have?"

Jim looked at his watch, then turned his back on the small office they were in to listen in the direction of an assembly area farther down the hall of the police headquarters building.

"I'd say you've got five or ten minutes. They're about halfway through the scheduled commendations. You're supposed to be last. I'll run back and check. In the meantime, Craig, can you get this guy put together?" Jim joked as he smiled and left Danny and Craig alone.

"It annoys the shit outta me that I can't even fit into my old dress jacket."

Craig sought to assuage some of his cousin's concern.

"I know. But think of how far you've come. Really. To put yourself in a position to get back on the job. You've come a long way, man."

Danny shrugged.

They were readying themselves for a public relations event, one that was typical of those that occurred every few months to recognize officers for performance in the line of duty. Family and friends would gather, along with a contingent of the press. Today was to be the surprise reintroduction of Danny Walsh into the Chicago police force. It had been well over a year since the events at the church had left him badly injured. Craig had been able to heal relatively quickly from the stab wound near his collarbone. But Danny's injuries had been much graver, and it had taken him until now to return to any semblance of his former self.

Using a cane, Danny crossed the room to retrieve the new jacket Jim had left draped over a chair. Craig looked him over. Danny had made significant progress, but Craig worried about the injuries he couldn't see.

"Just be glad you don't have to dress up in this fancy gear," Danny said. "You just get to wear a sport jacket to this show."

Suddenly self-conscious, Craig glanced down at the khakis, blue blazer, and white dress shirt he was wearing. "Should I have dressed up more? I mean, I don't know how these things are supposed to work."

Danny raised the arm that ended in a prosthetic hand and motioned dismissively. "Nah. You're good. I'm the one who has to look all shipshape in front of the superintendent."

Craig watched Danny begin to wrestle with removing the jacket from its sleeve. He could see the results of his cousin's long journey: several surgeries to repair his knee and leg, then a few more to reset his badly fractured arm. After he began to heal from the physical injuries, the mental ones emerged. Danny had become depressed and opened up to Craig about feeling as if he were a lesser version of himself. He had struggled to come to grips with having been robbed of the opportunity to have a lasting relationship with Emma.

Craig had been with him throughout the process. Infections had kept forming in Danny's arm, so badly injured by the Tourist. Continued complications ultimately resulted in Danny's forearm needing amputation and replacement with an advanced prosthetic.

Danny removed the dress jacket from its plastic sleeve and took off his old jacket, which was now too large for his frame. As he held the new one up and looked at it, he seemed lost in thought. He paused for a moment and exhaled deeply. Craig saw his eyes drift from the jacket he held to looking at his reflection. Craig could sense him struggling.

"Are you sure you're ready for this? I mean, rejoining the force full time."

Pulled out of his thoughts, Danny answered Craig's concern. "What? Yeah, of course. I didn't bust my ass to get all the way back here and not join, right?"

"And your dad? Are you sure you wouldn't rather have him introduce you out there? I'd totally understand if you would."

"No way. You and I have been to the edge and back. You're the one I want saying a few words about me returning."

Craig smiled and nodded his head.

Danny donned the dress jacket and was working to fasten its remaining buttons, pinning it against his body with his disabled hand while using the other to button up.

"Can I help you with that?"

Danny continued to work on it himself. "I got it. Believe

me, I've had a decent amount of practice over the last few
months."

Looking up and smiling at Craig as if to brush away any
concern, Danny said, "I mean, Jesus. If I can't get a coat
buttoned up, I'm sure as hell not gonna be worth a shit back
on the streets."

Craig smiled cautiously. He stepped behind Danny as the
two of them stood in front of a full-length mirror that hung
against a closet door in the office. As Danny worked to adjust
the fit of his new dress jacket, Craig went from looking at
his cousin's reflection to looking at his own. With a renewed
sense of purpose and confidence over the past year and a half,
Craig had embraced a regular exercise routine and healthier
habits. He was now seeing their beneficial effects reflected in
the mirror. He felt physically fit, like he was coming together
stronger and better than he had ever been.

The contrast between him and Danny seemed stark in the
mirror. The effects of all the damage Danny had sustained
from the attacks at the church had left him skinnier and
slumped. Even though Danny was several inches taller than
Craig, they now looked nearly the same height.

Danny stepped back and caught Craig looking at himself.
He grabbed up his cane.

"Now *you're* looking good, pal. Seems like you're happy."

Craig felt like Danny was intentionally steering the
discussion away from having to talk about himself. "I do feel
good."

"You and Lauren really seem to be getting along well. Was
she able to get out of work to come?"

"Oh, yeah. Said she wouldn't miss it. We should see her
out there."

"What I'm really curious about is whether Lauren's dad is

still gonna let the two of you move in together. I mean, he's okay with your freeloader status?" Danny smiled.

"Hah. Yeah. So far, so good." Danny was referring to Craig's leaving Grey, Parker, & Harris to take grad school classes and look for part-time work elsewhere.

"So, does she know about everything now?"

"Of course—she was there with us in Iowa," answered Craig.

"I mean about all of it. The power you have in your hands, what your dad told you, all that stuff you've called tactile whatever."

"Tactile transference. And no, not everything."

Danny looked puzzled.

"Baby steps, you know?" said Craig.

Craig had rationalized not coming completely clean with Lauren in a selfish way. Until he could understand the full extent of the abilities that had emerged in the church, and the clues to his family's past, he thought he needed to withhold the full truth, at least for her protection. He also appreciated that his relationship with her provided the sutures that bound the emotional wounds he had carried with him since childhood. He wasn't yet willing to jeopardize that by telling her everything, especially since he hadn't yet needed to use his abilities against any new supernatural stalkers, nor had he been required to re-create any crime scenes.

Nothing extraordinary had occurred since the events in Iowa. With Danny out of the force until now, there was no reason for Craig to attempt a re-creation. The respite had allowed Craig the opportunity to work on himself. He was coming to grips with a larger purpose he felt that he had, and he had taken the time to reevaluate his career and his health, and to pursue an inner calmness.

"Baby steps, huh?" Danny said skeptically. "So, what does that mean, exactly?"

"It means she knows *some* of what I can do. The re-creations at the crime scenes. C'mon, you and I went over this months ago."

Danny raised an eyebrow and asked, "So, you're telling me you haven't shared any more with her about the powers you have? And that they came from your dad?"

Craig shook his head. "Not ready to cross that bridge yet. Don't really want to scare her off."

"I don't know. She doesn't seem like she scares easily." Danny lowered his voice. "Have you been able to, you know, shoot those things from your hands again?"

"Nope. Don't you think I'd tell you if I could?" Craig looked down at his palms for a moment. "Maybe it was just some one-time thing in church? I don't know."

Craig turned away, not really wanting to pursue the topic. After all, this was supposed to be Danny's day. Craig had been perfectly happy the past several months not having to wade through all the curiosities that still ebbed in his mind.

"I guess I'm kind of glad that you haven't told her the full deal. You and I need to get to the bottom of it all. My getting back on the force can help with piecing things together." He turned back to the mirror and held the bottom of the dress jacket with his good hand as he used his prosthetic to pull down at his opposite shoulder, trying to turn the jacket so that it fit squarely.

"Let me help you, man," said Craig.

"No," Danny countered. "I mean, check this out."

He held up the prosthetic hand and, one by one, was able to bend each artificial finger inward toward the palm about half the distance a normal finger would function.

"Military grade, my friend. They've got the wires tied into the tendons in my upper forearm. So, I can get the fingers to move pretty decently."

Danny had shown Craig this functional ability before. It was important that it could operate in this way in order for him to be cleared for duty again. He continued. "Since she still doesn't know everything, we just have to be careful about how we go about researching your family's past."

All the questions Craig had kept in the back of his mind over the past year were coming to the forefront again. What did his abilities really represent? What foes was he destined to face now? Were there others like him? Did he know the full extent of his abilities? The questions were endless.

Turning to look at Craig, Danny said, "Am I pushing this on you? I mean, I just thought you were more determined than ever to fully understand it."

"Oh, I am. Honestly, it's been a little annoying that I haven't been able to learn any more over the past year. Kind of like it was just some crazy dream the way everything happened. I just feel that I need to be patient, is all."

Craig indeed felt an overwhelming curiosity at times, as well as an immense responsibility. He believed it was his responsibility to help good people, and to keep others like the Tourist from hunting them down.

"I know I haven't been much help at all on that yet. But now that I'm past all of the hospital shit, that's gonna change," Danny offered.

"You don't have to apologize. Besides, I've been trying to look through a few things in the file boxes to see if any other scraps of information turn up elsewhere."

"Nothing else you could find on that Council in the letter? Or the initials on it? What were they? C-O-I?" Danny asked.

Craig knew Danny was referring to the old letter of
condolence he had found, and the name of some Council to
which his great-grandfather belonged.

Shaking his head, Craig responded, "Nothing yet." He
took a deep breath as he closed his hands into fists at his sides.
"Is it crazy that I'm as eager to confront the rest of those . . .
things as I am to find out about what my dad represented?
And what it all means for me?"

"I don't think so," Danny replied. "Seems whatever you
experienced in the church and learned from your dad has
made you the one person best equipped to stop them."

Craig clenched his jaw as he nodded slightly. "Whatever
that Council was that the letter mentioned, I need to track
down what it was about." Craig looked away from Danny.
"But this doesn't have to involve you. It doesn't have to be
your quest too. I know we've talked about it, but don't feel
like you have to stay a part of this. I'm not sure where it will
lead. More importantly, I don't know to what it might lead."

Craig hadn't meant to speak as ominously as it had come
out.

"I guess I'd say the same thing to you," Danny countered.
"Being a cop, I've always had to be okay with facing off against
people who just wanna hurt someone. But this?" He pursed
his lips and looked equally serious for a moment. "What we
faced in Iowa wasn't just some killer. These stakes are a lot
higher. I know I used to give you shit for not wanting to be
involved in my line of work, but no one should have to sign up
for facing what we ran up against in Iowa."

"Agreed," Craig said. "But I feel like this is who I'm
supposed to be. This is what I want to do, and I think it is
what I *should* do. I'm not sure how or why I've been chosen

for this. Hopefully following where the letter leads will shed light on that. I'm ready to step up and face whatever comes next."

"You know that I am all in on this with you. Wherever it leads . . . " Danny trailed off as he smiled and looked past Craig, intrigued about what they might learn.

There was a light tapping at the door, and then Jim opened it. "Hey, boys, you've got just a few minutes. After the next round of applause, that will be your cue to come down the hall and wait at the side of the stage. Danny, you're to take a spot next to the superintendent. Craig, just wait off to the side until he introduces you. After that, you say a few words about Danny. You both got that?"

Danny nodded. "Got it, old man. We'll be ready."

Leaving the depth of their discussion behind, Craig sought to refocus on the event. "So, I guess we get ready to unveil you, huh?"

"Right, okay."

As Danny reached toward the chair where he'd placed his cane, Craig noticed several tags affixed to the sleeve of the new dress jacket that covered his cousin's prosthetic arm and pointed them out.

"Shit," said Danny. "Thanks, Craig. That'd look real cheesy if I walked out there like that. Hold on a sec." Using his other hand, he withdrew a pocket knife and opened it with one hand.

"Just hold on," said Craig. "There's probably some scissors around here."

"I got it. I got it." Danny seemed to be growing anxious, apparently worried they'd be late. Trying to use his prosthetic hand to pin the tags against his jacket and draw taut the plastic string that affixed them, he struggled with holding it in such a way that he could use his other hand to cut them free.

"Here, come on, Danny. Just let me get this for you."

"Craig, I got it."

Craig reached down anyway and pulled the string out tight so Danny could push the knife blade through it. His good hand shaking, Danny pushed the knife too hard. As it severed the plastic string that held the tags, it continued on and sliced into the top of Craig's hand in the fleshy part between his thumb and index finger.

"Ouch!"

"Oh, shit. Goddamit, Craig. I'm sorry."

The cut was deeper than either of them had initially realized. Instinctively, Craig clasped his other hand on top of the cut.

"How badly did I get you?" Danny asked.

"I'm not sure. It felt pretty deep."

They both looked down to see a steady flow of thick blood drops begin to fall from inside his covered hand.

"Oh, man. Let me get you a rag or something." Danny tossed the knife on the chair and limped toward the desk, where he found a box of tissues. He quickly retrieved it and started pulling several out, ready to hand them to Craig in order to arrest the bleeding.

A rush of anxiety suddenly spread through Craig's chest as he realized they were mere moments from going out into the assembly, and he was worried whether they would be able to tend to his injury in time.

Danny stood in front of Craig, clutching several tissues. "Dude. Take these. Apply some pressure to it."

"Wait," Craig said. The burning pain from the cut was

beginning to dissipate. The droplets of blood that had been falling from inside his clutched hands stopped.

"What's it look like? For real, we gotta get our asses out there in a minute," Danny pushed.

Craig slowly lifted his hand away from the cut. It looked like a fairly deep wound, about an inch long, between his thumb and first knuckle. It was red and creased with blood. But miraculously, the laceration looked to be sealing itself, like a zipper coming together. In a matter of seconds, as they both stared in disbelief, the cut was completely closed. The only visible sign that there had been a wound was the drying blood that creased the inside of Craig's palm.

Danny was the first to speak. "Craig. What . . . the . . . hell?"

Craig looked at his cousin. His eyes couldn't have been wider. Words escaped him, and he could only shake his head from side to side in amazement. A loud round of applause from down the hall startled them and Danny tried to spur them into action. "Here. Take the damn tissues and at least get the blood off your hand."

"But Danny, what the heck just happened?"

"Right. Total curveball, no doubt." He placed his hand on Craig's shoulder. "I'll help you figure this shit out. But I need to know quickly whether you want to try to go out there. I get it if this has thrown things off too much. But if you can do this, we need to go now. What do you say?"

Forcing himself to be resolute, Craig replied, "Yes, of course. That's what today is about. We can figure out later what just happened."

"Okay. Thanks. This means a lot to me," Danny said, snatching up his cane as Craig hurriedly wiped his hands clean.

"Let's get out there."

They made their way toward the assembly room, forty or so feet down a hallway. In the few brief moments it took to traverse the distance, Craig felt a flood of fresh anxiety enter his chest. He couldn't understand how the cut on his hand had healed itself on its own. Had he always been invulnerable to injuries from others? That didn't make sense to him as he thought back to times in the past when he was involved in scuffles or when he broke a wrist in martial arts or, even recently, when he was injured by the Tourist in the church. None of what he had just seen with his hand made any sense against what he had experienced in the past.

They turned the corner into the assembly, and Craig took his place along the wall while Danny walked over to stand near the superintendent of police at the podium.

Craig looked out at the scene in front of him. He, Danny, the superintendent, and several other officers in dress uniforms were on a stage that opened onto a small auditorium. It appeared to have room for about a hundred people and was half filled. Toward the back, Craig could see at least two local television news cameras pointed at the podium, recording the event.

Craig was nervous. He was already a little uneasy about speaking publicly but had resolved to do it out of respect and gratitude for Danny. Seeing the cut on his hand miraculously heal before his eyes had shaken him even more. The superintendent seemed to be introducing him, but Craig couldn't focus on what he was saying—stage fright was quickly overtaking him. His eyes scanned the crowd. After a few seconds, they found Lauren seated a few rows from the front. Their eyes met, and he saw her flash a wide grin at him.

But seeming to sense his discomfort, she raised her eyebrows in an expression of concern.

Craig glanced over at the superintendent. He still was not really following his words, but he could tell that his introduction was almost over. Looking back out at Lauren, he watched as she gently waved one of her hands in a way that would be nearly imperceptible to anyone else who might be watching her. Immediately, all the nervousness that had built up inside him released, like a sink whose drain plug had been pulled. Amazed and feeling only relief, he looked into her eyes. Puzzled, he raised an eyebrow as he stared out at her. In response, she flashed him a wide, warm smile, and winked.

He heard clapping and saw the superintendent turn toward him with a welcoming gesture. Craig nodded in acknowledgment, smiled to the gathered crowd, and strode confidently to the podium.

Turn the page for a sneak peek at the next novel in the Relentless Enemy Series:

THE INVICTUS

Available Fall 2021

The older man leaned in. His voice was calm but his eyes narrowed, intent on conveying concern.

"We don't yet know enough about this newest one. But we do know that one of our brothers has fallen. That brings our numbers to half of what they have been. With both losses occurring just within the last century."

The other man, sitting across the small table, sought to assuage his concern. He spoke in a deep baritone. "Relax. We don't know whether it was just carelessness on our brother's part or that the bastard got lucky somehow." His large frame fidgeted in his seat; he seemed uncomfortable about resigning himself to what had happened to his brother. He clasped a pair of massive hands on the table in front of him. A flash of light glinted off the gold signet ring that adorned one of his fingers.

"This doesn't give you pause?" The older man questioned.

"Not at all. Look at our progress. Their numbers dwindle, do they not? And even if ours have been halved, the effects of our work have been undeniable—and ever increasing."

A sternness now entered the older man's voice. "Nonetheless, we should not understate the loss we have sustained. The gravity of that has drawn you and me together for this meeting, such as it is. The first we have needed in such a long time."

"Agreed." The larger man began cracking the joints in his

knuckles. "But you and I have an advantage that the other two did not. We remain well protected, well concealed. Our approach is more surgical, more selective. Until the end, when they finally understand but lack the ability to change their fate."

As if gaining more confidence, he continued: "And unless this new follower is more educated in exactly what he faces, he doesn't yet understand how different we are compared to the others. He won't stand a chance once we have him within our reach. Don't naturally assume that his ability is any more advanced than the others, or that he would be foolish enough to try to seek us out. He'll naturally assume that we resemble our brothers. This is the advantage we retain until we learn more about him and how we choose to confront him."

A harsh smile creased the wrinkled skin of the older man's face. He leaned back in his chair, now appearing more at ease. "Yes, of course you are right. It provides me great confidence to know that you and I have built, within our organizations, elements of both protection and subterfuge. The ability to hold our ground until the very last moment will be critical in drawing out and destroying this one. So long as we are able to work together."

"As we always have, when it has been necessary," replied the other.

The smile on the older man's face began to dissipate. "But we should also remember that whoever this new actor is, he is different from any of the others we have faced over the preceding millennia. We should maintain our vigilance."

Across the table, the larger man straightened up, his chest seeming to grow. "When the time comes, we will deliver our most punishing blows until he falls."

"Yes. We need only stay coordinated in how and where

we find him, and how he is to be eliminated. Have your men learned anything at all from their contacts in Chicago?"

"Not much yet. Only his first name. 'Craig.'"

ABOUT THE AUTHOR

An author, professor, and financial executive, Keith Goad lives in Indiana with his wife. He received an undergraduate degree as well as an MBA from the Ohio State University. In addition to serving as a financial executive, Keith had also taught as an adjunct university professor for over 15 years.

Relentless Enemy is Keith's first book of fiction in what will be the Relentless Enemy series. The inspiration for this series is drawn from the real-life, personal histories of Keith's father and grandfather.